MW01128964

An Allie B---

Woof at the Door

by

Leslie O'Kane

Book Four in the Series

Copyright 2013 by Leslie O'Kane

Digital edition published in 2013 by O'Kane Ink
Current print edition published in 2014 by O'Kane Ink

To Cindy Miller,
my ever-so-wonderful friend.

Chapter 1

Sometimes I feel slightly tense when I ring a new client's doorbell. This time my mental flags were fluttering wildly. Nothing seemed out of the ordinary, so why were my instincts screaming at me to run?

The property itself appeared to be standard fare for the newer north-Boulder neighborhoods—small lot size and a large two-story house with earth-tone siding and trim. Two red-and-white "Beware of Dog" signs were posted on either side of the surrounding six-foot cedar privacy fence, and from inside the house, the deep, muffled woofs hinted at a large dog. The barks sounded normal. If persistent.

I shored myself up and rang the doorbell. The door swung open, and my jaw almost dropped. The tall, forty-something man before me sported shoulder-length blond hair. His striped headband featured a large peace symbol, centered on his forehead. He wore pink-tinged octagonal wire-rimmed glasses halfway down his nose, an electric-blue satin shirt, and orange crushed-velvet bell bottoms with brown pockets.

Was this Rip Van Winkle of the Sixties?

He peered down at me, scoffed, and, over the loud rhythmic woofs of the large dog behind him, said, "You'd better not be Allida Babcock."

"Actually, I am," I replied with as much of a smile as I could muster. Due to his disdainful facial expression, I silently formed a personal credo: *People who wear bell-bottoms shouldn't criticize others' physical appearances.* Including their height. Or lack thereof. "You must be Tyler Bellingham."

"Shut up, Doobie!" he called behind his shoulder at the barking dog, which, of course, ignored him. "Actually, I go by Ty. As in Tie-dye." Making no move to invite me inside, he shook his head, still studying me. "No offense, lady, but you sure you can handle this? My dog coughs up things that are bigger than you."

Stifling a sigh of frustration, I ran a hand through my short sandy-brown hair and focused my attention past him at the constantly barking dog. Doobie was a mixed breed—of very large origins. He probably weighed around one-hundred-forty pounds. He appeared to be mostly mastiff and Chesapeake Bay retriever, with, judging by his fur's black-and-brown pattern, a few Doberman genes thrown in. As with a standard Doberman, his ears had been clipped. We locked eyes for a moment, and I said with authority, "Doobie, sit."

He stopped barking and followed my command.

"Good dog."

Ty, I noticed, had a bit of a paunch overhanging those hip-hugging bell-bottoms of his. I looked up at him. He was a good foot taller than me, which put his height at six feet.

"There are dog trainers here in Boulder who make house calls, Mr. Bellingham. Odds are, they'll be taller than I am. If you would rather—"

"No, that's okay," he said, stepping aside and holding the door for me. "Your friend, Beverly Wood, recommended you highly. She lives right next door."

Not surprisingly, the dog sprang to his feet and resumed his barking. I stepped inside and was temporarily staggered at the overwhelming sickly sweet fragrance of incense. Though largely drowned out by Doobie's barks, sitar music played from an enormous stereo system on a cinder-block shelving unit that took up one entire wall. A slab of flagstone served as the coffee table. Other than the stereo shelves, none of the furnishing was more than two feet high. This room seemed to have been decorated for trolls. Trolls with a taste for futons, beanbag chairs, and lava lamps.

Ty was staring at me, and I wrenched my attention back into our conversation. "Beverly and I went to high school together."

"That's what she said." He chuckled and, to my extreme annoyance, used his hand and arm as a leveling stick to measure how high the top of my head was compared to his chest. "But when she said you were a dog shrink, I didn't realize she meant you'd be pre-shrunk yourself." He laughed—a loud braying sound.

"I'm going to need background information on Doobie." To my curiosity, Doobie was not barking at me, but rather had rushed over to the living room window, put his paws on the sill, and was now barking out the window.

I called him, and he obeyed, albeit slowly. The dog had numerous scars. If this dog was being abused, "Tie-die" here had just hired himself the wrong "dog shrink" and was soon going to be sorry for what he'd done to his pet.

While assuring Doobie that he was "a very good dog," I stroked his fur, making a mental audit of his extensive injuries. My own hackles were rising. Doobie's ears had almost as much scar tissue as fur. While pretending to be simply stroking his neck, I lifted the dog's chin and checked the soft flesh along his teeth. The edges were jagged, a tell-tale sign that he'd been in a dreadful dog fight. During fights, dogs tend to bite through the skin surrounding their own mouths without realizing it.

Having lost his patience with me, Doobie pulled away and returned to his compulsive-sounding barking out the side window. I straightened and glared at Ty Bellingham. "Your dog's been in at least two serious dog fights. Has he ever been—"

"He was all scarred like that when I got him last December from a Dog Rescue outfit in Nevada. He was a stray. Probably had to fight for every scrap of food he got, till I came along."

That was plausible, but Ty had a long way to go yet to gain some credibility. Acquiring background information on the dog could wait. If Doobie cowered or shied away whenever Ty approached, I would have my answer.

"Mr. Bellingham, could—"

"Call me Ty," he corrected.

"Could you please call your dog?" I asked, unwilling to be on a first-name basis until I felt relatively certain he wasn't an animal abuser.

"Call him?" he asked as if utterly perplexed. He gestured in Doobie's direction. "He's right there." The man was either extraordinarily dense or deliberately evasive.

"I'd like to see how quickly he responds to you."

Ty sighed and slid his hands into his velvet pockets. "Doobie! Come!"

The dog ignored his owner and continued to bark. In the meantime, Ty showed no frustration with his dog's insubordination, just raised his own voice and repeated the command. After four ever-louder commands, Doobie finally deserted his post and trotted over to us, with an occasional bark over his shoulder, as if he greatly resented this interruption.

Ty pointed at the floor. "Doobie, sit. Sit!"

The dog's haunches barely touched down, then, without awaiting further command, he rushed back to his noisy post at the window. I rapidly reevaluated. Doobie was not behaving as if he were an abused pet, but rather a woefully untrained one. Moments earlier, he'd responded to my commands. That meant the problem was due to his not viewing his master as the alpha dog. I still felt uneasy, but was willing to give Ty the benefit of the doubt. Although this "benefit" might only last until I could contact the dog rescuer to verify Doobie's condition at time of adoption.

Ty fidgeted with his blond tresses and gave me a sheepish smile. "He's a spirited animal."

"Does he always bark this persistently?"

"Not usually." He glanced at Doobie. "Don't know what's gotten into him today. Ty gestured at the expanse of oversized pillows on the floor. "Why don't we have a seat?" He immediately sat down Indian style on the hardwood floor. "These furnishings are all from my store, 'Way Cool Collectibles.' We have a 'Far-Out Furniture' division."

Perhaps the dog-and-owner authority problem was related to Ty's devotion for the sixties. Ty might have a hey-like-do-your-own-thing attitude regarding his dog. I sat down on a chartreuse beanbag, which tried to swallow me alive, sweeping me over backwards in the process. Perhaps Way Cool Collectibles used marble-shaped beans. With a struggle, I bobbed back up and regained my equilibrium, glad that I was wearing pants and not a skirt.

Mostly to cover my embarrassment, I snatched up a four-inch high ceramic gold-painted Buddha that had been having an easier time at sitting on the floor than I was. "This is one of your collectibles?"

"Yes. Be careful. That piece is forty years old. I could sell it for well over a hundred dollars."

A hundred dollars for a palm-sized gold-painted Buddha? His store should be renamed 'Really Rad Rip-offs.' I set down the ceramic piece. "When we set this appointment, didn't you say that your wife was going to be here, too?"

He shrugged. "Something came up."

Uh-oh. Lackadaisical dog owners don't make for good partners toward the successful treatment of their dogs. But, I reminded myself, I had chosen to come here today because I wanted to help Beverly; Doobie's barking was driving her nuts. For her sake, I'd give this my best effort.

I delved into my standard questionnaire designed to gather insight into the dog's problem behavior. Ty answered the standard opening questions: no kids; he and his wife were joint owners of the dog; the dog obeyed both of them equally, which, in this case, meant he disobeyed them equally.

Just as I was getting into the more revealing questions about the dog's daily routine, diet, and reward system, Ty rose and asked, "Would you like some tea? I'm getting myself some."

I hesitated, having seen reruns of the Smothers' Brothers' "Tea With Goldie" segments, in which "tea" was a euphemism. "To drink?"

He headed toward a doorway that was delineated with strings of brightly colored plastic beads. With a parting-of-the-seas gesture, he went through the beaded doorway. I intentionally lingered to observe the dog's behavior. Also to give myself time to get out of this ridiculous beanbag. As soon as his master left the room, Doobie perked up and galloped through the doorway, the bead strings clacking and swinging to and fro in his wake. I followed and was not at all surprised to find myself in an avocado-colored kitchen. Despite the old-fashioned color scheme, it featured a modern island, complete with a grill. Above this structure was a massive oven hood that looked as though it might be able to suck up anything airborne, regardless of size.

Doobie had immediately rushed to the back door and tried to push through a dog door. Finally accepting that it was locked, he whined at his owner, who ignored him and continued to rummage through a cabinet. "I had to lock him inside. The neighbors have put up quite a stink about his barking."

Beverly, the friend from my old days, was one of the neighbor's who'd complained. Ironic that even though I was close to two decades younger than Ty, my "old days" were the nineties, which made them considerably more recent than Ty's current days. Doobie's barking, Beverly had told me, got her Beagle barking, and set off a chain reaction throughout the neighborhood that had resulted in more than one "disturbing the peace" claim against Doobie.

"How long have you lived here?" I asked.

"Ten years." Ty filled a cup with water, dunked a tea bag in it, and slid the cup into a modern convenience: a microwave. Mr. Tie-Dye was a hypocrite.

"Do you know how old Doobie is?"

"The rescue folks didn't know exactly. Like I said, he was a stray. By now, he's about four and a half. And, like I told you over the phone, my wife and I didn't used to have any trouble at all with barking or anything else till about three months ago."

"A sudden change in a dog's temperament often indicates a health problem. You told me you took him to a vet last month. Did they find anything?"

"Nope."

"Anything significant happen three months ago?"

He shrugged. "Nothing. Not a thing."

"You didn't change jobs or change daily schedules?" I prompted.

He shook his head. The action seemed to shift his hair slightly off-center. "Not at all. I run my own store at the mall, and my wife and me take turns there. When business is good, we're both there, but generally, we only need one person to run it. You ever shop there?"

"'Fraid not."

He smirked at me. "Figures. You're too young to appreciate it. You probably missed the sixties entirely."

Being thirty-two, that was obviously true, but I didn't want to go off on a tangent. "So you've been compensating for the barking by keeping Doobie inside. Is that correct?"

He sighed and nodded. "We've had to lock up the doggie door and everything. Makes poor Doobie nuts, but we've got to keep him away from the maniac who lives next door."

Since the house on the west was Beverly's and Doobie was barking at the window to the east, it was easy to guess which house he meant. "You told me that your neighbor has a dog, as well. Right?"

"Yeah. Big white fluffy thing with pointy ears. Looks like an albino huskie."

"A Samoyed."

"Whatever. That's the dog that started all this trouble."

"Is this Samoyed new to the neighborhood?" Such as acquired three months ago? I silently added. Samoyeds were not nervous dogs in general, and if this one was a "problem barker," it would be a first for me.

He shook his head, which re-centered his hair part. "No, but his owner seems to think just 'cause his dog's white, she's as pure as the driven snow in all of this. Let me show you something."

Ty unlocked the dog door, which looked comically small for the size of his dog, but Doobie slithered through in a heartbeat. For a moment, I wondered if Ty intended for us all to squeeze through this opening as well, but he opened a half-dozen deadbolts on the back door and finally had the people-sized door open. Apparently, Ty was very security conscious, which seemed unnecessary, given the furnishings. Then again, he did have that lovely Buddha collectible.

Doobie had rushed to the cedar privacy fence that separated Ty's property from that of the Samoyed's owner. Doobie sniffed along the length of the fence along the ground, where there was only the smallest of gaps.

"Watch this," Ty said, folding his arms across his satin-clad chest and pointing with his chin in the direction of the fence.

After a few more trips up and back along the fence, Doobie jumped up against the fence, managing to get his paws on two of the three supporting beams. He ladder-stepped his way up to get his muzzle over the top of the six-foot fence.

A deep male voice boomed, "Bad dog! Put your paws down and back away from the fence!"

"What the—" I muttered in amazement. I located a loudspeaker attached by a stand such that it was clearly inside this neighbor's fence, but aimed directly at Ty's yard.

"That's Hank Atkinson's doing," Ty said through clenched teeth. "My illustrious neighbor."

Hank Atkinson, I repeated to myself. The name rang a bell, but I couldn't quite place it.

"He works in security. Installs home-security systems, that is. He's got this motion detector set up so that anytime anyone so much as reaches an inch over the fence, that thing goes off."

Doobie whined, got down, then tried it again. Once again, the stern-voiced recording admonished him.

"I'm surprised your neighbor doesn't find that loud recording more offensive than the barking itself."

"Oh, I know. The guy's a crackpot."

This from such a fine source of mental stability. I'd glanced at Mr. Atkinson's house while checking addresses on my way to the Bellinghams'. It had seemed normal—gray siding with white trim—but then, so had Ty's house. "Is Mr. Atkinson's dog home now?"

"Beats me. Might be inside of the house. But, believe me, it's unusual that only my Doobie is barking. His dog is usually barking back every bit as loud. Tends to be the two of 'em going at it, and she's the female. She's the one that starts everything."

This was probably a sexist conclusion, but I was too busy pondering the situation to care. Excessive barking is often a sign of boredom or separation anxiety. Judging by what I'd seen so far, in Doobie's case it was likely caused by lack of training.

"Have you tried talking with your neighbor about your dogs?"

"Hell, if I could talk to the guy, I wouldn't have had to call you. He and I have a personal history."

"Does this 'personal history' have anything to do with your dogs?"

He let out a guffaw. "Not of the four-legged variety."

That could only be a misogynistic crack—unless "dogs" referred to his feet, which I doubted. Ty ignored my withering glare and continued, "Hank's a Nazi conservative, and he thinks I'm a hippie degenerate." He peered over the frames of his glasses and wiggled his eyebrows at me. "I'm hoping he'll like you. The guy thinks he's God's gift to women."

Regardless of Mr. Atkinson's personal appraisal of me, getting his perspective on the barking situation would be helpful. Doobie took another leap at the fence, and nearly managed to climb over the fence, which finally got a rise out of Ty. Joining the recorded voice, he cried, "No, Doobie! Down, boy!" Ty pulled the dog's massive back paws off the fence support beam, which caused Doobie to yelp as he fell onto our side of the fence. "Bad dog!" Ty shouted, yet, for the first time in my presence, he patted his dog. He glanced at me. "Let's go back inside the house."

I said nothing, watching with interest as Ty tried to coax his dog away from the fence. "Come on, boy." Doobie jumped up on the fence again. Ty grabbed his collar and needed every ounce of strength to drag Doobie back to the house. Ty's smile while doing so hinted that he was proud of the dog's disobedience.

Once inside, I leaned against the kitchen counter and watched the difficult procedure as Ty strained to lock the dog door despite his dog's noisy and furious attempts to bull his way through it. Afterwards, Ty bolted the series of locks on the door, then turned toward me, laughing. "See what I mean? He's really something to handle. You sure you're up for this?"

I stared at the gray eyes above those silly rose-colored glasses. "Do you want your dog to be trained?"

His smile faded. "Of course. I hired you, didn't I?"

"Out of duress. You're afraid the authorities will take your dog unless you get his barking under control."

He scowled. "All right, yes. You got me. I believe in letting everybody do their own thing. I'm a free spirit—" he indicated his clothes—"as if you couldn't figure that out for yourself. That's why I chose Doobie in the first place. He's got a lot of energy, and he can handle himself real well. I don't want to break his spirit."

"Do you consider training a dog 'breaking his spirit'?" I asked pointedly.

He hesitated, but finally frowned and muttered, "Obviously I've got no choice in the matter. I need to be able to control Doobie, or those whiney neighbors of mine are going to see to it that he's declared a nuisance. Can you get him to quiet down enough to suit the neighbors, without turning him into some kind of a Hush Puppy?"

I resisted a smile. "The only way I can do that is if you're willing to assert yourself as his master."

"Fine, fine. We'll buy into the whole dog-obedience scene, if that's what it'll take." He sighed as he stared at the ever-barking Doobie. "I sure wish you could tell me what's going on today, though. He's never barked quite this bad before. It's gotta be Atkinson's dog. Maybe she's in heat, or something."

That was the first sensible thing Ty had said—an assessment which reinforced my core issue: Without the dog owner's full cooperation and approval, there was little chance my program would succeed. I did my best to explain this to Ty, who assured me he understood and that, even if he disagreed "on principle" about my wanting to train dogs, he would still comply fully with my instructions.

During the rest of our hour, I discussed the standard ways that Ty would need to assert himself over Doobie. Ty also needed to tone down his dog's aggressiveness, which meant giving Doobie a lower-protein diet, more exercise, and staying away from rough-housing and tug-of-war games. Ty nodded throughout, but I could tell that, underneath that silly wig of his, my words were falling on deaf ears. Secretly I was putting my hopes on his wife's assistance, but she never arrived. Not a good sign.

After our hour was up, I headed next door to Hank Atkinson's house to find out if Ty's hunch about the Samoyed being in heat was correct. Preoccupied, I almost bumped into an elderly man on the sidewalk, who had bent down to tie his shoe and was partially hidden in the shadows. The man let out a howl of protest at our near collision.

"I'm sorry, sir. I didn't see you there."

He merely glared at me, cleared his throat noisily, and shuffled off down the street. Apparently this was not the friendliest of neighborhoods.

Hank Atkinson's front door was wide open, except for the thin screen door. A dog was whining.

I peered through the screen. No dogs were within view, though the whines sounded like a dog was just on the other side of the doorway. A pair of male voices were coming from the next room, which, if the general layout was the same as Ty's house, would be the kitchen. I rang the doorbell.

A gray wolf charged through the house, straight toward me.

Chapter 2

I gasped, automatically putting a hand over my exposed throat. All that separated me from the wolf was a thin screen. The wolf could leap through that in the blink of an eye.

I stood my ground and hoped the wolf was domesticated. In any case, if I turned and ran, I would only trigger chase-of-prey instincts. The wolf stopped at the other side of the door, and we stood staring at each other.

What was going on here? There was no way Ty Bellingham's description of his neighbor's "white fluffy" Samoyed could have actually referred to this wolf.

A male voice chuckled, and I was vaguely aware of a figure in the shadowed inner doorway behind the animal. "I see you've met Kaia, our local celebrity," said the man. "Don't worry. He's perfectly harmless."

"That's nice to know," I replied, though I was fully aware that was a false statement on his part. Kaia had his teeth and his claws intact, so while he might be completely domesticated, he was not harmless. Nor, for that matter, was any canine.

The man stepped into view alongside the vigilant wolf. He was in his sixties, rather dumpy looking with tobacco-stained teeth and a week's worth of gray whiskers. He wore unbelted and low-riding brown pants, and a stained light blue T-shirt. Was this the neighbor Ty Bellingham had implied was a skirt chaser? If so, he must be deceptively fleet of foot.

"Are you Hank Atkinson?" I asked, recalling a joke that if this was "God's gift to women," I hope He kept the receipt.

"No, that would be me," a second man said from the background. The first man stepped aside to allow Hank access to his own door, but kept a watchful eye on me over Hank's shoulder. Hank Atkinson was in his forties, strikingly attractive with reddish-brown hair graying at the temples. He wore khaki shorts and a denim shirt with rolled-up sleeves that accentuated his muscular, stocky frame. "And whatever you're selling, I don't want any." He started to shut the door on me.

"I'm not a salesperson. My name is Allida Babcock. I'm a dog behaviorist. Do you have a couple of minutes to discuss your dog with me?"

"Sammy?" he rolled his eyes. "Why? Are you in the market for a used Samoyed? If so, this might be your lucky day."

"No, actually—"

"So. You're a dog behaviorist, eh?" He gave me a salesman smile of his own and leaned against the door frame. "Maybe you can answer some questions. I'd been hoping to breed my Samoyed to Kaia here, but it looks like that's not gonna happen. She backed herself into a corner and is protecting herself for all she's worth. Can she tell Kaia isn't a dog?"

"Yes, and she might be frightened. Some female dogs can be very discriminating when it comes to mating."

Actually, I silently considered, I'd known of many instances where female dogs had rejected male dogs, albeit in those cases that immediately came to mind, the male dogs were of the same or smaller breeds than the female. I'd had no experience whatsoever when it came to mating dogs with wolves, but, it was logical to assume that his dog was frightened. I sure would be.

The man who'd first come to the door chuckled again. "How d'ya like that? Your Samantha thinks she's too good for Kaia. Ain't that just like your typical dame?" He jabbed Hank in the shoulder.

Hank stiffened, but made no reply.

"Why'n't you invite the lady in?" He gave me a sly smile, "'Less you're afraid of being in the same house with a wolf." He laughed again, then added, "And I ain't talkin' 'bout the four-legged kind."

Charmed, I'm sure.

"Come on in." Hank opened the screen door. "It's not as if you'll be seeing anything illicit going on, damn it all."

I stepped inside, keeping a wary eye on the wolf, who returned the favor, his nostrils flaring as he checked me out. Kaia, the two men, and I shared a relatively small square of hardwood flooring that marked the entranceway to a nicely decorated living room. The air bore an unwashed-dog odor. I couldn't identify its source, but I was betting on Hank's human visitor. I glanced over at him. He blatantly gawked at my chest. Was he hoping my blouse would suddenly spring open like the doors of a cuckoo clock?

I heard another whimper and glanced to my left, along the front wall. Except for her head, which poked out from around the edge of the love seat, my view of the Samoyed was blocked. She had a few square feet in the corner of the living room between a roll-top desk and the love seat. She was whining and clearly ill at ease, staring at Kaia, who, in turn, seemed utterly indifferent, showing more interest in me than in her. If Sammy was truly in heat, Kaia was strangely unaffected.

"That's my Samantha, over there." Hank frowned as he looked at her and crossed his tanned arms across his broad chest.

"Are you sure she's in heat?" I asked.

"Nah, but she will be any day now," Hank said. "Thought I'd go ahead and have her meet her future mate. They don't seem to take to one another. Was giving them a preliminary intro to each other a bad idea?"

"No, but ideally, this initial introduction and their future meetings should be in the male dog's—" I paused and corrected myself— "in the wolf's...home. By doing this in the reverse, you've put her in a defensive position toward Kaia. She's compelled to defend her home from him, which isn't conducive for mating."

Hank's guest guffawed. "That bitch doesn't want to get into any position for Kaia, if you ask me."

Hank shot a glare in the man's direction and said, "'Fraid it isn't possible to do this at Kaia's place."

"You have discussed all of this with Sammy's veterinarian, haven't you?"

"Er, no. Maybe I'd better do that. I got to admit, I don't have much experience with dogs. She's my first. Owned her for less than two years. She's been acting strange the last few weeks. Kind of stand-offish. Does she look all right to you?"

I took a step toward her, and she immediately let out a series of warning barks. She was clearly set to defend herself, if necessary. "I can't examine her under these conditions. She might let me get closer, though, once Kaia's gone."

I glanced at the other man, who was apparently the wolf's handler. For the dog's sake, I needed to find out what was going on here, and that meant forcing myself to be pleasant to this rather disgusting person. I held out my hand to him. "I'm Allida Babcock."

He took my hand, his palm rough and calloused. "Larry Cundriff. Pleased to meet you, miss." He held my hand a little longer than necessary.

I resisted the urge to wipe my palm on my slacks. "Are you Kaia's owner?"

"Me? No, no. I just...work for the owner, that's all." The question had put him ill at ease. Something wasn't above-board here.

"Has he or she got a license for owning an exotic animal?" I asked, watching the wolf, which was making

himself at home. He had leapt onto a small off-white
sofa across the room from us.

"Sure, he does."

"What's the owner's name?"

The man cleared his throat and ran his fingers
along his whiskered chin. "No offense, miss, but uh,
what's it to you?"

"I'd be interested in speaking with him or her
about purchasing a pup," I lied.

He grinned. "Ah, well. In that case, you'd be better
off making the arrangements through me. That Damian,
he's a real straight arrow. He won't sell a wolf pup to
anyone without first checking that you've got a suitable
home and licenses and all that crap."

"Nevertheless, could I get his number?"

Larry made a show of patting his pockets and
shot a nervous look at Hank, still standing beside him.
"'Fraid I don't have one of his cards. Not on me. Sorry."

"What's his last name?"

"So, Hank," Larry said, pretending not to have
heard my last question. "What do you think? Think it's
about time to, uh, pack it in?"

Hank nodded. "You might as well take Kaia home.
I'll be in touch when the time comes."

Larry whistled and patted his thigh. The wolf
gracefully leapt off the couch and allowed Larry to slip a
choke collar around his neck. "Pleasure meetin' you,
miss. An' like a said, if'n you want yourself a wolf pup,
you talk to me. Hank here knows how to reach me."

It didn't take a genius to figure out that Larry had
some insidious deal going, perhaps behind the back of
the wolf's owner. "Damian" likely didn't even know that
Larry was studding Kaia out. I needed to learn Damian's
last name, without raising Larry's or Hank's suspicions.

I decided I'd have a better chance of getting
answers from Hank, who would likely suffer less
ramifications if caught. I followed a step behind Hank,
but remained silent as Larry took Kaia out through the
kitchen and into Hank's three-car garage, where a plain

steel-gray van with tinted windows was parked. The two men loaded the very amiable wolf into a cage in the back of the van, then Larry took off, Hank shutting the garage door after him. Strange that Larry's vehicle would be parked inside Hank's garage. Apparently, they didn't want to raise neighbors' curiosity by leaving the van in the driveway.

Hank led me back through the kitchen. Despite Ty's words to the contrary, Hank hadn't been at all flirtatious toward me so far. He did walk with something of a swagger, though. His bearing hinted at his having considerable pride in his muscular, if somewhat compact, physique. "So, can you take a quick look at Sammy for me?"

"I'd be happy to." The dog was still where we'd left her. I got a slightly better view of her, enough to see that she was surprisingly plump. She'd been lying down, but immediately sat up when we entered the room. I stopped in the center of the living room. "It'd be best for me to give Sammy the chance to get comfortable with my presence and come to me," I explained.

He nodded and plopped down in the same spot on the couch that the wolf had recently abandoned. Hank splayed his legs and laced his fingers behind his head, taking up as much space as possible as he regarded me at length.

"Larry called Kaia a 'local celebrity.' How come?"

He widened his eyes and stared at me. "Oh, now, surely you've seen my commercials, right?" He gave me a full-wattage smile, his perfect teeth contrasting with his tanned skin. "'Safe and sound, thanks to Hank's'?"

"Oh, right," I said, playing along. I watched television only irregularly, and less often than ever, now that my temporary living quarters had put my mom in control of the remote. "So that must be the wolf in your commercials."

He gave me a broad grin, his chest visibly puffing with pride. "That's right. Kaia circles me during the commercial, and then sits next to me."

"And Kaia's owner? Is he there as you're shooting the commercials?"

Hank's smile faded a little. "Yeah, he's usually just out of view of the camera, behind the couch or right next to the cameraman."

"What's Damian's last name?"

He frowned and rose slowly. Though he wasn't tall—five-eight or so—he strode toward me in a John-Wayne sidle, looped his thumbs into the waistband of his shorts, and rocked on his heels. "Look it, little girl, I'm not doing anything illegal here. It's true that Damian doesn't know about my arrangement with Larry to stud Kaia. Damian doesn't treat his employee half as well as he treats his animals. The only way Larry can make ends meet is when someone like me slips him a hundred bucks or so. And, you're sure not going to see Kaia complain."

If I ever hoped to learn Damian's last name from Hank, I needed to keep myself in check and not be baited into an argument. "That much is certain," I murmured noncommittally. My thoughts raced. Maybe I didn't have to learn the owner's identity from Hank. I could ask around till I found a friend who'd seen these commercials and could tell me when they were broadcast. Then the television station might be able to give me the name of the commercial's production studio, which would know who the wolf's owner was.

Hank's Samoyed finally felt secure enough to gingerly venture a couple of steps out from her post in the corner. I knelt and said softly, "Hello, Sammy. That's a good dog." She cautiously approached, sniffing at me. She walked with a stiff-legged gate and was panting. She lay down on her back in the submissive position the moment I was in reach of her. I obliged and rubbed her tummy, surprised to feel telltale bumps and swelling.

Talk about "inexperienced" dog owners. Couldn't he even tell that his dog was pregnant? A veterinarian would likely be able to give a more accurate estimation than mine, but by my best guess, this dog could be as much as sixty days into her sixty-three day gestation period.

Admittedly, my dog skills are better than my people skills, especially when it comes to tactfulness, but I at least knew not to blurt out, "You idiot!" Plus, if the loudspeaker system on the fence was there because of Doobie's jumping into Sammy's yard, I had a feeling that the neighborhood discord was about to intensify. "Have you noticed changes in your dog's physical appearance in the last few weeks?"

"You mean her weight gain?" Hank barely glanced at her. "She's always been pretty plump, though. I just figured she's getting her winter coat in a little early. She's a good outdoors dog." He frowned. "At least she was, till that worm, Bellingham next door, bought that mutt of his."

"From a dog rescuer, right?"

He scoffed and shook his head. "Ty told me that he bought Doobie from a private party. But you can't believe anything that jackass tells you."

Ty might have lied about where he got his dog to explain Doobie's scars, which might also mean he'd lied about his dog's origins.

At the mention of Ty Bellingham, Hank's demeanor was growing more hostile by the moment. "He sent you over here to check on me, right?"

"No, actually, I came over because his dog was barking at your house so persistently. He must have picked up on the wolf's scent."

"That's not all that miserable mutt's going to pick up on, if I have my way," Hank said under his breath.

"What do you mean?" I tried to conceal my automatic bristling at his threat to a dog. It wasn't Doobie's fault that his owners hadn't trained him to be a good suburbia dog.

"If you ask me, that menace should be put to sleep. And I mean Mr. Tie-dye, not the dog."

"Did you hook the loudspeaker up to the fence because Doobie was jumping it?"

Hank spread his hands. "I have to do something. I don't want that fleabag over here. Damned thing can actually jump over a six-foot privacy fence. Course, once it gets into my yard, it can't get back out, so we're stuck with the damned thing all day."

Uh-oh.

He eyed me. "So, tell me, Miss Babcock. In your—" he rolled his eyes—"expert opinion, is Sammy sick?"

I gritted my teeth and rose. "No, she's not sick. She's—"

"Good. Listen, I hate to kick you out, but I'm a busy man. If you'll excuse me..." he swung open the door and stood by it, gesturing that he wanted me on the other side.

Our relative positions—his standing by the doorway as I stood up— sparked a memory. Now I knew why he seemed so familiar to me. Softball. My co-rec team played in the same league as his. Last week, he'd rudely rushed in to take premature possession of the dugout after our game ended, bumping into me in the process. His lack of even a lip-service apology had won him instant membership in my mental AA—Arrogant Asshole—club.

The heck with mincing my words. I strolled past him and out the door, saying, "Sammy and Kaia won't mate because she's already pregnant."

Hank followed me onto the porch. "What did you say?"

"Sammy is pregnant. In fact, my guess is that she's expecting any day now."

"But...But that isn't possible! She's supposed to be in heat this month!"

Though his having belittled my area of expertise made me feel more like spitting at him than speaking civilly, if I stormed off now, Hank might take his frustrations out on his dog. While counting to ten, I turned, then said calmly, "You miscalculated and missed that event by two months or so."

"Oh, shit! Two months ago, I was in Dallas for.... But my wife was here. She never said anything about Sammy being in..." He called over his shoulder, "Paige? Paige?" He started to go back inside, then stopped, muttering, "Must be listening to her stupid self-awareness tapes. Damned things make her deaf to the outside world!" He leveled a finger at me. "You sure about this?"

I nodded. "With outside dogs like Sammy, you need to be somewhat vigilant. It's not impossible for you and your wife to have missed the signs." Though it did speak volumes about how inattentive Hank and his wife must be about their pet. A dog's cycle lasts about three weeks, and the Atkinsons had decided to breed her, so they should have been watching. Were these people aware that there was a world outside their own front—and back—doors?

Hank pounded his palm with a fist, eyes darting as if he were making desperate mental calculations. "That bastard!" He brushed past me and marched down the sidewalk toward Ty Bellingham's house.

Feeling somewhat responsible for Hank's agitation, I followed, his long, athletic strides forcing me into a trot. "Mr. Atkinson, just because Doobie can jump your fence doesn't necessarily mean he's the sire."

Hank pounded on the door, ignoring my lame attempts at distracting him. I joined him on the porch. Doobie was barking at a feverous pitch and had put his huge paws against the front window sill so that he could see us.

"It could have been another dog, even from an entirely different neighborhood. Some male dogs, once they pick up on a female's scent, will literally jump through glass to—"

"Bellingham! Get out here and face me, you miserable chicken-livered piece of dog crap!"

"If Sammy was out in your yard while she was in heat, it's possible that any dog could have—"

Hank shot me a furious glare, letting me know that the subject was closed, and pounded again. The vibrations rattled Ty's windows. Meanwhile, Doobie maintained his fever pitch.

Ty opened the door and slipped out, leaving only the screen door shut on his massive dog.

"You...you...miserable—"

Despite Hank's sputtering fury, Ty looked at me and said, "Thank you, Miss Babcock. You must be quite the skilled negotiator. Look at all the progress you've made at mending fences between me and my neighbor."

Hank jabbed Ty with his finger. "That piece of crap, flea-hotel, ugly dirt-bag goon you call your dog knocked up my Sammy!"

Ty blinked a couple of times, then said calmly, "The powder puff on four paws is pregnant?"

"That's right, jerk, and you better wipe that smile off your face!"

"Whoa," Ty said, lifting his palms and taking a step back. "'Fraid you got the wrong daddy dog. It couldn't have been my Doobie." To my horror, Ty surreptitiously snapped his fingers behind his back while he was speaking. "And even if Doobie was the sire, let's keep this in perspective. We're talking about a pair of dogs, not a knocked-up daughter."

He now had a grip on the handle of the screen door. The otherwise untrained Doobie instantly went into a fighting stance, hackles raised, muscles primed to leap. He let out a rumbling growl.

This was trouble. There was nothing I could do to stop an attack on Hank if Ty sicced his huge dog on hi.

"Hank! Ty!" I pointed at the dog, trying to warn Hank, but he ignored me.

"Perspective?!" Hank shouted, his face beet red and sweaty. "I'll tell you about perspective, you moron!" He kept an eye on Doobie, and backed down the steps. "You ruined everything! I was going to mate Sammy with a wolf! You owe me five thousand dollars! That's what I planned to make on this litter alone! Then I was going to get a steady income out of breeding the females!"

"There's no way I'm going to pay that kind of money," Ty scoffed.

He squeezed back inside through his door. He stood beside his still growling dog.

"Oh, you'd better believe you're going to pay!"

Ty slammed his front door on Hank's words.

"You'll pay, all right! Otherwise, I'm going to kill you!"

Chapter 3

My heart was pounding from the near miss of a horrible altercation.

I looked at Hank. "You realize that Sammy can be bred again safely in another year to eighteen months. As long as this is only going to be her second or third litter, that is."

"Her previous owner already bred her three times," he replied through gritted teeth.

"This is all for the best, Hank. It would have been enormously irresponsible of you to sell Wolf Dogs as pets to the average owner. That could have had hideous consequences for all concerned. One bad bite, and you could have been sued and lost your home-security business."

Hank glared at me, lifted his chin, then pivoted on a heel and marched back into his house. I hesitated on the porch, wanting to make sure Ty wasn't going to sic Doobie on Hank after all before I dared leave.

Just then, an orange VW van neared. Its curtained windows bore peace signs. On one side was a mural of unrecognizable content. Perhaps the artist had painted it while the van was still in motion. Not surprisingly, the vehicle pulled into Ty's driveway. Out stepped a very pretty blond woman in her mid- to late-twenties. She wore a tie-dyed T-shirt and multicolored skirt, sandals, and at least twenty beaded necklaces.

As the woman came toward me—up the front walkway at a remarkably slow pace—Ty opened his door again and joined me on the porch. He smiled and said to me, "That went well, don't you think?"

As comical as he looked in his hippie garb, his making light of such a serious issue infuriated me. "Mr. Bellingham, you had better think twice before you sic your dog on anyone. Someone will be badly injured, you'll get sued, and Doobie will wind up being put to sleep!"

Ty merely laughed at me. "Now, would I do such a thing? He gave me the peace sign with both hands and waved them in the air. "Peace, love, peace, love."

"Don't test me, Mr. Bellingham. My client loyalties are squarely with the four-pawed sector."

"Oh, hey, wha's happ'nin'," the woman drawled to me, finally having reached the porch. Her eyelids were drooping and her smile was so lazy looking I half expected to see drool on her chin. "I'm Chesh, short for Cheshire. Ty's ol' lady."

"It's nice to meet you," I said, which was perhaps my biggest lie of the day. The woman's perfume mingled with the incense smells emanating from the house. The combination made me want to hug a pine tree. "I'm Allida Babcock. I had an appointment a little over an hour ago to help you and your husband with Doobie's barking."

"Heavy," she said with a slow smile and nod.

"Who's minding the store, Chesh?" Ty asked.

She glared at her husband. "Hey, cool it, man. Check your sun dial, babe. It's closing time."

"Since when do we close at one p.m. on a Saturday?"

"Speaking of barking," I interrupted, "I strongly suspect Doobie was picking up on the scent of a new animal next door, which might have been behind all his barking today."

"New animal?" Ty asked, the eyes behind the pink, octagonal glasses suddenly sparking with interest. "Was the wolf from Hank's commercial at his place?"

His question took me by surprise. With all the animosity between those neighbors, it was odd that Ty watched the man's commercials, let alone cared about Hank's four-pawed visitors. "Yes. Shall we set another appointment for—"

"Damn it! I wish I'd known. I've been dying to see that wolf in person!" He leveled a finger at his wife. "Chesh. Make yourself useful and set the next appointment with Allida for us. And, this time, be there! I've got a couple phone calls to make." He shut the door, leaving his wife standing beside me on the front porch.

My cheeks warmed out of embarrassment for her sake. I was appalled at Ty's abusive treatment of his wife—even if she did seem to be either on drugs or rarified air. "Groovy, daddy-o," she muttered under her breath. She looked at me and put her hands on hips.

Suddenly dropping her strung-out persona, she said, "I'm sorry I couldn't make our appointment, Allie. A clerk called in sick. Here's the deal. Ty's got some macho ego-trip regarding the dog. Actually, with all dogs; hence, the obsession with Hank's wolf. I've been training Doobie as best I can behind Ty's back, but there's only so much I can accomplish. Ty wants us to treat Doobie like a wild animal. The thing is, though, if this keeps up, Doobie's going to take a bite out of the next cookie-toting Girl Scout. Can you help us?"

I was so dumbfounded by the abrupt change in her demeanor that the question took a moment to register. "Frankly, I can't do all that much to train your dog without your husband's cooperation. I can get him to behave in my presence, but as soon as I leave, he'll revert to his old behaviors."

"You're referring to Doobie's behavior, not Ty's, right?"

"Right," I repeated, though my answer had been obvious. Even if I wanted to train her husband, a suggestion I found repulsive, the dog was certain to be a better student.

She pursed her lips and nodded, grabbing the doorknob. "I'll talk to him. Can you come back tomorrow, same time?"

"I guess so," I said, as she stepped inside her house.

Adopting her strung-out attitude once again, she slurred, "Outta sight. See ya then, babe." She winked at me and shut the door.

"I've stumbled into 'The Twilight Zone'," I muttered to myself, then headed toward Beverly's house, where I was now a few minutes late for lunch.

Why, I pondered during my short walk next door, had Beverly never mentioned to me that her next-door neighbors were sixties-hippy-wanna-bes? She and I had been getting reacquainted over the past couple of months, mostly through our being on the same softball team. A friend of mine had recruited me and then asked me if I knew of any good female pitchers, which had immediately brought Beverly Wood to mind; she'd been a terrific pitcher in high school.

Come to think of it, Beverly had been running a cute ad on the radio for her construction company. In a wordplay on her last name, the slogan was "Hit Nails, Miss Wood." She might know the production company that did the wolf commercials. I might be able to get the name of the wolf's owner after all.

Beverly was expecting me, and, in fact, was standing by the screen door, which she swung open for me.

"Allida, hi!" She swept me into a hug, which was a bit awkward, because when it comes to height, I'm a Dachshund to her Greyhound. I'd gotten to know Beverly when we were high school seniors together on our basketball team. At five-eleven, she was our center. At five feet, I was a guard, and earned my position by dribbling and passing, and shooting only when I was wide open. Not to mention my dogged defense.

Beverly had long curly strawberry-blond hair that I envied shamelessly, and angular but attractive features—blue eyes, a crooked nose. Today she was wearing some sort of an ankle-length cotton dress of an Indian pattern that looked as though it could have come from Ty's store. Her little dog, Beagle Boy, was barking away at me, but he stopped as soon as Bev released me. I knelt to greet him; he wagged his tail as I scratched him behind the ears. B.B., for short, was a typical Beagle—affectionate, curious, energetic, and with an outstanding sense of smell that led him to be highly distractible.

"Allida, what's going on next door? I didn't mean to eavesdrop on my neighbors, but there was quite a bit of shouting a little while ago. Were you involved?"

"Only peripherally," I said, rising, though her dog clearly would have gladly let me pet him forever.

"Figures. I never did know you to back down from a confrontation. Was that Hank who was shouting at Ty like that?"

"'Fraid so. Hank Atkinson thinks Doobie got his dog pregnant."

"Uh-oh. Hank's been planning to breed Sammy. That's just going to make things even worse between the two of them."

Assuming "the two of them" had meant Hank and Ty, I said, "If that's even possible. I wish you'd warned me how bad things were between them."

"Didn't I?" Beverly said. She grabbed my arm and gave it a squeeze. She always was the enthusiastic touchy-feely sort back in high school, and the years hadn't dimmed her spirit. "So did you talk to your mom yet about hiring me to remodel her kitchen?"

"Yes, but she says the kitchen is her least favorite room in the house, so—" I imitated my mother's low voice— "'why spruce it up and dupe people into spending time in it?' Sorry, Beverly. Once my mom makes up her mind, she practically never changes it."

"Nor does she want to change her kitchen. Ah, well. My business is doing fine. I was just hoping to crack the Berthoud market."

I had to laugh. "Oh, right. The big booming metropolis of Berthoud?" Berthoud was one of the few towns even remotely near Boulder that had remained small. At almost an hour's drive from downtown Boulder, it was too long of a commute for most folks.

She raised an eyebrow. "Hey, don't knock it. Small towns are the best. You do a good job in one person's kitchen, her neighbor hires you, and then another. Next thing you know, you've got more jobs from one small community than you could have gotten from an entire city."

"Hmm. Maybe I should be on the lookout for difficult dogs in Berthoud."

"Absolutely. And check out the condition of their kitchens for me, while you're at it. I can always use more customers wanting a kitchen makeover."

She led me into the dining room, where she had already set out an impressive luncheon spread. I'd seen deli bars with less selection, and I told her so.

"Oh, pish," she replied, patting me on the back for some reason. "This is all just leftovers from a brunch I hosted yesterday. We'd better eat up before E-Coli sets in."

"Well. On that note, Bon appetite."

She giggled. "Just make yourself a sandwich." Then she rubbed her hands in excitement. "So, Allida, we're finally alone. Tell me all about you and your cutie."

I hesitated, honestly having to piece together that she meant the man I was seeing and not one of my two dogs. "Russell Greene? He's very sweet, and I like him a lot, but we've only been going out seriously for a couple of months, and we still have a few problems to hash out."

"Problems?"

"For one thing, he hates dogs. He's afraid of Pavlov."

"Your German shepherd? Why? I thought you said she was really gentle."

"She is. But Russell's brother got attacked by a neighbor's German shepherd right in front of Russell when he was just a little boy. He's got quite a phobia, and he doesn't want to see anyone professionally about it. He thinks he can just get over it by himself."

"Have you slept together yet?"

The years hadn't softened Beverly's characteristic bluntness, either. Even my really close friends hadn't asked me that, but then, they knew me well enough to surmise the answer. "Not yet."

"Once you do, that'll motivate him right into therapy."

"Oh, thanks a lot!"

Beverly laughed heartily and gave my shoulders a squeeze. "I didn't mean it the way it sounded. I just meant that soon he'll do anything to keep you. So, what else is new?"

"I came face to face with a purebred wolf a few minutes ago."

"Over at Hank's place?"

"You knew about that?"

She nodded. "He told me about his plan to have white wolf-dog puppies."

While we spoke, I'd created a tasty-looking ensemble of a sandwich and took a seat. Beverly grabbed a huge handful of lettuce, wedged it between two slices of rye bread, and took the seat across from me. Beagle Boy attached more hopes to me and spillage from my meat combo than to his owner and her lettuce, and rested his chin on my feet.

I was mildly surprised that both Ty and now Beverly knew about Hank's wolf. After all, Hank had even hidden the wolf-handler's van in the garage. Although, now that I thought about it, he probably did so to prevent Larry Cunriff from having to walk the wolf up Hank's suburban sidewalk.

Beverly took a bite of her lettuce sandwich and, in between noisy chomps, said, "That's quite a wolf, isn't it? Belongs to this guy, Damian Hesk, who has a ranch east of I-twenty-five. He's got two other wolves, too."

"You know him?"

"Oh, sure. I've even been to his house."

This news captured my full attention and I scooted to the edge of my seat, anticipating deserting my sandwich to jot down an address. "Where does he live?"

"Quite a ways out east. He's got hundreds of acres out there. I've got his card around here someplace. I'll get it for you." She left the room, but called from around the corner, "One Saturday a month, he does tours for small groups, and Hank set one up for his neighbors. So a whole batch of us went last month."

"Probably not Ty Bellingham, though. He and Hank probably avoid each other, right?"

She returned with a business card, which I slipped into the breast pocket of my blouse. "Actually, they managed to set aside their differences long enough to both be there. Not that they spoke to each other. They didn't come to blows, in any case, which is something of a triumph."

How odd. Ty had said that he'd been "dying to see the wolf in person," and yet, apparently, he already had seen the wolf. "Does Damian own just wolves?"

"No, he's got a regular zoo license, just doesn't have his place open to the public. He also has lions, tigers, and bears."

"Oh, my," we said simultaneously, and chuckled.

My envy at the thought of "hundreds of acres" to keep numerous animals was making me greener than my host's sandwich. For now, all I could do was call Mr. Hesk and hope he'd be willing to show me his facility. Maybe he owned dogs, too, and I could work out some kind of a barter arrangement. It would be fascinating to see well-cared-for exotic animals, especially wolves.

"Do you know this Damian well enough to call him now and introduce me to him over the phone?"

She took another bite of lettuce and gave me an exaggerated shrug. "I guess. Thing is, though, he said he travels quite a bit on weekends, so I doubt he's home. He has a—"

She was interrupted by shouts from outside, in the direction of Ty's house. A woman was screaming, "I'll get you for this!"

Another murder threat?!

"Oh, crap." Beverly dropped her sandwich on her paper plate and hopped to her feet. "It's Paige Atkinson. That woman is not stable!" For some reason, Beverly not only leapt to attention, but charged out the door, leaving Beagle Boy yapping in her wake.

From what I'd seen of the neighbors so far, if Beverly singled out only Mrs. Atkinson as "not stable," the woman must be swinging from the trees. I followed Beverly out the front door.

Ty and his wife were out on their front lawn, confronting Hank and a woman I took to be Hank's wife, dressed in a peach-colored tailored suit. She grabbed a handful of Ty's long blond hair. In the blink of an eye, she had yanked the wig off Ty's and proceeded to whip him with it.

"Paige! Stop!" Beverly yelled.

At the sound of Beverly's outcry, Hank's wife froze. With Ty still cowering, hunched over to protect himself, Paige turned in our direction.

"You!" she cried, pointing at Beverly. "You whore! Get out of my sight!"

It was all I could do to keep silent rather than speak up on my friend's behalf, but she gave me a slight headshake, so I bit my lip. Meanwhile, Paige threw Ty's hairpiece onto the ground and whirled back around to face Ty. "We're going to sue you for every last lava lamp you own! Then we're going to have that rotten dog of yours neutered, whether you like it or not!"

"You'll touch Doobie over my dead body!" Ty yelled. He glanced back at his house, where Doobie's muffled barks were rattling the window.

"Suit yourself!" Paige marched back to the sidewalk, nose in the air.

During all of this, Hank was merely watching his wife assault their neighbor and didn't raise a finger to stop her.

Cheshire, too, had remained a passive audience, but now that the fight was over, she sauntered to Ty's side. "Wow, man. She was like, totally whacked. Are you all right, babe?"

"Fine." He looked much better without his wig. In fact, if he were in normal attire, he might even be a handsome man. Ty retrieved the silly looking hairpiece and slapped it back on his head. His cheeks were bright red and his expression was one of barely suppressed rage. "Show's over, everyone." He re-centered the wig, which I couldn't help but notice had the peace headband sewed on as a permanent attachment, then he stormed inside his house.

Chesh looked back over at us, flashed us the peace sign, and followed her husband inside.

Hank, meanwhile, tried to throw his arm around his wife, who shoved him aside and marched ahead of him. "I told you this whole idea of breeding Sammy to a wolf was stupid!" she snarled at him. "Now look what you made me do!"

Ty came back out onto the porch, holding a snarling and all-but-rabid-acting Doobie by the collar. "Hey, Hank! You and your wife ever ambush me like that again, and you're dog meat!"

Chapter 4

Paying no attention to Beverly or me, Ty pulled his dog back inside and slammed his door. Still only halfway to their own house, Hank and his wife froze. Hank's face had paled such that it lost most of its tan. He smoothed his mustache, staring after Ty, then met my eyes and pointed at me. "You're my witness." He and Paige walked home, the swagger now absent from Hank's gait.

My stomach fell. I had visions of my business going up in smoke, the spoils of war between the neglectful owners of a Samoyed and that of a former stray, egged into being dangerous so that his owner could feel like a big man.

I looked at Beverly, expecting her to voice her reaction to her neighbors' bizarre behavior. Her cheeks had colored, but she turned away without another word and headed back inside her home. I trotted after her. She held the door for me, but then merely reclaimed her seat and continued to eat her lettuce sandwich as if nothing had happened.

I followed Beverly's lead and resumed eating my lunch, but my stomach remained in knots. I mentally paged back through all the conversations I'd had with Beverly since I'd returned to Colorado five months ago. All she'd ever said about her neighbors was that their dogs' barking had become a major nuisance. I could maybe see her not mentioning to me that these people had peculiar tastes in apparel and furnishings. Perhaps neglecting to mention that they and their other neighbors were in the habit of threatening to kill one another. However, I was utterly perplexed as to why Beverly never thought to say, "Oh, by the way. One of my neighbors tends to refer to me as a whore. Pay her no mind. She's a little unstable. Also, this dog that you're about to work with is being trained as a man-eater, so you might need to be careful."

"You and Paige Atkinson don't get along?" I asked as casually as I could.

Beverly shrugged. "She's obsessively jealous and can't stand the fact that her husband's living near an unmarried woman. She assumes that every woman who exchanges a friendly word with a man is trying to get him into the sack."

"Why do you allow her to treat you that way, without so much as a word of protest?"

Again, she shrugged and did not meet my gaze. "I feel sorry for her. Imagine what a horrible life she must have to be incapable of believing men and women can even be friendly acquaintances, let alone friends. She's just not worth the effort."

"And yet she was worth the effort to rush outside and try to break up a fight between her and your six-foot-tall male neighbor?"

Once again, Beverly's cheeks reddened. She pushed a stray lock of reddish-blond hair away from her forehead. "She's crazy, and there's so much bad blood between her and Ty, I'm always afraid it's going to...splatter over onto me."

I grimaced at the image her words brought to mind. Although her explanation made some sense, it struck me as only a partial truth. She'd felt no need to intercede when she heard Hank and Ty shouting at one another. Maybe guilt had motivated her into action during Paige's outburst. Beverly was well aware of how attractive she was and had been something of a flirt in high school. Perhaps Paige's jealousy was not without cause. She'd been divorced for five years now and claimed that she'd sworn off marriage, but not men.

"Beverly, I have a certain liability here. As Hank Atkinson put it, I witnessed Ty threatening to let his dog attack Hank. And as a dog behaviorist, I'm in a position to know how dangerous a—"

Beverly was already shaking her head. "Ty is all bark and no bite. He'd never actually sic Doobie on anyone. I got to know him somewhat when I was doing his kitchen."

"You remodeled his kitchen?"

Nodding, she polished off the last of her lettuce sandwich. "That was a tough job. Try getting all-modern appliances in an avocado color these days. And, see, since their divorce—"

"Since whose divorce?"

"Paige's and Ty's." Her eyes widened as she looked at me. "Didn't I tell you?"

I shook my head. "Obviously, that piece of information would have stuck with me."

She blinked a couple of times, letting this omission of hers register. "No wonder you're so confused. Their hatred toward one another must have seemed completely nutty, without knowing that they used to be married."

Apparently, one should come to expect "nutty" behavior from former spouses. "So Paige used to be Ty's wife, and then she remarried and moved right next door to her ex?"

"Hank and his first wife got a divorce a few years back. She got the kids and their vacation house up in Vail. He got the house in Boulder. And, I guess, when he and Paige decided to marry, he wanted to stay put."

That must be the "personal history" that Ty had referred to as unrelated to four-legged dogs. "No wonder the two men don't get along." It also went a long way toward explaining why Paige Atkinson was willing to beat Ty Bellingham over the head with his hairpiece, ostensibly all because of a pregnant dog. "So, you felt you needed to defend Ty from his ex-wife? Why?"

She pursed her lips and said nothing.

"Beverly, it feels to me like you're sitting on top of a powder keg here. While I was standing right next to him, Hank threatened to kill Ty. And we both heard Ty's threats toward Hank just now. What if you're wrong about Ty's making good on his words?"

"I'm not," she said firmly, refilling her iced tea. She winced a little as she set down the glass pitcher, then massaged her shoulder through the fabric of her Indian-print dress. "Ty Bellingham talks before he thinks. We've had our share of problems in the six years we've lived next door to each other, not to mention the arguments that erupted when I was doing his remodeling. But believe me, Allida, Ty loves Doobie more than anything. He'd never risk letting his dog bite someone and wind up getting put to sleep."

I wished I could share my friend's confidence on that last point, but what I'd seen so far of Ty Bellingham told me she was giving him too much credit for self-control. "If Ty does sic that dog of his on Hank, somebody's going to get very badly hurt. Personally, I don't want to get caught in the middle, and I don't want you to be, either."

She reached over and patted my hand. "This will all blow over, eventually."

"Maybe, but so do tornadoes, and they do a lot of damage in the process."

Beverly made no comment. Why was I having such a hard time getting through to her? She was staring forlornly at the wall in the direction of Ty's house. A worry popped into my head, which I hoped was unfounded: Was she in love with Ty Bellingham and blind to his glaring faults?

"Have you been dating anyone lately?" I asked.

She chuckled and batted her eyes. "No, why? Got any guys in mind for me?" She leaned back in her chair.

"Actually, I just gave you the number of the best-looking eligible man I've met in ages."

It took me a moment to decipher this statement. "Damian Hesk?"

She nodded. "I did some of my very best flirting with that man, but he showed no interest. Apparently he's only attracted to furry four-leggers."

Just then, somebody opened the front door without knocking. A female voice called, "You ready to go, Bev?"

Beverly pushed back from the table and hopped to her feet. "Oh, shoot. I lost track of the time. Come on in, Rebecca."

A pretty woman entered, the lines in her face and freckles indicating too much time spent in the sun. She wore dust-covered overalls and a T-shirt, her long, wavy brown hair pulled into a pony tail. Her pleasant features were unadorned with makeup. She clicked her tongue when she saw Beverly. "You're not even dressed, yet."

Feeling awkward at being the only one still seated, I wiped my hands on my napkin and got to my feet. I had the feeling that Rebecca's arrival meant lunch was over.

"I know," Beverly replied. "Our lunch got interrupted by a fracas next door."

Her features tightened. "At Bellingham's?" Without waiting for an answer she muttered under her breath, "I hate that guy."

A pained expression passed across Beverly's features. "This is Allie Babcock." She swept her hand in the direction of her new guest. "This is my business partner, Rebecca Henders."

She gave me a big smile and shook my hand, her own surprisingly strong. Her nails were so short they must have been chewed off. "You're that dog psychologist Beverly told me was going to be working with the shitheads in her neighborhood."

"Rebecca!" Beverly scolded.

Her smile fading, Rebecca turned to Beverly and said, "But that's exactly what they are. That Ty Bellingham is an abusive bastard. He treats his wife worse than his dog. And after what he—"

"Rebecca!" Beverly said again under her breath, casting a sideways glance my way.

She stopped abruptly and gave me a sheepish smile. "Sorry. I need to keep my opinions about these things to myself."

"About what things?" I asked.

Rebecca furrowed her brow, then looked at Beverly, and said with a shrug, "About other people's obnoxious neighbors." Her cheeks colored and she stepped back. "Listen, Bev, I'm gonna go wait for you in the truck. It was nice meeting you, Allie."

"Nice meeting you, too," I replied, puzzled. The unpleasant thought that my old friend might have set me up somehow were starting to tug at me. I watched Rebecca leave, then immediately turned to Beverly, who was already well into the process of clearing the table. "Beverly, is it my imagination, or was she about to accidentally blurt out something you didn't want me to hear?"

Beverly flinched ever so slightly and turned back to face me, her arms full of sandwich supplies. "It's nothing personal," she said gently. With a slight toss of her head, she indicated I was to follow her into the kitchen, and she led the way into a room of cherry, slate, and brass that could shame the kitchen of a five-star restaurant.

"Ty and Rebecca had some serious disagreements over the quality of her work on his kitchen project," she explained. "I wound up having to redo the job at no charge. It causes nothing but friction whenever Rebecca insists on bringing the subject up." She stashed the food in the refrigerator, then turned to face me and gave me a sad smile. "I've got to go change into my work clothes. Allida, I'm so sorry. I don't normally work on Saturdays, but we ran past our completion date on one job, and if we don't finish it now, we'll be late starting the next one, and on it goes. One big line of uncompleted dominoes."

"Oh, it's fine. I've got another house call to make myself." Which was true, but did nothing to address the bigger problem here; thanks to Beverly's referral I'd found myself with a hornet's nest firmly planted on one foot.

She walked me to the door. I stopped and searched Beverly's features. What I saw there was simply the face of someone I truly liked. She probably did have a "thing" for Ty Bellingham, hard as that was to understand. But that really didn't affect me. If there was anything seriously amiss between her and the Bellinghams, Ty would never have taken Beverly's suggestion to hire me. That is, not unless he was so intent on getting revenge against her, he wanted his dog to eat her friend alive. But that was just being downright paranoid.

"Thanks so much for lunch, Bev."

She smiled. "We'll have to do this more often, now that you're going to be in the neighborhood anyway."

And a fine neighborhood it was, I thought sourly. "Thanks also for the referral. At least, I guess I should be thanking you."

Her typical friendliness returning, she gave me a hug. "See you tonight."

"Tonight?"

"At softball. You are coming, aren't you?"

"Absolutely." Witnessing these altercations today had affected my mental calendar; I was normally reliable, not scatterbrained about my commitments. With just a couple of weeks left in the season, our team was undefeated, which was saying something. Softball was popular in Boulder and quite competitive.

Beverly opened the door for me. "Don't worry, Allie. My neighbors have their minor eccentricities, but are perfectly harmless."

Perfectly harmless. Those were the same words Larry Cunriff had used to describe his wolf. And I was equally skeptical about Beverly's neighbors.

I made a decision. Tomorrow I would make a thorough evaluation of Doobie, and of Ty and Cheshire's ability to control him. If I still felt there was a serious possibility of someone getting hurt, I would notify animal control immediately. It would break my heart to play such a key role if the end result was that Doobie was put to sleep, but I would have no choice if Ty was unwilling to rein in Doobie's deadly potential.

The Atkinsons probably didn't need me to warn them off of Doobie in the meantime, but there was no sense in taking chances. I trotted past my car and knocked on their door. This time, no wolf greeted me, but rather, Paige Atkinson. She flung her inner door open, put her hands on her hips, stared at me through the screen and demanded, "What?"

The wolf had been more pleasant.

"Mrs. Atkinson, we haven't been introduced. I'm—"

"I know who you are and what you do for a living. Why are you here?" Up close, I couldn't help but notice how oddly shaped her nose was. It was thin until just above the nostrils, where it rounded out noticeably. Not unlike the long, skinny beakers we would heat over Bunsen burners in high school chemistry labs.

"I just wanted to make sure you understood not to take Ty Bellingham's threat about his dog too lightly. I'm going to—"

"Oh, please!" Paige said, giving her dark hair a haughty flip. "That dog is every bit as impotent as his owner. He'd never actually attack a human being." She looked me up and down. "I'm surprised that, as a dog psychologist, you couldn't recognize that for yourself. You musn't be very good at your job."

She shut the door on me.

Chapter 5

"I hate these people!" I said under my breath as I marched down the sidewalk to my car. Poor Beverly, having to live in this neighborhood! And to think, she'd summoned me because of a barking dog. Noisy animals were one thing, a minor irritant that can be resolved. Bitter, hateful humans were quite another matter. Beverly's house may be lovely, large, and expensive, but give me my mom and her little ranch-style house out in the sticks of Berthoud any day.

As I got into my car, I glanced toward the mountains, where huge gray clouds now loomed, rapidly overtaking the sky. My appointment was on the southwest side of Boulder with a seven-year-old yellow Labrador named, ironically enough, Sunshine, who was afraid of thunder. This fairly common problem is one of the hardest behavior problems to cure, and Boulder has more thunderstorms than any place in the country. To make things worse, Devil's Thumb, the pricey neighborhood in the foothills where this Labrador was located, tended to get the very worst of the storm fronts. Last fall, Sunshine had been in the room when a windstorm had caused one of their large picture windows to implode. Since then, Sunshine had jumped through windows twice, desperately and blindly trying to "escape" from the storm.

I arrived at Sunshine's house and spoke to her sweet, elderly owners. As I'd predicted, the desensitization program we were using was meeting with only partial success. I'd given Sunshine's owners an audio tape of thunderstorms, which they were playing at increasing volumes, counterconditioning Sunshine by offering her treats when the taped noises began. We needed a good month or two without full exposure to a storm for the treatment to work, but we didn't have that luxury. I'd decided to try a homeopathic treatment as well and came armed today with phosphorous pellets.

A thunderstorm began just a few minutes after I arrived. Sunshine went berserk, and her owners opted for the pellets. I showed them how to drop the pellets into the back of Sunshine's throat, the important aspect being to "wear gloves when handling the phosphorous" and "radiate confidence" when handling the dog. Sunshine was drooling and an emotional wreck after the first dose, but calmed down after the second.

By the end of our appointment, Sunshine's owners were singing my praises—enthusiasm which I tempered with warnings about relapses and a rehash of instructions for how they should do this on their own next time.

As I pushed out the door, they thanked me profusely, which normally made me feel better than it did now. Although the storm front had passed and the sky was clearing, my mind was clouded with thoughts of Doobie and Sammy, and with the inexplicable behaviors of their human counterparts.

By now, I had so many things to think about that my head was spinning. Next I wanted to drop into my office and call Damian Hesk, even if I'd only be able to leave a message. No doubt, my tattle-telling wouldn't sit well with Hank Atkinson, but then, his breeding a wolf without the owner's knowledge didn't sit well with *me*.

To my surprise, Russell Greene was leaning against my cherry-red Subaru. His Volvo was directly behind my car, which I'd parked in the circle a short distance from my clients' home. I wasn't expecting to see him and had no idea how he'd found me here.

I'd become more and more physically attracted to Russell over the last several weeks that we'd been dating. I now thought of him as possessing a "compact" build, rather than his being short—and my being guilty of the pot calling the kettle black. He was five-six, with shiny dark brown eyes and hair, and he'd recently shaved his mustache, after I'd told him that I wasn't especially fond of it. He was wearing dark shorts and Birkenstocks, and a light yellow Izod shirt, but he'd stitched a cloth Band-Aid over the alligator. Although he'd explained to me the last time he wore this shirt that the Band-Aid was to avoid the preppy look, to me it just looked as if he were announcing an injured nipple. But it was his shirt, not mine.

"Surprise," he said by way of greeting.

"Hi. Weren't you going to go rock-climbing this afternoon?" This was an avid hobby of his that held no interest for me, but then, my acrophobia balanced my love for dogs, which he did not share. His loss, of course.

He looped his arms around my waist and kissed me. I felt the familiar and wonderful stirrings and quickening of my heartbeat whenever he held me. "Yeah, but I cancelled. It's our three-month anniversary. I thought we'd get an early start celebrating."

"Three months?"

"Since our first date. Remember? The basketball game in Denver?"

"Of course I remember.' I ran my hands over the bumpy fabric of his shirt, taking care to avoid the Band-Aid, and teased, "The Nuggets won easily. The final score was ninety-eight to seventy-six."

He chuckled and brushed an errant lock of hair back from my forehead. "And is that all you remember about our first date?"

I shrugged. "What else was there? Like the fact you were wearing jeans, a white Oxford shirt, and a red tie? That you bought me a hot dog, popcorn and a flat Pepsi? That you impressed me with how insightful you were as we discussed why we were both still single? That you wanted to meet my cocker spaniel afterwards and were appalled when I told you that I also own a German shepherd?"

He merely chuckled again, his eyes riveted to mine, his breath warm against my cheeks.

"Who notices stuff like that?" I continued. "I was just into watching the game."

"I see." Russell was still smiling, but for the first time in my recent memory, he was blushing. He dropped his gaze, which drew my attention to his sexy, thick lashes, and said shyly, "So, can I maybe convince you to come over to my place now? We've got six hours till our softball game tonight, and that might be just enough time for what I have in mind."

Automatically, I stiffened and pulled away slightly. It was all I could do not to blurt out an "Oh, shit!" at Russell's unfortunate timing. We'd discussed the fact that neither of us were the bed-hopping type, and, furthermore, I'd told Russell straight out that I would never sleep with someone I wasn't also seriously considering spending my life with, which was why I'd had only two lovers and was single at age thirty-two. Such an old-fashioned stance tends to cut down on one's repeat dates. But Russell was such a great guy and had been so loving toward me that lately, I'd recently admitted to myself that I might be ready. Soon. Just not now when I had my mind full of wolves and potentially vicious dogs.

Russell studied my expression, and his face fell. "I knew you'd say no."

"I'm not saying no. I'm just saying not yet. I can't right now. I've still got a lot of work to do."

"Really?" His tone sounded disbelieving. "Because I called your mother, and she told me this was your last appointment for the day."

"Since when did you stop taking me at my word and start double-checking with my mother?" I straightened and grabbed my keys out of the front pocket of my dark blue slacks. "It's true that I don't have any more appointments, but I do have phone calls to make, and I need to put my thoughts together regarding a new client."

"I could go back to the office with you and wait."

Though he was an electrical engineer and our professions were vastly different, we shared an office suite in downtown Boulder. That was how we'd met. Last April, I'd answered his ad for office space in the Boulder Daily Camera.

"That would be too distracting. I'd better go. I'll see you at the softball game." He looked so disappointed, it was painful to meet his gaze. My annoyance with him instantly evaporated. "Sorry, Russ. It's been a weird day."

"Plus, you don't want to share your troubles with me. Whenever things go wrong for you, you pull into yourself and push me away."

I hesitated, unsure of how to respond. Wait a minute. Wasn't it supposed to be the guy-thing to withdraw within one's cave and the gal-thing to want to talk endlessly about feelings? If this was "life as a guy," it was no fun. Nor was the female's role of feeling shut out. This is why I prefer communicating with dogs, rather than people. Dogs live in the moment. People aren't even necessarily experiencing their current location or whomever they're with, let alone the particular moment in time.

"Russell," I began, my voice even to my own ear much sterner than I'd intended, "it's the middle of the afternoon, and weekends are my busiest time. I just...wasn't expecting to see you so soon. I'm sure if I followed you to one of your meetings with your clients, you'd feel the same way."

"No, I wouldn't. I'd be thrilled. But you just don't feel the same way about me that I do about you."

Oh, damn it all! I was thrilled. Not in the set-off-firecrackers, throw-me-on-the-floor way, but still. Did I have to explain myself? Right when I was looking at possible lawsuits myself as the "trainer" of a borderline killer dog? "Don't do this right now, Russell. Please."

The muscles in Russell's jaw were working. "I'm crowding you, aren't I? Sorry. You'd think I'd learn."

He threw open his car door, got in, then drove off without another word.

I got into my car and headed back to my office, alone. What had just happened here? Was this my fault? Had Russ backed me into a corner that I was defending just as vociferously as the Samoyed?

Maybe it had just been too long between romances for me. Everything felt so forced and out of sync all of a sudden.

After an hour in my office, all I had to show for it was one phone call to Damian Hesk—I'd left a message on his machine—and a lot of pointless ruminating. I'd tried to call various dog-rescue places in Nevada as well, but gave up after ten minutes on hold at the third attempt. Truth is, I wanted to keep my phone line open, just in case Russell called, having already gotten his machine several times.

There was something to be said for the canine style of this whole mating ritual. Sammy could just back her rear end against a wall and tell Kaia, "Hey. I don't care if you're a wolf. You're too late, buster." And you certainly weren't going to see her pining that "Doobie never calls. He never brings me flowers." Nor, for that matter, do female dogs go eight years or so till they finally choose to send out some come-hither signals.

The phone rang. I snatched up the handset as the first ring had barely sounded. The moment I said hello, a distraught woman's voice said, "Allida? Thank God. This is Beverly. Some terrible dog fight is going on next door. Please come help."

"A dog fight?" I repeated, rising and grabbing my keys. "In Ty's yard?"

"No, inside their house. At least, I think that's what's happening. I don't know for sure. There are all these...snarls and whines. I heard shouts, too."

"Shouts? Do you think Ty is home?"

"I don't know." Beverly was so upset, I could barely understand her, but she continued, "Cheshire's van is gone. I tried to call over there, but there was no answer. Maybe I should go knock on the door."

If Ty was in the midst of some dog fight between Doobie and some other unfortunate canine, I doubted he'd take the time to answer the door. "I'll get out there as fast as I can, but by then, it'll probably be over." Dog fights usually only last a few minutes. I hung up, grabbed two of my sturdiest leads and choke collars, and bolted through the door and into my car.

I drove as fast as I could without being a menace, all the while wondering what I hoped to accomplish. Even if the fight was still going on by the time I arrived, it was extremely risky to try to break up a dog fight. Invariably, the person gets badly bitten in the process, and if both dogs were large, I'd be physically unable to separate them. The best course of action was to startle the dogs—drop a platter right next to them—and work like mad to get the dogs separated and under control in the second or two that followed.

When I pulled into the driveway, Paige Atkinson was pacing on the Bellinghams' front porch. Still wearing her peach-colored pants suit, she rushed toward me as I got of my car, bringing the leashes with me. "You need to go in there! A few minutes ago, I think I heard Ty cry for help!"

"Did you call the police?"

She shook her head, all the while sputtering, "I didn't know what to do. Then Beverly told me you were on your way." It was surprising that these two women could even communicate that much to each other, but Paige continued without hesitation, "She's waiting for you by Ty's back door. Something's terribly wrong. I think Sammy might be in there."

"Your Samoyed? But how can that be? She can't jump the fence in her condition."

"Nevertheless, she's missing."

"Is Hank home?"

"No."

"Are you certain he didn't take the dog with him?"

"No, but he was so upset today, he said he was going to bring her over to the Bellinghams'. That they could take care of her and the pups till they were born."

What an idiot! This couple deserved one another! "I'll see what I can do." There were no noises whatsoever emanating from inside the house now. "How long has it been quiet like this?"

She gestured at me to hurry to the back yard. "I don't know! Just get Sammy out of there!"

The heck with my ex-husband; just save my dog. I opened the gate and trotted around the house to the backyard. I understood the sentiment, but for heaven's sake! She'd heard the man call for help!

Beverly was sitting on the redwood deck by the dog door, rocking herself, her face drained of all color. "Beverly? Are you all right?"

She shook her head. "I can't fit through the dog door. There's blood everywhere. Fight's over. I keep hearing this noise. Whining and scratching sounds. I think one of the dogs got locked in a closet."

"That means somebody has to be home." I had visions of Ty Bellingham badly injured and collapsing as he finally managed to get one of the dogs closed off in a separate room. If one dog was in a closet, a second dog could be loose and in a crazed state, and might attack the first person who went inside.

Beverly shook her head, still apparently in shock. She was wearing work boots, shorts, and an orange blouse over her T-shirt that made her unkempt blond hair look reddish. "Paige and I were banging on both doors. Nobody answered."

"What about the shouts you heard? Paige said she thought she heard a man cry for help a little while ago. Ty could be in there, passed out from blood loss."

She just shook her head again. "All that blood."

I was really losing my patience. "Did you call the police, Beverly? Didn't anybody call the police?"

My question snapped Beverly out of her numbed state. "Paige told me she was calling! Just before I came back here and tried to get through the dog door."

"She told me she didn't call!" I cried in exasperation. "Damn it! Ty could be in there bleeding to death while we're out here bickering about whose going to call nine-one-one! I'll go in and use Ty's phone!"

I pushed the little plastic flap fully open. From my position flat on the deck, I could see that there were indeed blood splatters all over the kitchen floor, which grew ever denser farther from the door. My vision, however, was blocked by the kitchen island.

Keeping a tight grip on the dog leashes, I got my arms, head, and finally shoulders through the door, which was a tight fit, the thick fabric of my teal-colored T-shirt snagging in the process. I needed to move quickly. I was absolutely defenseless in this position and would look like prey to a dog inside. This was as risky an entrance as I could possibly make. As Beverly had described, I could now clearly hear the sounds of a dog straining to escape some inner confines of the house.

While I was halfway in, Beverly said, "Allida. Be careful."

I made it inside and stood up, surveying the gruesome scene around me with as much detachment as I could muster. Blood splatters and paw prints had come from the other side of the kitchen island. Almost unwillingly, I followed the crimson trail toward the beaded entranceway. I had to grab onto the countertop for support at the horrific vision at its other side. I had never seen so much blood in my life, and I felt woozy.

It was Ty. He was now wearing a long black wig instead of his blond one. He was bare chested and barefoot, wearing only his bell-bottoms. He was on his side, curled in the fetal position. His exposed cheek sported three bright red, finger-wide marks that appeared to be grease paint. It was as if Ty's features had been graced with Indian war paint.

I steeled myself as best I could with the intention of feeling for his carotid artery, but I realized it was too late. Ty was dead. His throat had been slit.

Chapter 6

Against my will, I studied Ty's body, horrified and yet mesmerized. Part of me was screaming that my eyes were playing tricks, that if I looked hard enough, the horror would be exposed as some elaborate Halloween-style hoax.

This was crazy. Ty's arms and chest were covered with scars, as well as by fresh claw and bite marks. Ty's pants were ripped in numerous places, the accompanied jagged wounds there all too apparent. Yet the cuts on his fingers were straight lines, as if he'd defended himself against the knife-wielder.

How could Ty be dead—stabbed to death, I was certain—yet wounded from bites and claw marks all over his body? Had he been attacked by Doobie, closed him up in a closet, then gotten stabbed to death in his kitchen? That made no sense. The scars on his arms appeared to be healed bite wounds.

"Allida?" Beverly called. "Is everything all right?"

That had to be the stupidest question I'd ever heard. "No, it's Ty. He's dead."

Beverly shouted, "Paige. Why didn't you call the police! Allida's in there, and she says Ty is dead."

"Oh, my God!" Paige cried. "I'll go call now. I thought my dog might be inside. I didn't want the police to shoot her."

What was wrong with these people? What kind of an idiot hears a dog growling, a man cry for help, and phones a dog psychologist instead of the police! A better question: What kind of an idiot dog psychologist enters a house under these circumstances?

I spotted an old-fashioned black phone on the wall on the other side of Ty's body. The telephone cord below it had been cut. Ty was beyond help, and I needed to get out of here. There could still be a second dog, who at this moment might be on the other side of whatever door the locked-in dog was behind.

I started to head for the back door, but my vision grayed. I closed my eyes for a moment, willing myself to summon the strength to leave this horrible place without vomiting or passing out.

Just then I heard a rumbling growl, coming from the direction of the living room. Oh, good Lord! Was this Doobie? I whirled around toward the sound.

It was a wolf.

I gasped, feeling my blood turn to ice water.

The wolf considered the body his kill. That also meant he was worried I might steal it from him. I had to get away from Ty's body.

"Twenty feet" popped into my head—some obscure fact about the distance wild animals instinctively registered as a sufficient distance for other animals to maintain. Or was it twenty yards? Meters?

My heart in my throat, I backed away from Ty and from the wolf, being careful not to look him straight in the eye, which the wolf would take as a direct challenge. Crap! If anyone ever needed a bigger kitchen, this was the time. This room was too small to allow me the distance I needed from Ty's body.

Petrified, I backed to the opposite corner of the kitchen, along the same wall as the door, bumping into the refrigerator. Still facing the wolf, I smoothly boosted myself up on the counter. The wolf could easily leap up here after me. I could only pray that he wouldn't.

The wolf was still standing in the beaded entranceway of the kitchen. If he'd flown to the attack immediately, I'd be history. He had to have been checking out whatever door Doobie was behind till he heard me in the kitchen.

I struggled to keep from panicking—to think of a means of escape. I would have to get down on the floor and flatten myself to make it out the dog door. Might as well make a general announcement that I was wolf bait. Nor could I make it to another room in the house. Wolves can run some forty miles an hour, and there was no chance of my sneaking out the doorway when that damned beaded curtain started clacking.

The wolf took a couple of silent steps toward me, his muscles moving in perfect coordination. I was about to die at the claws and jaws of a graceful, beautiful animal. Small consolation. This wolf had a slightly darker coat and was smaller than Kaia—but I wouldn't want to stake my life on my belief that this was a different wolf from the one I'd met. Was this wolf domesticated?

Doobie, in the meantime, was making a relentless racket from the other room. I had no idea if this was going to drive the wolf into a greater frenzy or, with the possibility of Doobie making a flank attack, distract the wolf from attacking me.

The wolf padded closer. I flattened myself against the cabinets. A growl rumbled in his chest. His muscles were primed to spring at me.

"Allida?" Beverly called, pushing open the dog door a crack. "Are you coming out?"

The wolf started to head toward the dog door. I couldn't let him get out! He'd dash through that opening and maul Beverly before she had any idea what hit her!

"Get back, Bev!" I hollered. "Block the dog door!"

I had the two sturdy choke collars in my hand, which would do me no good as long as the wolf was set to attack me. If I could get the lead on him, I might be able to stop him from heading through the dog door.

"What's going on?" Beverly yelled, but also let the dog door swing shut behind her.

"There's a wolf in here!" My hands were shaking so badly I dropped one leash. I crouched down on the counter and, with trembling hands, managed to loop the leash through the facing handles of the side-by-side refrigerator/freezer.

In the seconds that this action took, the wolf growled at me. He seemed torn by competing instincts, by judging who was the greater threat to steal his prey—me or Beverly on the other side of the dog door. He took the triangular approach and trotted over to Ty's body, keeping menacing yellow eyes on both me and the dog door.

Growling and in a stealth-like crouch, the wolf darted back toward me. I stood up again, still on the counter.

Dear Lord, help me! How could I have been so stupid as to get myself into this mess!

Beverly called again, her voice choked with emotion, "Allie! I can't just leave you in there alone with a wild animal! Tell me what to do!"

As she spoke, the wolf paced in a small circle between the door, the body and me. He was extremely agitated, panting and salivating. The other animal locked in a back room was now making more noise, too. I didn't know how Beverly could help me and was afraid my answering would spur the wolf into taking the offensive.

The police would be here soon. If this wolf was domesticated, I might be able to wait this out. If not and the wolf attacked, he could quickly shred me. Plus, Paige had already lied once about contacting the police.

I scanned the room. I needed a net, a tranquilizer gun, and a steel cage. Beside me were a blender and a toaster. There was a butcher knife on the counter above Ty's body. Even if I could reach that—which I couldn't from here—I didn't like my chances of fending off this wolf with a knife.

I had to tilt things for the wolf in favor of the dog door, while still allowing Beverly to keep it shut. "Beverly! Count to ten, then throw something through the door, and brace it shut again."

I said a silent prayer. My heart was pounding so hard it felt as though my chest would explode. My hands were trembling terribly. I made as big of a noose-like circle with the collar of the tethered leash as I could, holding it open before me with trembling hands. My throat was the bait that would tighten the noose, and heaven only could help me now.

The wolf sprang toward me.

Just then, Beverly hollered, "Ten!" Her shoe came flying through the entrance and whacked against a cupboard, sounding like a gunshot.

It's too late, I thought.

And yet the wolf flinched a little and hesitated in his charge toward me. I slung the noose over his head and threw myself out of his path, staggering sideways along the counter.

He snarled and snapped at me, but the leash held, keeping him tied to the refrigerator.

"I'm coming out," I cried and dove through the dog door and was soon panting beside Beverly, who was all set to whap me with her other shoe. When she saw it was me and not the wolf, she dropped her shoe.

"What the hell happened?" she cried as I struggled to get to my knees. She grabbed hold of me by the upper arms and shook me. "What was a wolf doing in Ty's house?"

"I don't know! I wouldn't have gone in there if I'd known he was there!"

"Did the wolf kill Ty?"

"No. He was stabbed."

The full realization of what I'd just seen and experienced hit me full force. I felt nauseated, dizzy with fear. If that wolf had been fully set on attacking me, I never could have survived.

Someone had unlocked Ty's dog door. The same person who'd stabbed him? Who'd put the wolf in the house? I'd come so close to getting mauled! "Thanks, Beverly. You saved my life."

I flinched automatically as the gate flew open. Paige came running up to us. "I called nine-one-one," Paige said. I must have looked as horrible as I felt, for her jaw dropped when she saw me. "What happened in there?" she asked.

Hank Atkinson came sprinting through the gate after her. "Are you women all right?"

Their pregnant Samoyed trotted along behind them on a long leash.

"We found Sammy," Paige said, giving me a weak smile as she pushed a handful of brown hair behind her ear. "Just like you said, she was with Hank all along."

"Never mind about the damned dog!" Beverly yelled at Paige. "Where are the police! Why aren't they here yet?"

"For God's sake, Beverly! I just called them thirty seconds ago!"

In the background, I heard the screech of tires as someone threw on the brakes. Meanwhile, Beverly gaped at Paige and cried, "Thirty seconds ago? What are you talking about! You left here at least five minutes ago and you said that—"

Hank interrupted, "Beverly, please calm down. If Ty's dead, who cares if the police are here in five minutes or in fifteen?" Hank, I noticed, had changed clothes since I'd last seen him. He was now wearing gray sweatpants and a T-shirt.

Beverly was angrier than I'd ever seen her. She towered over Paige Atkinson, who backed up in the face of her fury. "Allida was nearly killed by a wolf! Whatever problems you might have with me, you had no right to—"

"Hank?" The male voice came from the other side of the fence. The gate banged open, and a man I'd never seen before approached. Probably another neighbor.

Great. The troops had arrived after the fact and were determined to start up another war.

"Damian," Hank said. "I thought you were out of town."

I did a double-take. This was the wolf's owner. He was in his late thirties or so and had such a large, muscular build he even dwarfed Hank's powerful frame. He had a cleft in his chin and wore tight-fitting jeans and yellow T-shirt. His hair was light brown on the sides and sun-bleached on the top.

"I was, but I checked my phone messages and turned around," he said. "Someone named Allida Babcock left me a message about you and my wolf. Now I can't find Larry Cunriff anywhere, and Atla is missing."

"Atla?" he repeated.

"My wolf! She's missing!" He looked angry enough to flatten Hank with one punch. "She's my least well-mannered animal. She's not used to being around humans. She's dangerous. Do you have her?"

"Of course I don't have—"

"She's in there," I said. All along, I'd assumed the wolf was a he, but then, I'd had other things on my mind than checking for the wolf's gender.

"In someone's house?" Damian hollered.

"She's tied to the handles of the refrigerator. I don't know how long that will hold, though."

"Christ!" He knelt and pushed at the doggie door. "I can't fit through that door." He rocked back on his knees and pointed at me. "You! Get in there and unlock the door! I need to get my wolf in a cage before she or someone else gets hurt."

"Too late for that," Hank said. "Seems your wolf already killed Ty Bellingham."

"Oh, Jesus," Damian murmured. He grabbed both of my shoulders. His blue eyes seemed to see right through me. "Please, just let me inside the house so I can try and get her out of there! If I have to break a window, she might go completely berserk."

He was right. "I'll crawl through and unlock the door for you."

I got down on my elbows and knees to crawl through the small dog door. I couldn't. For the first time in my life, I was paralyzed with fear. I felt furious with myself for my weakness. There was no reason for me to feel this now. The wolf was securely tied. I'd already faced that horrifying scene in the kitchen once.

I could hear Atla's frantic struggle inside. He needed to get her out of there before she choked herself on the chain or ripped the handles clear off the refrigerator and freezer doors.

"Get in there! You're the only person small enough to fit through the opening! Now go!"

I propped myself up and vented at Damian. "Look it, buster! I don't know you from Adam, but you're a complete jerk!"

"Lady, that's what my ex-wife used to say, but it isn't getting us anyplace right now!"

Police sirens were growing louder. They would break through the kitchen door and wouldn't hesitate to shoot the wolf dead. For Atla's sake, I had to act now. Whatever had happened tonight, it wasn't her fault. Some fool had brought her here. Who? Ty?

I took a deep breath, gritted my teeth, and wriggled through the door, mentally telling myself not to look at anything, just to stand up and immediately throw the locks on the back door.

I got in and stood up. The smell of blood and death made me gag.

Atla was whining, definitely still breathing, despite her choke collar. My back was to her as I threw the locks, determined to do this fast. From deeper inside the house, Doobie was still thrashing about and trying desperately to get through the bedroom door.

Just as I fumbled with the last lock, there was a strange noise from the direction of the refrigerator.

It sounded for all the world like a bolt ripping loose from the door handle.

Chapter 7

The lock was stuck. I leaned against the door and finally forced its turn-style mechanism open. I turned to check on Atla. A blur of gray came at me. A hot-poker shock of pain raced up my arm as Atla sank her teeth into my left hand. I screamed in agony. The door bashed into me, and Damian rushed into the room.

"Atla, no!" he yelled. She instantly released her grip on me, which sent another shock wave of hideous pain through my body. Damian grabbed hold of her leash just above the collar and was strong enough to lift her front paws off the ground.

I took a couple of staggering steps, my vision blurred with pain. I gripped myself tightly around the wrist. I looked at the injury. She'd caught me in the fleshy part of my hand. The puncture wounds had begun to bleed. The pain was searing and relentless.

"You okay?" Damian asked, straining as the wolf started to pull him toward Ty.

In the corner of my vision, a quick view of the shocked faces outside the door registered on me. "What happened?" a female voice called. Beverly's voice, I realized.

"I'm okay," I immediately shot back. A by-product of my being small and young-looking for my age was that I couldn't tolerate being coddled, even when it was justified.

"I've got to get her out front to my van," Damian managed to tell me, straining with his physical effort at keeping the wolf under control. He paled when he and the snarling wolf reached the far side of the kitchen. "Oh, Jeez," he murmured, staring down at Ty's body. Frenzied by being near the body, Atla snapped at Damian, who held so tight to the leash that only her back paws were on the ground.

In a remarkable show of strength, Damian managed to half lift the struggling wolf through the beaded entranceway. "Get the front door for me," he barked over his shoulder. "I've got to load her into the van and get her caged. Now. Before the police burst in here and shoot her."

In a strange, almost out-of-body state, I managed to obey, stepping around the body and after Damian and the wolf. We crossed the living room. He held his wolf at bay as I staggered past him toward the door. The room was dark, the heavy curtains on all windows drawn tightly shut. The room was empty. No bean bags, lamps, collectibles. Had the house been burglarized?

Working with my good hand, I got the locks to operate and looked back into the room as I pulled open the front door. Along the wall of cinderblock shelves, the stereo and TV were still in place. A tripod was set up in the back corner, no camera in sight.

Outside, Damian was instructing a pair of startled officers and another pair of male paramedics to let him pass. "Just let me get her locked up. The van's got a built-in cage." Damian's vehicle was a dark blue and again had tinted windows, similar to the steel gray van that Larry Cunriff had used a few hours earlier.

One paramedic opened the back doors of the van for him and then dashed aside. Damian was strong enough to hurl the wolf up and into the van.

I made my way down the steps toward them in a dazed state. Beverly had rounded the house and was on the sidewalk talking to one of the officers. When she saw me, she trotted toward me, ignoring the policeman beside her telling her to stop. In the corner of my vision, I could see the Atkinsons heading through the gate with yet another uniformed officer.

Feeling faint, I shut my eyes for a moment and saw a vision of Atla, her blood-soaked ruff and paws.

Beverly rushed to my side. "Allida! What happened to you? You're bleeding!"

"The wolf bit me. Not bad, though. I'm current on my tetanus vaccinations. I'll be all right."

She yanked off the long-sleeve blouse that she'd been wearing jacket-style over her T-shirt and wrapped it around my hand. The policeman had stepped beside us. "Officers? She needs medical attention."

"Miss?" one of the officers said. "We need to speak to you. Would you come with us, please?"

I glanced down at my injured hand, which was throbbing. Blood was already soaking through Beverly's blouse. "Okay, but could you give me a ride to the emergency room while we're at it?"

The next couple of hours passed in that same kind of semi-conscious state my brain seems to put itself into when I've got a really bad flu. The EMTs put some butterfly bandages on my wound, then took me to the emergency room at Boulder Community Hospital. Although having policemen as companions won me a lot of strange looks and a pariah-like treatment from my fellow patients, it didn't seem to get me a doctor any sooner.

Despite my trauma, the officers asked me questions, and I answered them, while garnering random images from my surroundings. A nurse was criticizing the EMTs over something about my butterfly bandages. The family in the cubicle next to mine, distraught over their little boy's head injury. The loud, elderly woman on the other side of me complaining in a thick German accent about how slow the doctor was in arriving. The pervasive masking odor of antiseptic that I was certain was now permanently embedded in my nostrils.

Then the doctor came bearing bad news. A wolf can't be observed for a mere ten days for rabies the way domestic animals can. I would have to undergo both the two rabies immune globulin shots—today's and in another three days—plus the full set of vaccinations. This meant a total of five vaccine applications; three this week, then one in two weeks, and my last in four weeks. That meant treatments to the wound itself as well as turning my butt into a pin cushion for extremely long needles.

Once my stitches were in place, my hand bandaged, and I was able to sit without crying out, the officers took me to the station house on 30th Street. We went through the very same lengthy set of questions that I'd already answered while in the hospital. I told them, once again, that it was clear to me that Ty Bellingham's death had come not from teeth or claws, but from a knife. The police, in turn, made it clear that, for my own safety in case a killer had hoped Ty's death appeared to be from the wolf, I was not to share this observation with anyone.

Eventually, I'd talked my throat raw. Then it was all I could do to convince them that I was capable of driving myself, if they could just bring me back to my car in front of the Bellinghams' house.

An officer drove me in a patrol car. There was still no sign of Cheshire's orange VW. The property was now surrounded with yellow crime-scene plastic tape, its perimeter teeming with onlookers. Having arrived in a squad car, four or five people rushed toward me and started shouting questions at me. A microphone was shoved in my face and the shutter of a camera clicked. I said nothing, kept my head down, got into my car, and drove away without a glance in my rearview mirror or any real thought of where to go now.

I was a couple of blocks away before a realization hit me: I had told Beverly Wood that Ty had been stabbed to death. There was no harm there, though. She was a friend. I'd just have to tell her not to repeat this.

The thought of Beverly allowed me to gradually make the connection that I was supposed to be at the softball game. The game had started at six forty-five, and was now probably half over.

I wouldn't be any good to my team anyway. My thumb was throbbing despite the anesthetic. If the key to mankind's success was opposable thumbs, I was halfway toward being a lower life form. Certainly a life form that did not play softball.

My mind and emotions in a tailspin, I drove toward the ball fields. I needed to tell Russell what had happened. Otherwise he might think that our minor spat had kept me from even showing.

I drove right through the red light on Valmont and was extremely lucky that my only consequence was a blast from another car's horn and its driver's one-finger salute. My heart raced, shocked at my having made such a potentially dangerous mistake, but at least this jarred me back to full alert. All I wanted to do was go to sleep and forget today had ever happened. The thing was, though, every time I closed my eyes, I had a vision of the wolf, Atla. Each time, I felt a horrible rush of fear that rattled me to the core.

All that kept me going was the image of myself in Russell's arms. The hell with being strong; I'd never been as frightened in my life as I'd been in that kitchen. If Russell proved willing to console me, I would let him. I arrived at the ball fields east of town, parked, started up the long sidewalk toward the back field.

Stazio Field was a tribute to concrete and chain-link fences. Other than the softball fields themselves, there was remarkably little grass, the xeriscaping featuring heavily mulched gardens and lots of rocks. It's a peculiar part of town, just outside the major population centers, and isolated by its geography—trees and craggy hills where the gravel pits are located. A softball island, of sorts. The lights were already on, though they weren't necessary. It was barely even dusk.

The field my team used was the closest to the parking lot, and I walked up the paved hill along the fence. Our team was up to bat. In a bizarre coincidence, Hank Atkinson's team was playing against us. They were all wearing their Hank's Security Systems T-shirts, which all bore their team name: The Wolves. Hank was their pitcher. I scanned our dugout as I neared and saw Beverly and Tracy. It finally dawned on me that Beverly would have told everyone about my close encounter with the wild kingdom.

I didn't stop to speak to my teammates in the dugout. Still watching for Russell, I slowly made my way along the fence. He was just stepping up to the plate. He, too, was obviously watching for me, because he stalled before entering the batting box, reseating his cap as he surveyed the bleachers.

He spotted me, and his face registered relief, but did not light up the way it always used to at the sight of me. Instead he immediately glanced down at my bandaged hand, then turned his attention to the pitcher and got ready to swing.

Beverly was on deck and had just selected a bat when she saw me. She rushed up to the fence that separated us. "Allida, hi! Is your hand going to be okay?"

"Yeah, thanks." I gave her a wave with it. In the meantime, Russell took the first pitch, which was a called strike. "Your shirt's seen better days though. It's in a plastic bag in my trunk."

Meanwhile, Tracy Truett heard us and dashed out of the dugout and up to me, her hard-rubber cleats against concrete giving her a jock-like swagger. She was a large, wide-shouldered woman. Her spiked, dyed-blond short hair poked out below the rim of her cap. The overall effect resembled a baseball cap squashed onto the end of a long-needled pine bough, but no one with any instincts for self-protection would dare laugh at her.

She rushed up to me and said with her usual gusto, complete with waving arms, "Beverly told us what happened. Holy Moly, Allida! What are you doing here? If I'd just done battle with a wolf, I'd be in Margueritaville by now!"

"I wanted to see Russell." He took a wild swing at a pitch, missing the ball entirely. Normally, he was a good player, but he was already behind in the count oh-and-two.

She gestured with her chin in Russell's direction. "What did you do to that poor boy?" By Tracy's standards, her voice was quiet, but I wasn't at all sure that Russell couldn't overhear. "Even before Beverly got here and spilled the beans, he's been barking at everybody—worse than your noisiest clients."

He swung again and struck out, which is not easy to do in slow-pitch softball.

Tracy groaned. "He can't play worth a damn, either. Go talk to him." As she spoke, she'd put her hand on my shoulder and was gently pushing me toward the dugout. "We're losing, eight to four. Can I put you in at second base?"

I held up my bad hand. "I can't get a mitt on this hand, let alone hold a bat. You'd better put me on your disabled list for the rest of the season."

"Oh, shoot! Beverly told us you were bitten, but I forgot." She stared at my bandages. "Damn! It would have to be your glove hand. Tell you what, I can put you in at rover next week, and we'll just cover for you."

Her tendency to focus exclusively on herself and on the immediate matter at hand—so to speak—was just her typical behavior, and I wasn't offended. I deserted all pretense of resistance and returned to the dugout with her, and Russell came over to me. He sat down beside me, but avoided my gaze.

"Jeez, Allida," he said quietly, shaking his handsome head. "I can't believe this. You could have gotten yourself killed." He sighed and finally studied my face, his eyes full of worry. "Are you all right?"

"I'm fine. Just a bit shaken. It seems so strange the way everyone's here, including me, as if nothing had happened. Hank's playing for their team. He's Beverly's neighbor, who was feuding with the guy who was killed."

"Which one is Hank?" Russell asked, scanning the defense.

Whether or not it made sense, the feeling that this was all Hank's fault suddenly overwhelmed me. Somehow, my emotions had decided without my brain's consensus that the wolf never would have been in Ty's house if not for Hank and his television commercials. I wanted my team to beat the crap out of his team.

I gestured at the fit-looking red-haired man on the mound. "The pitcher."

"Him? That guy's a bigot."

"He is?"

"Yeah. He hates short people. As if he's some sort of towering giant. He made derogatory remarks about my height during his at-bats."

Russell was our catcher. Since he was always in a squatting position during opponents' at-bats, it was really odd that anybody would tease him. He rarely engaged in those hey-batter-batter taunting of the other team members, and I'd never heard him complain about an opposing team's behavior.

Our batter hit a double. I got to my feet and cheered with abandon as Beverly rounded third base and ran home. I almost forgot my injury and clapped, but remembered in time, and rushed out of the dugout to give her a right-handed high-five, along with some of our teammates. She had to lower her hand to reach mine. Afterward she put her arm around my shoulders, and we returned to the dugout together.

"I'm so glad to see you here, Allida. I feel so guilty. I should never have called you in the first place. Now I wish I'd called the police. I honestly wasn't sure that those were human shouts I'd heard, they'd sounded so...." She let her voice fade and shuddered. "I thought they just had another dog there, or something."

"It wasn't your fault, Bev. Do you have any idea who could've gotten the wolf into Ty's house like that? Did you see a gray van with tinted windows, or anything?"

"No. I already told the police. I didn't see or hear anything. But then, I'd only just returned from my contract job when I heard those noises next door."

"That's right," I said, just now remembering how strange that timing was. "You'd only left your house a couple of hours earlier with Rebecca. Why were you home so soon?"

She clicked her tongue. "Rebecca and I got into an argument just after you left. We wound up going to the site in separate cars, and once we got there, we agreed it'd be better if I just reassured the homeowners that everything was going fine. She finished most of the work alone."

"I see," I said, though I didn't really. Why rush out of the house on a Saturday if this was a one-person job? "Too bad for Ty's sake you weren't home earlier. The killer might have parked right in his driveway." Though I felt ashamed of myself, I was testing her. She merely nodded, her lips pursed, giving me no insight.

We took our seats. Russell was used to witnessing my jock-like sports mentality emerge at games, but even he was watching me with raised eyebrows, as if surprised at my exuberance in the light of today's events.

Just then, Hank threw a brush-back pitch at our batter, which, considering this was slow-pitch, could not have been accidental. This was a female batter, because by co-rec softball rules, men and women alternate their at-bats. The umpire reprimanded him, and he held up a palm in a mock apology, chuckling all the while.

In unison, our male contingent shot to their feet and shouted their protests. Russell pointed at Hank. "Hey! Watch yourself!"

Hank ignored us and threw the next pitch, which was a strike.

"Did you see that?" Russell asked me in disgust. "What a jerk! He threw that ball right at Cindy's head!"

He sat down on the edge of the bench beside me, but stared at Hank, muscles primed to charge the mound if he threw another brush-back.

"I agree. Hank's acting like a total idiot. But it would have been an equally asinine thing to do to a male batter."

"No, this is way worse. He knows Cindy won't punch him out, though that's what he deserves."

"Oh, come now. If he were actually to have deliberately hit Cindy with that pitch, what do you think would have happened? He'd have had every guy on our team, and perhaps even on his own team, charging the mound. It would have been much safer to throw at a man."

"The guy's a turd," Russell grumbled as if he hadn't heard me. "The first inning, he got into the batter's box, kicked dirt in my face, and said if I didn't like it, I could blame my parents for my short genes. Then he hit the first pitch over the fence."

In the meantime, our batter was not so fortunate and popped up to Hank, ending the inning. As the rest of the team grabbed their mitts and headed out to their positions, emptying the dugout, Beverly slid over beside me and patted my knee. "You hangin' in there okay?"

"Sure," I said. "How about you? I'm surprised you can even begin to concentrate after what you just went through."

She winced a little and rose. "There wasn't anything I could do for Ty by sitting home. I needed to get out of there and get my mind off him." While backing toward the pitcher's mound she gestured at the opponents' dugout. "Hank's here, too."

"I noticed, but then, there was certainly no love lost between him and Ty."

"He didn't do it, you know, if that's what you're thinking. Hank would never do such a thing." She pivoted and walked to the mound.

Why would she defend Hank? Earlier this afternoon, he'd threatened to kill Ty, who threatened him back. He also had access to the wolves. Plus, the fact that he was a poor sport might carry through to his daily behavior.

The hairs at the back of my neck rose as I got the uncomfortable feeling that somebody was watching me. I whirled around in my seat and saw a dark-haired woman in a peach pants suit. Paige Atkinson. She must have been in the ladies' room when I arrived. Even from a distance, I could see her complexion was blotchy and tear-stained, her eyes red. Maybe the concept that her ex-husband was dead had sunk in.

In the corner of my vision, I noticed that Hank had left his teammates. He rounded the fence behind the plate, heading my way. He walked right in front of his wife in the process, seemingly without noticing. He looped his fingers through the chain link behind our dugout.

"Allida. What did you tell the police about me?"

His face had an unnatural sheen to it, and there was a familiar fragrance. Cocoa butter. Maybe he was trying to enhance his tan. "In reference to what?"

"The murder, of course," he snapped. "Did you tell them about our argument earlier today?"

"Of course," I repeated back to him.

"I'm innocent. I didn't let that wolf loose in his house."

"I'm glad."

"Ty probably swiped the wolf all on his own. He had this thing about dogs. Seemed to think being with a big, strong dog compensated for his small...inadequacies."

"Did you ever know Ty to arrange a dog fight?" I asked.

Hank shook his head. "Not that I saw for myself, but then, it's not like he'd have given me an invitation. He knows I'd have had him arrested on the spot."

A large man from their team rose and gestured gruffly in our direction. "Hank! Come on! You're in the hole!"

Hank hesitated, started to say something to me, then jogged toward his teammates.

For the first time since we'd met, Paige Atkinson smiled at me and held my gaze, as if she, too, had something she wanted to say. I'd already formulated a negative opinion of her and didn't relish spending time with her, but I was curious as to why she seemed to be trying to establish friendly contact with me. I left the dugout and sat down next to her.

"I'm glad to see you made it here," she said. "I wasn't sure you'd even be back on your feet. This is all...such a terrible shock."

Strange that she hadn't seemed all that shocked when it was happening, that she'd dragged her feet about calling the police while her ex-husband might have been screaming for help. "You...didn't have a key to the Bellinghams' house?"

Immediately she tensed and her eyes grew fiery. "You've been talking to Beverly Wood, haven't you? That bitch told you about my having been married to Ty, didn't she?"

"My *friend* Beverly, who is not a bitch, mentioned it, yes. Remarrying and living next door to your ex is the kind of thing people tend to talk about."

She turned her head and glared at Beverly on the pitcher's mound. "Next time you talk to her, you might want to mention that, no, I don't have any keys to Ty's house. He changed the locks. But I happen to know that *she* still has a key from when she and her lesbian friend were supposedly working on his kitchen."

I really hated what felt to me was no more than an assumption that Rebecca was a lesbian because she worked in a male-dominated field and didn't wear "girlie" clothes and makeup. But I was more concerned with the non sequitur about the kitchen remodeling. "Supposedly?" I repeated.

She had set her jaw and shot me an angry glance. "Don't get me wrong. They remodeled his kitchen, all right. But knowing what a slut Beverly is, I doubt they confined their activities to just the one room."

I didn't know what to say, so I sat in silence, my stomach topsy turvy. It was appalling to me how much hatred there was in this world. Life was short enough anyway without having to waste so much energy on rancor and hate. Why stay in a house next to your ex and live a cold, vindictive existence?

Then again, her problem was now solved. Maybe she'd killed Ty.

Hank came up to bat. He started to swing and tried to stop his motion when he realized that the pitch was too high. It landed behind the mat, and the umpire ruled it a ball. Russell protested vehemently and appealed to the in-field umpire at first base, who agreed that Hank had swung through. Hank shot Russell a dirty look and grumbled something under his breath that I couldn't hear, but, uncharacteristically, Russell flipped some dirt on Hank's shoe as he got back into position behind the plate.

Hank shook the sand off his shoe and hollered to Russell, "Hey, pipsqueak. Don't mess with me! I'm a former Arizona Wildcat! I've played against tackling dummies that were tougher than you!"

"Oh, give me a break," I moaned. Men and their games! I was one of the more competitive women I knew, having played college basketball myself. We threw elbows, too, but rarely called our opponents names. Until afterwards in the locker room.

Paige, too, clicked her tongue, as if disgusted with her husband's outburst. "He used to be a college football hero. Never lets anyone forget it."

Hank hit a monster shot that drove our left fielder to the fence. Hank raced around first and then second base, just as our fielder made a terrific catch. Russ hopped to his feet and cheered, taking a couple of steps down the third-base line.

Hank didn't slow, though he was out. He rounded third base, lowered his shoulder and barreled into Russell, who hit the ground with a sickening thud.

Chapter 8

I rose, horrified. Beside me, Paige Atkinson
gasped. Her hands flew to her face. I raced down the
concrete stairs, darted through our empty dugout and
onto the field. By then, most of our team as well as a
few members of Hank's team had circled Russell.

I shouldered my way through the cluster of
concerned onlookers. Russell was on the ground,
groaning. At least he was conscious and breathing.

Hank, meanwhile, had stopped just past the
collision on the third-base line. He had a grin on his
face. Loud enough so everyone could hear, he leaned
over Russell and said, "It was an accident. Sorry. But
you shouldn't have been in the base path."

"And you shouldn't have been barreling down the
baseline toward him!" I knelt, filled with rage at Hank
and with empathy for Russell. His face was contorted
with pain. "You knew full well that you were already
out!"

"Was I? Oh, Jeez. I didn't realize."

"She's right, you asshole!" Tracy shouted. I looked
up. If anyone on our team could take out this thug, it
was Tracy Truett. "Russell's filing criminal assault
charges against you!"

That statement drained the cockiness from
Hank's mannerisms. He gestured at our leftfielder, who
had trotted in-field to join our useless crowd. "I thought

he dropped the ball. Guess I did make a mistake." He glanced down at Russell again. "Sorry. I got too caught up in the excitement of the game. Good thing you're so short, or I might have broken some of your ribs."

It was all I could do to stop myself from screaming at him, "You want to see something short?" and kneeing him in the groin.

By then Russell, his forearms crossed over his midsection in obvious pain, had managed to sit up. The umpires were talking to him, telling him to stay put while they got an ambulance, but Russ shook his head emphatically and struggled to get to his feet while avoiding touching his hand down for balance. My heart lurched at the sight of him in so much pain, straining so mightily to save face. If I thought he'd have let me, I'd have thrown my arms around him and cried on his behalf.

Several of Hank's "Wolves" spat vitriolic remarks at Hank, even though he was their captain and team sponsor. Hank threw up his hands, shouted, "It was an accident," and returned to his dugout. The crowd began to disperse as Russell slowly made his way off the diamond.

To my surprise, Beverly was uncharacteristically crying and repeating: "I'm so sorry," to Russell, shooting hateful glares in Hank's direction.

When no one else could overhear, I headed to Hank's dugout and muttered to him, "Your claiming that this was an accident isn't fooling anybody. That was an asinine, cowardly thing to do! You may be taller than him, but he's twice the man you'll ever be!"

A couple of the men on our team flanked Russell as he made his way out of the playing field through our dugout. He waved them off, and the umpires called out for everyone to return to their positions. We already had one extra female player in my spot. Another male player was sent in to sub for Russell at catcher. The game would go on. No damage done. Just a brief injury time-out.

Again to my surprise, Beverly said she couldn't continue as pitcher. She dried her eyes and swapped positions with Tracy on second base.

In the meantime, I trotted back across the back of the dirt in-field and into our dugout where only Russell remained as he collected his belongings. I felt horrible for him. He was determined to pretend that he wasn't in agony, but his face and forehead were dripping with sweat from the effort. Wordlessly, I rubbed his back.

"The bastard broke my collar bone!"

Not knowing what else to say, I muttered stupidly, "Maybe it's just a sprain."

"I've had a broken collar bone before! I know what it feels like!" He had scooped up his small canvas athletic bag from underneath the bench in the dugout and waved off my attempts to take it from him. "I got it," he muttered gruffly.

Paige met us as we exited the dugout. She had paled and her hands were trembling as she tried to hold back her hair, which the breeze was blowing toward her face. "I am so sorry, whoever you are," she said to Russell. "I don't know what gets into my husband sometimes. Just send me the bill, and I'll cover the cost of your medical care. Allida knows my address."

"Nice of you," Russell replied as pleasantly as he could under the circumstances.

She gave him a tight-lipped smile and me an embarrassed nod, then she turned on a heel toward Hank's dugout.

I watched her walk away, wondering what, if anything, she'd say to her husband about this. I had a gnawing feeling in the pit of my stomach that this was just the beginning—merely battle lines being drawn. This seemed to be caveman stuff, wolves and clubs, and I'd somehow sparked a prehistoric blaze in the awful people that Beverly happened to live near.

Russell took a sharp intake of breath as he brushed against a fence post. I sighed, certain he wouldn't want me to embarrass him in public and shower him with words of concern. At the same time, my temptation to blurt out the words I love you was palpable and all but overwhelming. It was the truth. Yet the rational side of me was pointing out to my emotional side that I was currently a wolf-bitten murder witness. These strengthened feelings for Russell might merely be the byproduct of the trauma I'd just experienced. It was a long walk down a big hill to get back to the parking lot, and we were making slow time. Occasional pedestrians coming up from the lot eyed us with curiosity.

"Between you with your collar bone and me with my hand, all we need is a drum and a limping guy with a piccolo."

Russell glared at me as we shuffled our way to the exit. "Is that supposed to be funny?"

"Apparently not." We were nearing my car, but he kept going after I'd stopped. "Let me drive you to the hospital."

"No. I can drive," he called over his shoulder.

"Maybe, but certainly not well. For heaven's sake, Russ, you have a standard transmission. How are you going to shift if you can't move your right arm?"

He lifted his right elbow slightly, wincing in the process. "I can move it fine. I want..." He paused and scanned my face. His own was tense and damp with perspiration. "I want to be alone, okay?"

"Are you trying to punish me? Because that's what you're doing."

He ignored my words completely. It was tearing me up inside to watch Russell fumbling to get his key in the lock. He opened his door.

"Good luck. I hope you don't get into an accident on the way." It was a struggle not to start crying out of despair and frustration.

Fuming, I stood with crossed arms, watching as he stalled out twice just getting out of the parking lot. This was ludicrous! If I'd had a baseball bat in my hand, I'd have been sorely tempted to march back down to the field and pound Hank in the kneecaps until he admitted he'd injured Russell on purpose. It wasn't rational, but it felt as though Hank had targeted Russell because he knew about my relationship with him.

Tracy Truett came up to me just as Russell signaled and then pulled onto the street. "Tell me something, Tracy. Are testosterone and brain waves mutually exclusive?"

"Yep. Game's over. We lost. What a rip-off! The ump insisted we'd played for a full hour, but he didn't give us credit for the five minutes that Russ was...." She let her voice fade when she finally registered how very little I cared about our team's undefeated streak just now. "Is Russell all right?"

"No! He's got a broken collarbone! Why does everybody keep asking that stupid question when someone's obviously injured?"

"Whoops. I just pushed the wrong button."

"He wouldn't even let me drive him to the hospital. He can barely even move his right arm."

"That reminds me." She eyed my left hand. "How did you get your car here? Did somebody drive you?"

"No, but that's different." Granted, I couldn't say how it was different, exactly, except that Russell's injuries weren't treated yet, and I was the one offering the ride. And Russell, by God, should have accepted.

"The blind leading the blind. Rather, the righties driving the lefties," she murmured. She gave me a friendly jab on the shoulder. "Guess what, Allida? I just got the all-time greatest idea for what you can do to help out both yourself and our team sponsors."

"Sponsors? You mean, your radio station?"

"Yep. I'm putting you on the air during tomorrow's broadcast. I'll interview you, and you can talk about what it was like to come face-to-face with an untamed wolf."

"No way, Tracy."

"But a story like this will have all of Boulder tuning in. It's going to help my career immeasurably. You have to do it. Please?"

Tracy's saying "please" came up as often as the word "pantheon" did during the course of normal conversation. Nevertheless, I was steadfast. "Tracy, I'm not going to do that. Why would you possibly think that I'd be willing to?"

"Are you kidding me? To drum up business! You could use the free publicity." She spread her hands against the sky as if reading an imaginary banner. "'Dog Trainer Has Brush With Death From Wolf!'"

"You call that good publicity?"

She chuckled and whipped her cap off her head, her damp, kinky spikes still bearing the cap's imprint. "Oh, honey, in show biz, there ain't no such thing as bad publicity."

"Maybe not. But there is in the dog training business."

"Aw, come on, Allie. What could it possibly hurt?"

"No," I said through clenched teeth. I unlocked my car door. "And furthermore, I'm making a new policy for myself! The first time anyone assures me that something or someone is harmless, I'm running in the opposite direction!"

The moment my key was in the front door of my mother's blond brick ranch-style house, I could hear the dogs positioning themselves to greet me. Their hierarchy had undergone some changes of late. Sage, my mother's recently adopted male collie, had begun to exert authority over my dogs—Doppler, a male cocker spaniel, and Pavlov, my female German shepherd. Though physically the second largest, my German shepherd had been demoted to lowest rank, behind the two males.

I petted Sage, who wagged his tail slowly. Truth be told, I loved Sage almost as much as my own dogs, who'd been with me much longer. Sage was a noble animal, though not attractive by show standards. He had a wonderful sable coat worthy of Lassie, but he also had a bumpy Roman nose and one ear that had dropped while the other remained up.

Next, I knelt and greeted Doppler. Lacking the energy reserves to stay balanced, I sat down on the floor. It felt as though a train had hit me. My stitches were throbbing. I hadn't eaten in hours, but knew that my stomach was too knotted to keep anything down.

Surmising my mood, Doppler licked my face, which he knew under normal circumstances was forbidden. He was a handsome classically featured buff-colored cocker—big brown eyes, tapered muzzle. Patterns of white across his chest and tummy reminded me of cumulus clouds, which is how I came to name him Doppler, after the weather equipment, which was more apt than the names Cumulus or Cloudy.

My beloved German shepherd, Pavlov, had left the room and now came galloping back in. I looked up just as she rounded the corner and raced toward me, gripping the rawhide bone that she'd fetched to show off to me. To my horror, I had an image of being charged by a wolf. I gasped and flinched, barely managing not to cry out in fright.

It took me a moment to calm myself. Pavlov stopped in front of me, dropping the bone as an offering of her subordination. I threw my arms around her neck and buried my face in her fur. I could not let myself be afraid of dogs. Not of my own sweet shepherd, who would do anything for me. I was still in this position when my mother walked into the room.

"Allida, what's wrong?" she asked immediately.

By the time I looked up, Mom was sitting on the edge of the nearest seat, hands clasped in front of her.

There was no sense in keeping secrets from my mother. She knew me too well, and she would see my bandages soon anyway. I held up my injured hand. "A wolf bit me."

Her jaw dropped. "What were you doing getting that close to a wolf? Was this at the zoo?"

"No! What did you think?" I snapped at her. "That I was hand-feeding a wolf through the bars? My new client got murdered and...." I paused.

There was no way to tell this story in as few words as I was willing to waste on it. "His neighbor has a wolf, sort of. But the thing is, just for a moment there, when Pavlov came into the room, I was actually frightened."

I studied my mother's shocked expression. Facially, my mother and I were almost dead ringers, but she was six inches taller. Tonight, as she did most of the time, her gray-streaked long brown hair was in a braid. She wore a yellow terry-cloth bathrobe and gray slippers.

"Mom, do you know what this means?"

"No! I don't know what a single word you just said means! Somebody who hired you was murdered today? Is your life in danger?"

"No, just my livelihood." Not even eight hours ago, things were looking great for me. I'd been on the verge of the four-letter L-word with Russell Greene. Business was not exactly booming, but was at least thumping. My biggest worry had been whether or not I could find a house in Boulder county within my price range. I rubbed my forehead with my good hand. "Can I explain in the morning?"

"No! I have a student in the morning first thing after church, and this isn't a topic that I can be patient over!"

Mom was a flight instructor. She'd been an inspiration for my brother, a pilot for United. She'd inspired me, too, but not in the employment arena; I had a formidable fear of heights. Ironic that Russell was a rock climber and both of my immediate family members were pilots. The way things were going with Russell, though, it was hard to say if his hobby would matter to me for much longer. At that thought I sighed, then looked up and realized that my mother—who looked as though her internal time bomb might be set to explode—still awaited my reply.

Over a cup of Sleepy Time tea, I filled my mother in on all of the sorry events of the day, deliberately leaving Russell Greene out of the story entirely, knowing that was the one subject I wanted to discuss the most, and yet also the least.

When she puts her mind to it, Mom's a great listener, and she remained silent, nodded, or murmured exclamations at all the right places. After a long silence, she asked, "Did you see Russell today?"

I stood up, mostly to escape the weight of her eyes upon me. "Yeah. Can I get you some more tea?"

"I'll get it," she said, rising and whisking the kettle away from my reach. "I know you're something of a prude, but I assumed you'd be spending this weekend with Russell. Was I reading signals wrong?"

My cheeks warmed at being called a "prude" by my mother, but I decided to let it slide. "Maybe bad signal-reading runs in the family."

"He called earlier today." Mom was still probing, determined not to let it drop till she figured out what was going on between him and me. "I told him where you were. I hope you don't mind. He's such a doll."

I drank my tea, focusing on the surface of the water and avoiding Mom's eyes.

"You're awfully quiet, all of a sudden. Did you two have a spat?"

"We argued. Sometimes he just comes on too strong. I feel like I'm being smothered." The words that I'd wanted to keep to myself now burst forth in a torrent. "Then he starts pouting because things didn't go his way. It's not like I'm his mother. I don't want to have to coddle his ego, I want him to coddle mine. And yet I want to be the one to pursue, not to feel like he's chasing after me despite how rotten I am to him sometimes. You know? And then he got injured in the softball game. Says he's got a broken collar bone. This creep from the other team deliberately bowled into him. But Russell wouldn't even let me drive him to the hospital. Men are so stupid."

"They sure are. Of course, we women are equally stupid, just in different ways." She paused. "How did you get from the hospital, or wherever they stitched up your hand, to the baseball diamond?"

I set my half empty cup down so quickly the liquid sloshed into the saucer. "You're the second person who's brought that up, and there's no comparison. I accepted a ride to the hospital from the police when I was bleeding all over the place. Russell was being stubborn. I was just being resilient."

We sat again in silence. I felt too miserable at the moment to speak. Maybe I was wrong to blame Russell for not wanting me to take him to the hospital. Of course he hadn't wanted to lean on me just then; he had all but flat out told me shortly beforehand that he thought I meant more to him than he did to me. That wasn't true.

As if reading my thoughts, Mom quietly asked, "Do you love him?"

The unexpected question hit me like a slap in the face. "I don't know. I think so." My voice faltered a little. "Sometimes I desperately want to let him into my heart. It's just that...I can't survive another mistake, like I made the last time."

She knew what I meant. The last time I fully trusted a man with my love, he'd dumped me in favor of my best friend—my maid of honor at the wedding that never took place. I'd rather feed a wolf my other hand than face that kind of pain again. No wonder Russell and I were having troubles. He was attracted to a one-handed emotional train wreck.

"Honey, you can't withdraw from all men, just because you were bitten once, any more than you can withdraw from all dogs when one bites you."

I said nothing. Her words made me want to bang my head against the counter.

At length, Mom said, "Are you two going to break up over this?"

"I hope not. But I don't know. Maybe. We're at a crossroads in our relationship."

"Meaning you haven't slept together yet, and you don't know if he's the one?"

"Something like that." Technically, it was exactly like that, but it was bad enough discussing my love life with my mother without discussing sex as well. I pushed back my chair, the linoleum letting out a noisy scraping sound in the process. "I'm taking some ibuprofen and going to bed. Good night."

Somebody was pressing an ice cube against my cheek. I opened my eyes and gasped. A wolf! I bolted upright in bed, as the wolf changed in the blink of an eye into Pavlov, my German shepherd, who had nuzzled me on the cheek with her cold wet nose.

I wrapped my arms around my chest and struggled to regain my normal breathing pattern. In the middle of the night, I'd woken up in a sweat. In my dreams, my canine customers kept turning into wolves and lunging at my throat. Afterwards, I'd lain awake for hours, contemplating the previous day's events.

Pavlov let out one small whine and watched me with her doleful eyes, already detecting that my feelings for her were different. Doppler had run into my room, too, and now butted ahead of Pavlov in their self-assigned line of pettings. Doppler's stubby tail was wagging madly as I greeted him, then moved on to Pavlov.

"It's okay, Pavlov." In my so-many-dogs-so-little-time T-shirt, I dragged my weary body out of bed and petted Pavlov in her favorite spots, below the ears. "I'll get over this soon."

Dogs can sense what their masters are feeling before the masters themself can recognize these feelings. So I knew that Pavlov wasn't going to take my attention as a sign that all was well, but expected that she would take it as an appropriate "things aren't all that bad."

I have very little tolerance for sitting around moping and feeling sorry for myself. I hoped that last night's indulgence would suffice. In any case, I would now have to deal with insufficient sleep for the day.

I felt sufficiently confused and in need of answers to want to go to church. There's a small Methodist church here in Berthoud, and, while my mother is a regular, I always imagine that the minister spots me in a pew and says to himself, "Ah. Miss Babcock's here. Our resident foul-weather parishioner."

There were probably answers to be found in my prayer, but if so, I was unable to recognize them as such. If there was any one thing that could quickly put an end to my effectiveness as a dog behaviorist, it was fear of canines. While I was quite sure that all I needed right now was a brief vacation, my finances and my wet-behind-the-furry-ears business couldn't handle one at this time.

What was more, I always tended to trust my almost instinctive reactions to people and problems. I didn't know what to make of my resistance to Russell's advances, but I did know that it took a whole lot of love for a relationship to make it through the constant challenges of life. Russell had made it clear he thought I was "the one" for him. If he were my soul mate as well, would I be having these doubts?

Would I be attracted to Damian Hesk?

By the time I returned home, it was after ten a.m. The animal shelter would now be open. I decided I'd stop by on my way into town. I could ask them about the likelihood of a dog rescuer in Nevada allowing unfixed strays to be adopted.

I made the drive with my brain operating at half-mast. The warm air inside the animal shelter bore that odor of dog and cat urine that seems so strong at first it stung my eyes, but faded by the time the woman at the counter had a chance to say more than a quick, "Hi, Allida," to me. There were two men at the counter, as well, and they were doing a brisk business this Sunday morning—a lost dog and its tearful owner, a new adoption in process, and the constantly ringing phone.

In the last couple of months I'd gotten to know most of their full-time employees. I volunteer my dog-training talents there whenever I can afford the time. I exchanged some more brief pleasantries with the young woman, then asked, "Could you please check to see if you have a registration of a large mixed-breed dog within the last six months under the last name of Bellingham? He said he got the dog from a rescuer in Nevada."

I waited as she typed the information into her computer terminal. "First name 'Tyler'?" she asked.

"Not in the last six months, no. Only record we have of an adoption by Tyler Bellingham was almost two years ago. He adopted a purebred American Staffordshire Terrier from us."

"A pit bull?" I asked, incredulous.

"That's what it says here." Her brow was furrowed as she scanned the screen. "Dog's name was King. He was three years old, and his owners put him up for adoption when the woman was expecting. Didn't trust having one around the house with a baby. According to his owners, they hated to give him up."

"That's the only record of your dealings with Mr. Bellingham? And he didn't bring that dog back for re-adoption?"

"No, though I see complaints have been filed over the last three months about his dog's barking. Huh. That's a different dog...mixed breed. Is that the one you're asking about?"

"Yes. That was his only dog."

"Huh," she said again. "I wonder what happened to King?"

I thanked her and headed out the door for the Bellingham residence, determined to learn the answer to that question for myself.

As I could have predicted, had I stopped to think about it, the Bellinghams' house was still cordoned off with the yellow-with-black-lettering police tape. Where was Doobie? I parked on the street and got out of the car, listening for his barks. The neighborhood was silent. I walked next door and rang Beverly Wood's doorbell. Beagle Boy started to bark his repetitive shrill yip, but otherwise there was no answer. I spotted him through the front window and called, "Hi, B.B.!" which made him stop barking abruptly. He never looked behind him for Beverly—a sure sign that his owner wasn't home.

By the time I got back to my car, Paige Atkinson was standing beside it, arms crossed as she waited for me. Today she was wearing simple khaki shorts and a white T-shirt, looking much less formal than she had in yesterday's pant suit.

"Hello, Allida." She gestured at my cherry red Subaru. "I recognized your car. I hope your softball friend is okay?" she said, as if this last sentence were a question.

"I do, too. I haven't seen him since he went to the hospital."

"Hank is just sick about this. He was tossing and turning all last night."

I clenched my jaw and muttered, "Aw. Poor baby."

Paige ignored my unmasked hostility and asked, "Were you looking for Beverly?"

"Actually, I was just trying to find out where Cheshire Bellingham was."

"She's at her store. It's on Walnut, just east of Crossroads Mall."

Too incredulous to hide my reaction, my jaw dropped. "She opened her husband's store for business? The day after he died?"

Paige chuckled. "Surely you didn't think the woman would be mourning, did you? She didn't even like Ty, let alone love him. Their whole marriage was a farce."

"It was?"

"Absolutely." She searched my face. "Ty needed to a wife to maintain his image. You don't think for one moment that Chesh would have married Ty of her own free will, do you?"

"Why wouldn't she? You married him, didn't you?"

"Maybe so, but that was before—" She stopped abruptly, then furrowed her brow and gave me a visual appraisal, as if she were affronted that she'd apparently nearly let something slip, which she wanted to keep to herself.

The Atkinsons seemed to have an unending pool of hatred and acrimony to draw from in all matters regarding Ty Bellingham. That those resentful feelings might extend to Chesh didn't surprise me, but her decision to open the store did seem remarkably callous. The day after her husband and store co-owner died, she was still open for business as usual.

"I saw you ring Beverly's doorbell," Paige said. "She hasn't been here for hours. I saw her leaving with the police."

"The police?" I repeated. My heart immediately raced with worry for Beverly, but then I realized that she was probably simply giving her statement. At this point, she and Paige were the two best witnesses the police had as to what had transpired in Ty's house.

"We need to talk," Paige announced. "Do you have a moment?"

"I suppose so. What's on your mind?"

"Not here. Come inside."

That was not an appealing suggestion for me. If Hank was home, my temptation to hit him might be uncontrollable. Paige marched ahead as if I was at her bid and calling. She had already climbed to her porch before noticing that I wasn't dutifully a step behind. She gripped the railing, looked at me and said, "Allida?"

"You asked for 'a moment,' and that really is all the time I have to spare. How's Sammy doing?"

She shook her head and came back down the steps. "This has been the worst nightmare. Hank took her to the vet's last night. That was why they weren't here when all the commotion was going on at the Bellinghams' house."

So, Hank Atkinson was supposedly at the vet's when Ty was being murdered. That would be an easy enough alibi for the police to verify. "I see."

"There's nothing the vet can do about my poor Sammy. We were counting on white wolf puppies. That would have been so wonderful, you know?"

She blinked a couple of times, waiting for me to shower her with sympathy, but the sire of their Samoyed's puppies was way down on my priority list. I frowned and waited for her to go on.

She spread her arms wide and shook her head. "Now God only knows what ugly monstrosities we're going to wind up with."

"If it's any consolation, you wouldn't have necessarily wound up with 'white wolves.' Puppies' fur color is usually determined by the sire."

"Still, they'd be worth way more than these mutt-lings."

"Is that all you wanted to talk to me about?"

"No, there's one other thing." She blushed and drew nearer. In hushed tones, she said, "If I were you, I would put some distance between myself and Beverly Wood."

"Why?" I braced myself for the expected character attack on my friend, prepared to defend her.

"As I told the police, while I can't be one-hundred-percent certain of this—" she paused as if for dramatic effect.

My patience was wearing thin. "I really am in a hurry, Paige," I said in a near growl.

She pursed her lips, then said sharply, "Fine. I'll get right to the point. I spotted Beverly Wood coming out of Ty Bellingham's front door just before I heard all the noise of that dreadful dog fight. I think your good friend, the 'non-bitch,' Beverly, killed him."

Chapter 9

"You saw Beverly coming out Ty's front door?" I
repeated. To her nod, I protested, "But the front door
was locked."

"I told you. She had a key, supposedly so she
could get in to do those kitchen repairs."

"Wait a minute." Some thoughts finally registered
that should have occurred to me yesterday. "This isn't
making any sense. If Beverly had a key and you knew it,
why didn't either of you use that key to get in when Ty
was calling for help?"

"Beverly claimed she didn't have a key. She said
that her partner, Rebecca, had given it back to Ty when
the job was finished."

I had to squint a little, with the afternoon sun
right in my line of vision. Paige's strange, beaker-shaped
nose was in the air. My doubt regarding Beverly's guilt
must have offended her. "Only you think that she was
lying about having the key, because you saw her, or
another woman who looked just like her, coming out the
Bellinghams' door. Is that right?"

Paige gave her dark hair a flick. "Oh, it was her,
all right. That much is certain. I was just driving by on
my way home from shopping, and I saw her shutting the
screen door behind her. She came running up to me
and told me to call the police...that there was a dog fight
going on inside of Ty's house. She only did that to cover

up her crime. I went inside my house to call, but then I noticed Sammy was missing. In my concern for Sammy, I forgot to call the police."

"You forgot?" This was her second or third feeble excuse for not calling the police sooner yesterday, and I couldn't keep the sarcasm from my voice. "Didn't you put it on your To Do list?"

Paige ignored me and rattled on, "Anyway, Beverly gave me this big story, saying she'd merely opened the screen to knock on the door when no one answered the bell. But I'm almost certain I saw her pulling the door shut and locking it."

Beverly's version was plausible, I thought. During our phone conversation yesterday, just before I raced over here, Beverly had told me she was going to go knock on Ty's door.

"What possible reason would Beverly have to kill Ty?"

"A reason? Oh, how about the fact that he was threatening to destroy her and her business." On that note, she turned on a heel and headed back toward her house.

"Paige, wait!"

She stopped and turned back to look at me. Her features were tense and pale, in stark contrast to her dark hair.

"You must have your facts wrong. Yesterday she rushed out here to defend him when you and he were fighting."

"Oh, please! You think Beverly Wood wanted to defend Ty Bellingham? Ha!" She folded her arms across her chest and gave me a smile that bore only malice. "If she told you that, she's lying. She came out here to egg me on!"

"That isn't the impression I got. Beverly is a good person."

"Oh, please!" she spat out a second time. "First she broke up Ty's and my marriage by throwing herself at him. While she was screwing my husband behind my back, she installed that monstrosity of a kitchen fan and fed it my darling parakeet, Bluey. She claimed it was an accident, that Bluey got out of his cage while she was still testing the fan and got sucked up before she could react." She began to cry and dried her cheeks with the back of her hand. "All I know is, she was the only person who could have let my little baby out of his cage, and I never saw poor Bluey again!"

She lost her last semblance of self-control and broke into wracking sobs. I opened my passenger door, reached into my glove box, and grabbed a packet of tissues, which I handed to her. Still crying, she tore off the plastic wrap, got a tissue, and dabbed at her eyes.

I'd been in the pet business long enough to know what an owner's grief can do to a person. The death of Paige's pet was enough reason to unconsciously manufacture all sorts of sinister behaviors on Beverly's part—such as believing she'd seen Beverly emerging from a door that she had merely been knocking on. Or even having an affair with her ex-husband. Though it was ironic, to say the least, that Paige was more upset by this past event than she was by yesterday's death of her ex-husband.

"Um, Paige, anytime a pet dies, it's a terrible loss. But with all due respect, what does this have to do with why Beverly would want to—"

While I was speaking, Paige blew her nose and gestured with her free hand for me to stop. "What do you mean, 'anytime a pet dies'? Bluey wasn't killed by that exhaust fan. He would have been sent right through the ducts. I'm certain all that forced air just blew him so far away from the house, he couldn't find his way home. I know in my heart that Bluey is living a happy life with his adopted family. Wherever they may be."

No doubt they were living on the very same "big farm way out in the country" where cowardly parents sent their children's terminally ill dogs. "I'm relieved to hear that. Be that as it may, why would Ty want to destroy Beverly and her business?"

She clicked her tongue in impatience at my foolish question. "Hank asked me to marry him, right after the Bluey incident, so I moved in with him, and Ty latched onto that Cheshire catty little girl of his just to spite me. Ty's kitchen wasn't complete when Cheshire moved in. Beverly and her partner, that lesbian carpenter, had torn up part of the kitchen subflooring and had just set a small piece of plywood over the hole. Cheshire stepped on the plywood, it flipped, Cheshire fell and injured her back. She's been on pain killers ever since, and Ty is...was trying to get a huge settlement out of Beverly that would have cost her everything she's got."

"How long ago did Cheshire's accident take place?"

"Six months ago."

"So you've been married to Hank Atkinson for about six months?"

She stared at me for a moment. "Well, I don't see what that has to do with anything, but yes. Anyway, getting back to our original conversation, consider yourself forewarned." She thrust the wad of tissues, used and all, into my hands, then marched into her house.

It took me a moment to figure out that "our original conversation" meant her warning to me about my friend, Beverly. I sat in my car, checked my phone messages, and returned calls for a few minutes. If what Paige had told me was true, that explained why Cheshire seemed to act so drugged-out whenever her husband was there to witness her behavior around other people. Ty's lawsuit never had a chance of succeeding, though, because Chesh had dropped her ruse every time he wasn't present.

But some of Paige's assertions made no sense. Beverly Wood would never send me to work with a dog owner who'd brought a spurious lawsuit against her. She would have known that he could have found some cause to sue me, as well. And, once again, Ty Bellingham wouldn't have said, "I'm suing you, but I'll happily hire a friend of yours to work with my dog."

Still, what reason would Paige have had to lie to me about this? Whether or not someone had an active lawsuit against them would be an easy thing to check. Not that I knew how to go about doing so—but I could always call a lawyer friend to ask how.

For the sake of our friendship, I needed to sit down with Beverly and have a long chat. My desire to learn what had happened to Ty's adopted pit bull had fallen by the wayside during my conversation with Paige, and I decided to let the issue wait. Right now, I desperately wanted to see Russell Greene and remind myself what it was like to be with a nice, normal human being. Even if that particular nice normal human didn't want anything to do with me.

I headed off for my office, wondering what I'd say to Russ when I saw him. If a little time had brought him back to his senses, he'd be chagrinned at his own pouting and his stubbornness, and we'd be able to chalk this one up to experience and move on. There was probably a change or two that could be made in my behavior, too, but it was much easier to see what Russell needed to do.

Russell was one of the finest human beings I'd ever met. He wasn't dashing or adventurous, but steady, loyal, and amazing. I would never forget how he tried to act as my shield when my desperate attempts to save Sage's life had put me in a collision course with a murderer. Russell had done so even before we were officially dating. He was everything I'd ever wanted in a man...with the exception of our lack of some key common interests.

But, so what if I loved animals and he was afraid of them? So what if he had a passion for rock climbing that I can't begin to understand? Nobody ever said love was supposed to come in a perfect package. He could go off and climb his rocks while I went off to run my dogs.

I reached my office on Mapleton in downtown Boulder. I parked, my heart thumping in nervous anticipation as I spotted his car in the space beside mine. He'd gotten into the habit of working on Sundays, claiming that he could get more work done then because his phone wasn't always interrupting him. I never called him out on the matter, but had noticed that his working Sundays only began once we started dating, after he'd seen how busy my weekends were with work.

Our offices were on Broadway, in a semi-basement—"semi" because the building was partially carved into Mapleton hill. His office had a view of our cars' tires; my office, which he had to pass through to en route to his office, had a view of passing pedestrians' ankles.

I trotted down the steps and into my office and was greeted by the sweet fragrance of flowers. On my desk sat a vase filled with a dozen long-stemmed red roses. There was something about a gift of roses that immediately made me feel like Audrey Hepburn. When she was alive, that is. I glanced over at Russell's door. It was closed, which was somewhat unusual. He only closes it when one of us has noisy, barking customers.

Next to the sweet-smelling roses was a small card that read: I'm sorry. I acted like a jerk. Please forgive me, Love, Russell.

Pocketing his note, I rushed over to his door and knocked. He opened it and we stood there smiling at each other for a moment. Together we must have looked like a couple of overgrown children on Christmas morning. Wounded overgrown children, that is, for Russell's upper body was in a nasty-looking sling that kept his upper right arm pressed against his side, and my left hand was still in its impressive bandages.

"I'm sorry," he said. "I was being a jerk. Do you forgive me?"

"I'm sorry, too. I think we both said some things we didn't mean."

He said nothing, simply caressed my cheek with his unencumbered hand. "Rules are meant to be broken," he murmured, referring to our no-fondling-etc. policy. For obvious reasons with regards to a couple with occasional drop-in clients, we'd decided on a strict no-kissing-and-so-forth policy while we're in our offices. He kissed me gently. I felt distracted by not knowing where to put my own hands for fear of aggravating his injury, and we cut the kiss short.

Though I knew it wasn't the romantic statement the situation called for, I couldn't help but ask, "Is that sling as uncomfortable as it looks?"

"Yes, but at least I can take it off whenever the need arises." Russell returned to his chair, which was sitting suspiciously close to the door, as if he'd wheeled it over there to listen for my reaction to his flowers. "Is today going any better for you than yesterday?"

I pondered the question. Yesterday I had been attacked by a wolf, saw a gruesome murder scene, and argued with Russell. Today I'd been given reason to suspect my friend was guilty of that murder. Also, though, Russell had given me flowers. "Yeah, it's a little better."

"Good."

We both turned at the sound of the squeak my door makes when it's opened. It was just enough noise for me to hear most of the time but not so loud as to agitate a nervous canine. "Somebody's just entered my office. I'll see you later."

He gave me a wink and a smile and gingerly began typing on his computer keyboard. Watching him, my cheeks warmed and my heart felt as though it were doing some sort of tap dance. I wished yesterday had never happened—that I could have just said yes and spent the rest of the day with him.

I leaned through Russell's door to announce my presence.

To my surprise, it was Damian Hesk, the illustrious wolf owner. He looked, well, gorgeous in his tight-fitting jeans, loafers, and a green-and-brown plaid short sleeved shirt, the top two buttons open. Seen in the daylight, he had a fabulous physique, and his blond hair looked newly washed.

I started to shut Russell's door behind me, but he called, "Leave it open, Allida. It's getting a little stuffy in here."

"Allida?" Damian said, smiling slowly. He was standing with his hands in his back pockets, a step from the exit.

"Yes, hi, Damian. Come on in." I smiled, but inwardly felt like an idiot for noticing how attractive he was. Just an instant ago I'd been admiring Russell. I made a mental note to check my breakfast cereal's ingredients for Spanish fly.

"I got your business address from the directory." Damian seemed to have an interest in looking everywhere but directly at me. My office really wasn't all that interesting—the standard-issue filing cabinets, desk, chairs. It was strange how forceful and self-assured he'd been yesterday in dealing with the catastrophe, and how he seemed a little nervous now. Maybe he was the type who was only comfortable when he was outdoors. "I wanted to apologize for my behavior last night."

"Oh, you don't have to apologize."

"Yes, I do. Good God. I made you crawl through a dog door and caused you to get bitten by my wolf." His eyes finally met mine. His were very attractive dark brown, despite the blond hair. "I was just...so determined to get Atla out of there, I couldn't think straight."

Behind me, Russell cleared his throat. I turned and saw that Russell had followed me and was now standing in his doorway. "Hi, uh, sorry to interrupt, but I couldn't help overhearing." He furrowed his brow and studied Damian. "Did you just say that you were responsible for Allida's getting bitten?"

Well, if "true love" meant having schizophrenic mood swings, I was in love, because I immediately bristled at Russell's having interrupted someone giving me a private apology. Nonetheless, my upbringing took hold and I opted to introduce the two men. "Russell Greene, this is Damian Hesk. Damian owns the wolf."

"He *owns* the wild animal that viciously attacked you and killed your client?"

"Russell, that's—"

"Nice to meet you," Russell said, ignoring me. Despite the sling that his right arm was in, he started to extend his hand toward Damian, then winced. "You'll have to excuse me for not shaking hands."

"Quite all right." Damian straightened his shoulders. He probably outweighed Russell and me combined, yet he was perfectly fit. He turned his gaze to me. "Anyway, Allida, I realize I was out of line yesterday. I don't let my wolves into Boulder neighborhoods, and I'm completely opposed to suburbanites owning wolf hybrids. If I'd had any idea what my employee was doing behind my back, I'd have fired him on the spot. Maybe, if I'd caught on to him sooner, none of this would have happened."

"What did Larry Cunriff have to say for himself?" I asked.

A flicker of anger passed across Damian's handsome features. "Nothing. I can't find the guy."

"He's missing?"

"Hasn't been back to his apartment since yesterday, so far as I can tell."

I had the feeling that Russell was glowering behind me, but ignored it and asked, "Is that unusual? Did you notify the police?"

"No, and yes. It's not at all unlike Larry to disappear for a few days without telling anyone. But I did talk to the police about it, just because somebody had to have gotten Atla out of her cage last night, and if it was Larry, he's partly responsibility for a man's death."

My conscience gnawed at me. Damian apparently still believed his wolf had killed Ty Bellingham, but the police had asked me not to refute that for the time being. I said nothing, merely nodded.

"I'd better be going." He looked past my shoulder. "It was nice to meet you, Russell. And again, Allida, I truly am sorry. Let me know if there's anything I can do to make it up to you."

"Could you possibly give me a tour of your facilities sometime?" I blurted out.

He smiled. "Anytime." He reached into his back pocket, grabbed his wallet, and gave me his business card. "Just call. I'll introduce you to my dogs, too."

"What kind of dogs do you have?" I couldn't help but ask, though I could feel Russell grimacing behind me.

Damian grinned. "Two black labs and four mixed breeds."

Six dogs, plus however many exotic animals. Must be quite the menagerie. Mostly in jest, I said, "If you have any trouble handling the dogs, be sure and let me know."

He chuckled and said, "If I do, you'll be the first person I call. Hope to see you again soon."

Russell had returned to his office by the time I turned around. The air had a certain electric quality to it that reminded me of how things felt just before my former fiance and I were about to erupt into a big fight. I counted to ten, trying to put myself in Russell's place. If somebody had come into his office apologizing for urging him to crawl through a small opening with a wolf on the other side, I'd probably intrude on the conversation as well.

He was sitting at his desk, but had pushed his chair back from the keyboard when I entered his office. He didn't look up at me. "Allida, I wish you wouldn't flirt when I'm standing right there."

"I wasn't flirting!"

"At least be honest about it!" His eyes met mine, now, and they showed more hurt than anger. "You have the hots for this guy, and he's obviously everything I'm not! There's no way I can compete with"—he gestured in the direction Damian had gone—"the Brawny Paper Towel Man, short of joining the circus as a lion tamer."

"Well, before you do, you might want to note that all I said was that I wanted to come see his facilities. I was talking about the animal cages. I did ask him what type of dogs he had, but that just doesn't qualify as flirting in my line of work!"

"I heard every word you two said. I'm talking about the subtext. You're not being honest with yourself or with me if you think that's all that was going on. Didn't you notice the way he...?"

Russell stopped and combed his fingers through his hair. He winced as the action caused him to move his right arm. He kicked the drawer of his desk shut with a force that knocked his lamp over and rattled the picture frame above his desk. "I hate this. I hear words coming out of my mouth, and I don't like the guy saying them."

He paused and searched my eyes. With a sigh, he continued, "Maybe it would be best if we stopped seeing each other for a while."

"You want us to stop seeing each other?" I felt torn halfway between despair and fury. What was the sense in all these words we have at our disposal when I was incapable of expressing my feelings? "Then why did you give me the roses? Why did you kiss me ten minutes ago?"

"Why did you give another man all those longing gazes immediately after you kissed me? You obviously want the freedom to be with other men, so I'm making it easy for you."

"You don't know what I want!"

"Then tell me."

I hesitated. My throat was tightening and I doubted I could keep my voice steady if I tried to explain. The truth was, I wanted Russell, but with Damian Hesk's appreciation for animals. That wasn't going to happen, and it wasn't fair to either of us for me to wish it so. Instead of being honest, I called his bluff. "If you want to take a break, that's fine by me."

"I'll keep the door shut between our offices whenever possible."

"Good idea."

"Good. See ya." He shut the door.

I dropped down into my chair at my desk. The fragrant roses were making a mockery of me. In the short time since I'd left my desk, they seemed to have spread out to take every available inch of space. There was no sense in pretending to work, and I had over an hour till my first customer call was due at my office.

I decided to go to visit Cheshire Bellingham and ask about their missing pit bull. I stormed to my car, positively fuming. Somewhere in the recesses of my mind, it occurred to me that none of this was the way I'd wanted or expected for the conversation with Russell to turn out.

Or was it?

Part of me wanted to know more about Damian. Was I going to deny to myself that I was both attracted to and intrigued by the man? Maybe he was every bit as decent, gentle, and loving as Russell. Or maybe he was just a handsome, shallow guy who happened to love animals. Russell was right. It wasn't fair for me to be supposedly in an exclusive relationship with him, while secretly enticed by another man. I couldn't be truly in love with Russell and still have all of these doubts. That didn't mean I never *would* be in love with him, but I had a wandering eye that he'd picked up on. However lousy that might make me feel about myself, it was there and was undeniable.

While driving across town to Way Cool Collectibles, my spirits were sagging. I couldn't seem to shut out my thoughts about Russell. I decided to drown them out instead and tuned in my radio to Tracy's station.

"...that we're devoting this show to discussing wolves..."

"Damn it, Tracy! You drive me nuts!" I hollered and banged my steering wheel. This was so typical of her. There were a lot of things I truly liked about Tracy Truett, but her tendency to exploit local news for the benefit of her ratings was definitely not one of them.

"...have any right to own wolf hybrids. This comes on the heels of all the news about a wolf mauling a Boulder man, Tyler Bellingham. I understand our next caller has quite a personal connection to the story. Hello, Janine. You're on the air."

"Yeah, hello, Tracy." The woman's voice had a deep, almost reedy quality to it. "My ex-husband, Damian, is the owner of the wolf that killed that man. I just want to say that it wasn't the wolf's fault, it was Damian's."

"You blame your ex-husband for the man's death?" Tracy asked in incredulous tones.

"This whole thing was bound to happen, sooner or later. He never should have kept such a vicious animal alive in the first place."

Chapter 10

I turned up the volume of my radio so that I wouldn't miss a word.

"So let me get this straight, Janine," Tracy said. "You both knew that this wolf was dangerous, yet your ex-husband insisted on keeping him?"

"That's right. The wolf that did this, Kaia, was a vicious animal, yet Damian insisted on treating him like a poodle. He'd bring him practically everywhere he went. That's what busted up our marriage. The wolf bit my arm one day for no reason and should have been put to sleep. Damian refused to do it."

This had me so puzzled I pulled over rather than try to concentrate on both the conversation plus my driving. What I knew, but Janine apparently didn't, was that Ty Bellingham's throat had been cut with a knife, and that the wolf in question was a female named Atla, not the male named Kaia. And Kaia hadn't struck me as "vicious." Certainly not when compared to Doobie after Ty whipped him into attack mode.

"How did Kaia get into the victim's house?" Tracy asked next.

"You'd have to ask Damian that question. All I know is that the man is irresponsible. Now his inactions have led to somebody's death. My break's over. I've got to get back to work."

"Can I just—" Tracy paused. I got the feeling she was listening to a dial tone, which we in the radio audience couldn't hear. "We've got to take a commercial break now. My last question to Janine would have been 'Where is the wolf that did this right now?' For all we know, that wolf could be running around loose in Boulder. Perhaps that's a question we will all have to worry about, next time we're out walking the dog."

"Jeez, Tracy!" What a load of crap! Talk about playing up to people's fears and emotions. In a foul mood, I clicked off the radio, signaled, and pulled back into the traffic that snaked around the 29th Street Mall. I wondered idly where Janine Hesk worked, but reminded myself that locating her wasn't my concern.

What was my concern, due to my sense of professional duty, was to check into the missing pit bull's whereabouts. That discovery could verify my theory that Ty Bellingham had been staging some sort of wolf-versus-dog fight when he died. The police had acted noncommittal about that theory when I expressed it to them yesterday afternoon.

Suddenly, the image of Ty's living room returned to me with almost as much clarity as the physical view through my windshield. The furniture had been moved and the curtains drawn so that Ty could stage the fight, perhaps take photographs or video in progress. That would explain much of Ty's strange attitudes about dog ownership. He'd been building a champion dog fighter in Doobie and didn't want me to train the dog, for fear that it would curb Doobie's dominance instincts.

Then, yesterday, Ty or someone else could have nabbed the one wolf of Damian's that wasn't used to being around people. If my theory was correct, the killer could be a partner in the dog-fighting ring.

I had a little bit of trouble locating "Way Cool Collectibles," but finally did. It was at the tail end of a mall-ette, otherwise known as a "strip mall," but my coined term was nicer sounding. A little brass bell jingled as I opened the door and then stepped into a room so overloaded with cloying incense that it would immediately fell a canary.

The store had no shortage of customers—five, not counting me. I wondered if this was why Chesh Bellingham had rushed to open up the store despite her husband's death; her merchandise was collectibles, and few things made collectibles more valuable than the untimely and dramatic death of their previous owner.

Four of the customers were teenagers and seemed to be two couples who knew one another. They were giggling amongst themselves as they checked out the strobe light and the black light in one corner of the store. That corner was partitioned off with black velvet curtains, and it made me nervous when they shut the curtains behind them. There was also a very obvious wide-angle mirror on a stand in the corner above it, making it immediately apparent that the person behind the counter could see what was going on inside. Not that that would discourage anyone who wanted to "make out" in a store in the first place.

Cheshire was involved in a spirited conversation with an elderly man. If she recognized me, she gave no outward sign. I walked up to speak to her. Though the man was doing his best to keep his voice down, his face was red with anger.

"You listen to me! I know what you two did, and I want my money back! You hear me?"

"Mr. Melhuniak, I've had about enough of this! My husband died less than twenty-four hours ago, and all you can do is accuse him of ripping you off! Where is your compassion?"

"Where was yours when you two stole from me? Besides, you're the one who chose to open for business before his body was even cold! I've been patient enough! You know just as well as I do that Ty got exactly what he deserved."

"How dare you say—"

"Your husband has pulled these kinds of shenanigans in our neighborhood for the last ten years. It's high time somebody—"

She held up both palms and alerted him to my presence with her eyes. "If you'll excuse me, I have customers."

Drat! I was dying to know what kind of "shenanigans" Ty had pulled in the neighborhood.

The irate man gestured with his chin at the wide-angle mirror. "Yeah? And some of them are having quite the time of it in your spit-swappin' booth."

"Hey!" Chesh yelled in the direction of the booth. "You cut that out in there! Get out of here, now, or I'm calling your parents!"

"As if you're someone to talk," Mr. Melhuniak grumbled. "You'll be hearing from my lawyers! Count on it!"

The man flashed an indignant what-are-you-looking-at glare my way, then left, throwing the door open so hard the bell nearly came off its mounting. I recognized him. He was the old man I'd nearly collided with outside Ty Bellingham's house yesterday. The two couples emerged from the tiny corner, wearing I'm-so-cool smirks on their faces. They sauntered out of the store.

Cheshire cleared her throat, but otherwise seemed unfazed by what I'd witnessed. Today her long blond hair was in braids, and she wore a black armband over her loose fitting off-white blouse, and denim bellbottoms. "Allida. Hello. Welcome to our...my store."

"Thanks. I, uh, couldn't help overhearing your conversation." Nor could I help but notice that she was in one of her clear-headed moods. Was this because her husband was no longer around to insist upon her acting like a druggie? "Is everything all right?"

She gave a wave at the door where the angry man had just left. "Oh, you mean him? Sure. He's got this ridiculous notion that I"—she held up her hands and lowered her voice—"owe him something because Ty had cashed in on a valuable collector's set of Beatle statuettes that he was foolish enough to sell us at his garage sale. Like, what are we supposed to have done, warn him to get an appraisal before we buy stuff? It's both buyer- and seller-beware when it comes to garage sales."

"Mr. Melhuniak lives in your neighborhood?"

"Yeah." She pursed her lips and fidgeted with a lock of her long blond hair. "You'd think the guy would give me a break, considering I'm officially a widow now."

Meaning she was un*officially a widow 'til her husband died?*

Chesh appeared to be no more upset about her husband's death than she might have been by her van breaking down. Perhaps she meant by her comment that she wasn't the typical grieving widow—that their relationship hadn't been based on love. That wasn't my concern. As a canine advocate, I just wanted to find out if there was some sort of dog-fighting ring that Ty—and Doobie—had belonged to, so that I could do my part in putting a stop to it.

"What can I do for you, Allida?" Cheshire asked, leaning her elbows against the glass case that held a variety of tacky-looking figurines and paraphernalia.

"I was looking into Doobie's personal history, and I stumbled across a confusing piece of information I'm hoping you can clear up for me."

"If I can. And that reminds me. Now that I'm in sole charge of Doobie, we can train him out of his bad habits much faster, right?"

Ease of dog-training. Yet another reason not to mourn the death of one's spouse. "You still want me to work with Doobie?"

"Absolutely. I've got him at the vet's for the next day or two, which is good because the place where I'm crashing till the police let me back into my house is too small."

"Plus there's that darned messy kitchen to deal with," I grumbled.

Not picking up on my sarcasm, Chesh replied, "No kidding."

Doobie was at his veterinarian's. The dog had been in a fight with Atla yesterday. Of course he'd gotten hurt. Somehow I'd missed this obvious consequence. It seemed as though my brain were operating on a twenty-four hour tape delay. "Was Doobie badly injured?"

"Injured? No. Not at all. When I said he was at the vet's, I just meant that's where he's being kenneled for the time being. But I was hoping you'd start working with him right away, once I can pick him up. Maybe now he's learned his lesson."

"Learned his lesson?" I repeated with more than a hint of animosity in my voice. Did she mean that, now that he'd lost a dog fight and watched his owner get murdered, he might be easier to control?

The color rose in her cheeks. "I just meant that now that he's on doggie downers, he might mellow out."

"Doggie downers? I thought you said he was uninjured!"

"Well, yeah, but the vet had to give him something to get him into the cage. Doobie was completely out of control. You should have seen the state he was in last night when I finally got him out of that bathroom. He was frothing at the mouth. The vet was afraid Doobie might hurt himself."

I had to force myself to keep my voice calm. "Chesh, Doobie could physically be in a lot of trouble. Ty used to arrange dog fights for Doobie, didn't he?"

"No." I held her gaze, and finally she averted her eyes and added, "At least, not that I know of, for sure."

"Have you talked to the vet since you brought Doobie in?"

"Yes. Why?"

"I'm concerned about drug interactions. The owners of fighting dogs often put cocaine on the dog's nose. It drives the dog wild. That could have explained Doobie's frothing mouth and his overall agitated state. I don't have medical training myself, but if Doobie had cocaine in his system, it might have caused an adverse reaction to whatever soporific medication the vet gave him."

She listened carefully, her lips pursed into a thin white line. "Doobie's fine. I'm pretty sure Ty never would have done something like that."

That begged the question, though, of what despicable things Ty would have done. My mind's eye flashed again on that almost barren living room, except for a tripod in the corner. "Did Ty have some sort of black-market operation, selling photos or videos of dog fights?"

"God! No! That would be disgusting! He'd never pull something like that while I was around!"

This time, Cheshire was convincing. "There was an empty tripod in your living room. Got any idea where its matching camera is?"

"Ty sort of used to be into still photography."

"Did he own a video camera, too?"

She shook her head. "I don't think so."

But that just meant she might not have known what he was up to. Nor could he get away with being undetected as he staged fights in his suburban home. Unless...

"You must have a warehouse for your store merchandise, right?"

She nodded. "Down in Broomfield," she said with a wince, as if making the mental connection herself that this warehouse might be an ideal location to stage the illegal activity. She wrapped her arms around her chest as if protecting herself from the cold. "I hope you're wrong. Ty was the type of person who followed his own set of rules. If he did stage dog fights at his warehouse..." She let her voice fade away, then murmured, "The thought's just sickening."

"Is it possible?"

She nodded. "He had a hidden staircase that led to a basement. You have to move a panel in the back to find it. He claimed it was just his office down there, and that it was off-limits. I didn't even have a key. One day, though, I needed some cash and dropped in on him. Saw the basement. It was really weird. He did have a desk in there, but the whole rest of the room was partitioned off with these big ugly sheets of plywood set up in a hexagon. I asked him what was in there, and he just told me it was none of my business."

"So it could have been an arena?"

She said nothing, merely paled.

"I called the animal shelter, Chesh, to ask about Doobie's background, and—"

"Why would you ask them?"

"Because Ty told me he got Doobie from a dog rescuer in another state, and I was hoping they had some records or that Ty had registered Doobie."

She shook her head. "No, that's not true. Or, at least, that's not what he told me. Doobie was already part of the family by the time I met Ty."

That conflicted with what Ty had told me as I'd gathered the dog's background information. "So, when Ty was still married to Paige, they owned Doobie together?"

"I guess so. The subject never came up. He told me that Doobie was a stray he picked up himself when he was in New Mexico. Or Nevada. Something like that. He was nearly starved to death, so Ty brought him home with him to Colorado and, essentially, saved Doobie's life."

Chesh had no reason to lie. But why had Ty lied? To cover up for the fact that his dog was dangerous, perhaps? "What can you tell me about a pit bull that Ty adopted from the shelter last winter?"

She shrugged, her eyes wide in her confusion. "Ty never owned a pit bull. At least, not that I'm aware of. Doobie is the only dog Ty's had since I met him, over a year ago." Her smile seemed a little forced and her guise of casualness was fraying at the edges.

"The animal shelter told me Ty adopted the pit bull last December. Were you living with him then?"

"Last winter?" she repeated, rubbing down the glass showcase with a yellow dust cloth as she spoke. "I wasn't around much then, but Ty would have told me if he had another dog."

"Where were you? If you don't mind my asking."

"Pain therapy. An in-patient treatment. I'd injured my back pretty bad, thanks to Beverly's incompetence. She did some work for Ty and cut a hole in the flooring that she didn't mark off. I stepped in it and fell. Hurt my back."

"How is it now?"

"Oh, it's all healed."

"I'll bet you must have been on some pretty heavy-duty medication for a while there, huh?"

Her brow furrowed. "You're friends with Beverly Wood, aren't you? Sometimes the injury still flairs up. When it does, though, I take something, and I'm fine."

A middle-aged couple entered the store, and Chesh excused herself to assist them. I left, thinking to myself that if she had cause to marry a man she didn't love, she might have felt she had cause to kill him.

My opinion so far was that Ty had been a compulsive liar. Perhaps he acquired the pit bull as a sparring partner for Doobie. Ty might have tried to do the same thing with Atla. Maybe he couldn't swing staging a fight at the warehouse for some reason, so he opted for his living room. If my hunch that he took pictures was correct, the killer's image could be on those negatives, which meant the camera and film was likely in the killer's possession.

Could Larry Cunriff have killed Ty in some fight between the two men? If so, perhaps the only answer lay in finding Larry. That would be the police's job, of course, and with luck, they would nab him. Though the entire possibility of this dog-fighting thing had me so upset that the least I could do was try to learn more about it on my own.

I wandered to the opposite corner of the mall. It might prove handy at some point to learn how I could get in touch with Damian's ex-wife. She might know where Larry Cunriff was, and that information could prove useful to the police in their pursuit of Ty's killer. I dialed the radio station on my cellphone and asked to speak to Tracy Truett.

The receptionist put me on hold for a minute and an instrumental version of "Do You Know the Way to San Jose?" was piped into my ear. You'd think a radio station would have a more current selection. Nonetheless, there was nobody in my immediate vicinity, so I indulged myself by singing along until Tracy picked up.

"Tracy Truett," she barked into the phone.

"It's me."

"Oh, hi, Allida! You're on your cellphone?" she asked. "Does this mean it's important?"

"Yes." She knew I kept my cellphone off most of the time, because with canines' excellent hearing, a badly timed ringing or vibrating phone could derail my training. "I need you to tell me the number and business that Janine Hesk called you from."

She rattled off the number, which I jotted down. "She works at a place called Business Images. They're a consultant and advertising agency. You were listening to my show, eh?"

"Yes, I was listening, and it annoyed the heck out of me. You're barking up the wrong tree, here, Tracy. That wolf is very well managed, from what I can see. Don't mislead your audience like this."

"Let me put you on the air now, and you can tell my listeners all about what tree I should be barking up."

"No. Bye." I hung up.

I went back to my office. Russell's car was in the parking lot, but his office door was closed. This was ridiculous. He wasn't going to be able to escape seeing me forever.

I got on with my work. A customer brought in her woefully trained eight-month-old mixed-breed puppy. The woman had gotten so disenchanted with puppy kindergarten, she opted to use me as a training consultant, and I was happy to oblige her.

After they'd left, I returned the one phone call that had come in my absence. It was from a woman whose name, Henrietta Wilcox, meant nothing to me. She had given no information, just her number and a request to call her back. When she answered, I identified myself only as "Allida Babcock, returning your call."

"Is this the Allida Babcock who's a dog psychologist?" the woman asked.

As far as I knew, I was the only Allida Babcock in Boulder. "That's right. How can I help you?"

"My name is Henrietta Wilcox."

That much I already knew. She said nothing more, so I prompted, "Your dog is misbehaving?"

"Not exactly. In this case, it's more of what he's not doing. See, he's a Malamute. I bought him as a watch dog, but he won't bark."

"I see. You know, Malamutes tend not to bark very much. They really aren't ideal watchdogs." As a general rule, Malamutes are highly intelligent but have a strong independent streak that makes them hard to train, and they don't bark. Hence the "mute" in Malamute.

"Oh, dear. See, I adopted this dog a couple of months ago. I answered one of those 'free to a good home' ads in the paper."

Under the circumstances, just the mention of any "free to a good home" ad made me tense. There was no easy method to ascertain how "good" the home actually was, and, tragically, that was one of the ways trainers of fighting dogs could get "lambs" to lead to the slaughter.

Henrietta continued, "I made it very clear to the owners that I lived alone and was looking for a good watch dog, and they told me Titan would be perfect. What can I do?"

I thought for a moment. "Well, describe Titan's personality."

"He's...like a big pussy cat with people. He wants to be petted all the time, even by complete strangers. I put him on a leash, and it's all I can do to stay on my feet. He wants to pull so bad, he's like an old sled dog, or something."

"Do you want to keep him, even though he isn't much of a watch dog?"

"Yes. He's a great dog, it's just that he won't do a thing I say. But I figured, as long as he keeps an eye on the place, he's worth it. So I tested him. I had a male friend of mine from work 'break in' through my back door, and Titan didn't do a thing. Just ran up to the guy and licked his hand."

"Maybe Titan recognized the man's scent," I said, just to be optimistic.

"The problem with that theory is, two weeks ago, somebody actually *did* break in, and my neighbors told me they didn't hear Titan bark at all. Today I had a company install a security system. I'm hoping that that helps, but I'd still like it if I could get Titan to act at least slightly protective."

Surely this wasn't going to be Hank's Security Systems. "What was the name of the security-system company?"

"Hank's. You know, from the ad, 'Safe and sound, thanks to Hank's'? In fact, the owner, Hank Atkinson, is the one who recommended you."

"That was kind of him." Also inexplicably odd. Hank had given me no indications that he thought any higher of me than I did of him.

"Malamutes are such big, strong dogs, an intruder seeing one would probably be frightened and wouldn't know he was only risking getting a little dog saliva on him."

"Or fur. He sheds unbelievably."

Twice a year, dogs like Malamutes and Samoyeds "blow" their coats. "I can train your dog to bark in certain circumstances, if that's really what you want."

"Actually, I want you to train him to obey me. Can you do that?"

"Let me at least meet with you and Titan, and we'll go from there." We set up an appointment.

Russell opened his door just as I hung up the phone. Our eyes met, but he immediately looked away. "I'm just getting a cup of coffee. Didn't mean to intrude."

"I thought you gave up caffeine."

"I'm taking it up again."

"At two p.m. on a summer's day when the temperature's in the nineties?"

"I need some bad habits."

"So I've been replaced by a hot brown liquid that gives you a buzz, hey?"

Something flickered across his features that may have been a smile, but that might have been wishful thinking on my part. He saw that our coffee-maker was off and, in fact, hadn't been used for more than a week.

"It's not like I can avoid your office entirely, you know," he said. "Short of turning my little window into a second entrance, that is."

"Your customers probably won't approve."

"Not the pregnant ones. We could trade offices, if you want."

"And have my customers bring their dogs through your office and into mine? That won't work."

"I could find another office to rent, I suppose."

"I hope that's not supposed to be my cue to say, 'I'll find another office,' because if it is, I'm not moving out, Russell. I can't afford to, right now."

"No, neither can I. That wasn't... what I wanted you to say."

"Good. Then how about this. There's no need for either of us to leave. We can work things out between us, either way."

"Right. We can. I wish—" He stopped, his vision shifting to the glass door behind me. "Looks like you're about to get another visitor."

Beverly burst in. Her usually neat strawberry blond hair was now in a wild tangle and she was on the verge of hyperventilation. She rushed straight past Russell. "Allida, I'm so glad I found you. You're actually here on a Sunday."

"Most of my hours are weekends and evenings. Whenever the dogs' owners can be seen as a unit."

"Listen. I'm in big trouble." She paused, and looked at Russell. "I'm sorry to burst in here like this, Russell."

"That's okay, Beverly," he said. "I'm heading out, anyway. I'll be out of everybody's way in just a moment." He went into his office, grabbed his briefcase and struggled to lock his inner door behind him using only his left hand. "Good luck, ladies," he said over his shoulder as he pushed out the door.

Beverly watched this without a word, shifting her weight from foot to foot while she awaited the opportunity to speak to me in private.

The moment the door was shut, Beverly blurted, "Allida, you've got to help me. I just finished talking to the police. They suspect me."

"Is that because Hank's wife told them you had a key?"

"I'm scared half to death! The police think I murdered Ty!"

Chapter 11

Beverly paced in my small office, too distraught to follow my suggestion that she take a seat. My heart, too, was in my throat. Paige must have told the police about seeing Beverly leave Ty's house. The police might not yet be aware of how Paige's bitter outlook colored her perceptions.

"How do you know that the police suspect you? Did an officer flat out tell you that?"

She shook her head, her hands in perpetual nervous motion as she combed back her wavy strawberry blond tresses. "No, but they grilled me for a good two hours today. They found my fingerprints on the inside of the dog door. That must have happened when I reached in to try and see if I could fit through the opening."

"Why was the dog door open in the first place? Ty had locked it when I left, which was just a couple of hours earlier."

"I don't know, Allida." Her voice had an irritable edge to it. "All I know is, it was unlocked by the time I got there."

For the second time since she'd arrived, she came over to my chair and grabbed me by both shoulders. "Allida, I swear to you. I didn't kill him. I could never kill anybody."

"I believe you." That was the truth, but I had many issues surrounding how and why she got me involved with the Bellinghams. Before I could offer her my support or assistance, I needed to get those resolved.

"I'm glad somebody does," she replied. "The police don't seem to believe a thing I say. They think I killed him out of revenge or because he was suing my partner. But that's ridiculous. Rebecca's an equal partner, and he was suing her personally, not me. Rebecca's got—" She broke off abruptly then said, "More importantly, Hank hated him, and so did Paige. And then there's Chesh. I think she married him just to get his money. She might have killed him so she could inherit. Compared to everyone else Ty knew, I had the least reason to kill him."

The police would be basing their suspicions on evidence, not playing a guessing game of who had the strongest motive. She'd mentioned "revenge." "Paige seems to think you and Ty were having an affair. That isn't true, is it?"

"No, not really." She didn't act even slightly surprised by my question. She'd probably heard Paige's accusations straight from the horse's mouth more than once.

"Not really?" I repeated. When she didn't respond, I asked, "What does that mean?"

She grimaced and leaned back against my file cabinet. She still fidgeted with her hair, and her nervous motions revealed the small gold amulet around her neck. It was a peace symbol.

"Did he give you that necklace?"

Her eyes flew wide and she touched the pendant, then stashed it underneath the collar of her light green blouse. "No, he didn't give it to me. I just forgot to take it off. No wonder the police...." She let her voice fade.

She punched her thigh and started to pace again. "What an idiot I am! The police probably saw this thing and knew it came from Ty's inventory." She clenched her hands and brought them to her lips, meeting my gaze. "I bought it at his store, months ago. I was just trying to mend fences by buying some of his overpriced merchandise, but I wound up really liking the thing. It's light weight, and I hardly ever take it off." She stared at me, as if daring me to doubt her. "Ty and I weren't lovers, Allida. I didn't even like the guy."

Which was roughly what Paige had said in regards to Ty's relationship with his current wife. Ty had certainly been a strange person, sporting the accoutrements and slogans of the peace-love generation, all the while raising a fighter dog. It was hard to imagine that Beverly would find any attraction there.

"Beverly, there's something that I just don't understand in all of this. If you're really my friend, how could you knowingly get me mixed up with these people? All you ever said beforehand was that you needed my help with a neighbor's barking dog."

She winced and shifted her gaze. "I'm sorry, Allida. My lawycr had advised me not to say anything to anyone about Ty Bellingham. He wanted me to avoid the possibility of libel charges getting added on to the charges." She searched my eyes again, her angular, attractive face distraught. "The trouble with that advice was: I needed somebody I could trust to do a good job with Doobie. The whole situation had gotten so dangerous. I think Ty Bellingham chose such a big, aggressive dog specifically to terrorize me and my little beagle. Ty hated Beagle Boy for digging under his fence and pooping in his yard. His getting Doobie put a stop to that, but then Doobie nearly killed Beagle Boy in his *own* yard."

"You never told me that!"

"Didn't I?" She twisted at one lock of her hair, practically knotting it in the process. "Doobie jumped our fence one day. Beagle Boy managed to crawl under the deck where Doobie couldn't reach him. Fortunately, I was home at the time and called Ty at the store. He came and grabbed Doobie before he managed to get at B.B."

"When did this happen?" My agitation was rising, which I didn't bother to hide.

She finally took the seat that was stationed a short distance from my chair. "Two months ago. Just before softball season started, and I found out you were back in the area. Jeez, Allida. This is such a mess." Her eyes filled with tears, but at the moment, I was too annoyed at her bouts of selective memory to muster sympathy for her.

"That much I realize. But in order for me to try and help you out of it, I have to be able to understand you. There's a wide gulf between not slandering somebody and soliciting a friend to work for that person. You could—and should—have clued me in. It seems to me that you were so concerned about yourself and Beagle Boy, you gave no thought to the possible consequences I might suffer."

Her lip quivered, and her voice was choked with emotion. "I'm sorry, Allida." She got up, stuffed her hands in the pockets of her khaki shorts, and resumed her pacing. "A couple of years ago, I threw a neighborhood get-together. The night before, I'd had a fight with the man I'd been seeing and wound up having to host the party alone. I threw myself at Ty Bellingham. I never cared for Paige in the first place, and Ty was just...convenient and willing."

She sighed and ran her fingers through her hair. "I'm not proud of what I did, but we didn't even have sex. He'd had too much to drink, so technically it wasn't even an affair. I thought we'd put it behind us. Last year, he hired me to remodel his kitchen. In retrospect, I think he did that just to hurt Paige by throwing me in her face. By then she was having a none-too-secret affair with Hank. But, back then, I just figured he wanted to fix things between us."

Beverly's mannerisms while she was speaking were animated. She kept walking back and forth between the walls to either side of my desk. It reminded me of the behavior of a caged coyote I'd once seen at a zoo.

"Has it occurred to you that he might have hired you solely to set you up to get sued?" I asked.

"No, I'd like to think the whole law suit was valid initially. When he told me his fiance wrecked her back due to Rebecca's incompetence, my reaction was 'that's why we have liability insurance,' and I saw to it to fix his kitchen to his satisfaction."

Something was out of whack. Mentally, I tried to establish a time-line. It occurred to me that the impression that Paige had given me about the time of her pet's death wasn't in keeping with this story. "He called Chesh his 'fiance'? So Ty and Cheshire were already engaged, even though Paige's belongings were still there?"

She gave me a sly smile. "You heard about the Bluey Incident, I take it."

It was not really a question, but I nodded.

She rolled her eyes. "That was the world's most obnoxious bird." She started to chuckle. "Bluey went kerplooie."

The death of a pet is something I won't joke about. "Paige was obviously attached to him, and she thinks you let her out of his cage."

"She never accepted the truth about that being an accident. All I know is, I never touched the cage myself. I think Ty left it open before he went to work hoping it would fly off with Rebecca and me going in and out of the house all the time. Anyway, after the...bird hit the fan, Paige moved in with Hank before the kitchen remodeling was even complete, and Cheshire moved in with Ty. Musical chairs with your spouses, I guess."

"Did Rebecca approve of your handling of the disagreement with Ty?"

She shook her head. "Rebecca thinks I should have fought him tooth and nail, that she'd rather risk losing the business on legal proceedings than let someone get away with scamming us. But you have to know Rebecca as well as I do to understand how she thinks."

"Not to be overly self-centered here, but I still don't get why you got me involved. If you believed there was a possibility that Ty might have scammed you, why didn't you just tell me that your lawyer advised you not to mention your own troubles with the dog's owner? That would have been enough to forewarn me."

She spread her hands and gave me an expression of complete exasperation. "No offense, Allida, but it was just...a dog. It's not like I recommended you to do construction work on his place."

She paused and held my gaze as if she expected her pronouncement that "it was just a dog" was cause for instant empathy on my part. When I said nothing, she went on, "All that happened is, a couple of weeks ago, I went over to Ty's, knocked on his door, said, 'Ty, you've got to do something about this noise.' He says there's nothing he can do to get a dog not to bark. So I said, 'Here's someone top-notch for you to call who can help you,' and I gave him your card. In retrospect, sure, it was a mistake. But how could I possibly have known all this would happen?"

Her explanation seemed reasonable enough. "Have you talked to your lawyer about your fears that the police suspect you?"

"Sure, but the guy charges something like five-hundred-dollars an hour. That tends to make me want to keep my conversations with him as brief as possible. He referred me to a criminal lawyer, but I haven't talked to him yet. I got out of the interview session with the police and came straight here."

That struck me as odd, but I couldn't think of a kind way of asking why she preferred my counseling to that of a closer friend.

"What can I do, Allida? I've never been in any kind of legal trouble my whole life. Not counting Ty and Rebecca's lawsuit, that is."

"Really, there isn't anything you can do, except talk to this criminal attorney. He'll probably just tell you to sit tight and hope the police discover the real killer."

She nodded, her shoulders sagging as she massaged her neck. I remembered another possible suspect then, and said, "There was an elderly man at Ty and Chesh's store who says those two ripped him off. He was fit to be tied. I think he's even a neighbor of yours."

She perked up a little. "Seth Melhuniak? He lives in that yellow house with the white trim across the street, a couple of houses down. I didn't even know they were feuding. Seems as if everybody had some ax to grind with Ty Bellingham. I'm so sorry I got you into this mess."

That was at least the third time she'd apologized for the same error in judgment. "That's okay. In retrospect, I would rather be involved than see you go through all of this alone." At least, I think I would.

She gave me a hug, saying, "Thanks, Allida. You're a true friend."

I flashed on a time in a high school basketball game when her temper had led to technical fouls that cost us a close game. She'd worn me down then, too, with her incessant apologies.

Beverly noticed my roses and leaned past me to run a fingertip along the red petals. "These are beautiful. Who gave them to you?"

"Russell. Beverly, do you think it's possible that Ty was running some sort of a dog-fighting ring with Doobie as his...champion?"

She dropped back down into the chair. "That occurred to me, months ago, just because of the way Doobie chased Beagle Boy and was so scarred up. I never saw any proof of it, though."

"Did you ever see Ty with an American Stafford...with a pit bull?"

"No, I...." She paused and swept back her blonde hair from her face. "Wait. Several months ago I saw him getting a pit bull into his car. I happened to be outside, walking Beagle Boy, and I nearly panicked when I saw what type of dog Ty had. I think I said something to Ty like 'Getting a guard dog for your store?' And he said that it belonged to a friend of his and he was just dog sitting."

"Did he own Doobie, too, at the time?"

"Yes. But the two dogs weren't together. The pit bull seemed really mellow. Didn't even bark back at Beagle Boy. Ty drove off with the dog, and I never saw him again."

"I'm thinking that there was a dog-fighting ring set up in Ty's warehouse, but that he couldn't use the facilities last night for some reason, and so he moved the operation to his house. You said you were at Damian's property to visit the animals last month. Did you meet an employee there by the name of Larry Cunriff?"

"Yes."

"And did you ever see Larry and Ty talking privately?"

She gave a slight nod. "Toward the end of our tour. Ty had kind of pulled Larry off to one side and they exchanged business cards."

Aha! I could see no way that Ty reasonably could have gotten the wolf except through Larry Cunriff. Which, since Larry was now missing, might mean something terrible had happened to him.

"Allida, all I can say is, I'd give anything to go back and keep you from getting involved with this sorry mess. You always handled everything so easily, back when we knew each other in high school. You were always the one who took charge when things were falling apart in our basketball games. Truth is, I hoped you could come in and pull out another victory, you know? It seemed like a sign from above when I was being tormented by my neighbor's dog, and then, here you are, suddenly back in town and working as a dog psychologist."

Apology number four, I thought.

My next appointment waddled in. It was a very overweight woman followed by her equally overweight cocker spaniel. The woman looked up at Beverly, who'd risen, and asked, "Are you Allida Babcock?"

"No, that's me," I said. The woman's face fell as she dropped her vision to my eye level.

"I'm nobody," Beverly said as soon as the woman's eyes returned to her impressive height and attractive features. "Just a friend of Ms. Babcock's. Thanks for listening, Allida."

"Just a moment and I'll walk you out." Something had been puzzling me that I hoped Beverly could help me clear up. I turned to my client and said, "Please excuse me. I'll be right back."

She nodded and sat down gingerly on the chair Beverly had recently deserted. "That's okay. Take your time," she said in puffs, as if out of breath.

We let the glass door shut behind us. Beverly chuckled and said under her breath, "I'll bet I can take a wild guess as to what that dog's problem is. Just be firm with her. Tell her to put herself and her mutt on a diet."

I ignored her unwanted advice. Another question had occurred to me that I needed her to answer. "Beverly, you must have seen Ty with his shirt off, right?"

"Sure, two years ago. Not since then, though. Why?"

"Did he have a lot of scars on his chest and arms?"

"No, just on his back. He said it was from Paige's fingernails. Gotta tell you, that was a real turn off. When you're about to have sex with a guy, the last thing you want to hear about is how his wife does it, you know?"

"Not firsthand, no. I've got to get back to my client. Take care."

She pulled me into another hug, and then trotted up my concrete stairs. I wondered what was really going

on with her. I felt a pang of frustration and emptiness
while watching her leave and realized I felt the same
way about my conversations with Beverly now as I had
years ago—that she'd played a verbal game of dodgeball
with me.

I returned to my office and reclaimed my chair.

My client reminded me of her name and that her
dog's name was Rufus, then said, "As I told you over the
phone, my vet recommended you. He's advised me to
put Rufus on a diet, but you should see how Rufus begs
for food."

I watched Rufus beside his owner's feet. The poor
little dog was so overweight, he couldn't begin to get
comfortable on my linoleum floor, yet it was a strain for
him to keep rising and readjusting his position.

"I can't bring myself to deprive him of the one
thing he loves most in this world."

"Meaning food?" I asked. This was one of those
tricky areas where I have to work extra hard not to
offend the owner. My therapy work here had to be
geared toward the dog owner, not the dog.

"Yes. It brings him so much joy."

"It's also brought him poor health and a
shortened life-expectancy."

She pursed her lips and raised her chins.

"It is only natural to want to please your pet and
give him treats," I continued. "But a dog depends on his
master to protect him, as well as to love him. If Rufus
loved to dash through a four-lane highway, you wouldn't
let him, would you?"

In clipped tones, she answered, "I hardly compare
serving my dog prime rib with letting him run loose
through traffic."

Prime rib? Yum. I'd curl up at the woman's feet
for that myself, but it was hardly a healthy diet for a
dog.

We needed to back up and get the dog's
background information. In the process, I learned that
she did, indeed, feed three-year-old Rufus as she might

a carnivorous visiting dignitary—sirloin, rib, veal—
because "Rufus just likes those foods so much better
than dog chow."

I annotated a calendar for her complete with
dietary guidelines on how to wean Rufus back into a
healthier dog-like diet and exercise plan. A strange
offshoot of my work as a dog behaviorist had me
working as a dog dietician as well; some veterinarians
around town had recommended me when they ran into
brick walls with their patients' owners, such as this one.

The biggest problem was changing the owner's
mindset to fully realize that the words "love" and "food"
are not interchangeable. Toward that end, I dusted off
my standard your-dog-does-not-love-you-solely-
because-you-feed-him lecture, combined with there-are-
other-rewards-besides-food.

We worked on changing her reward system for the
dog from treats to hugs and pats, discussed the dog's
exercise regime, which at this point largely consisted of
running to the food dish. I espoused the virtue of
playing fetch and walking the dog and how much Rufus
would enjoy the exercise, as well as the chance to
investigate. I also told her that cockers were bred as
hunting dogs, not lap dogs; they need exercise. She left,
and we made arrangements to have bi-weekly
appointments.

I watched them leave and had the suspicion that
she was going to be feeding Rufus beef jerky in the car
on the way home.

My thoughts immediately returned to Beverly and
her predicament. My instincts were telling me that the
whole key to Ty's murder lay in the dog-fighting ring.
That would help clear Beverly of charges, since she
would have had no involvement whatsoever in such a
thing.

I called the police station and asked to speak with
Detective Rodriguez, one of the detectives who'd
interviewed me yesterday. Once he was on the line, I
reiterated my suspicions about Ty's use of Doobie as a

fighter and said that, because of his connection to the wolves, Larry Cunriff was almost certain to be the one witness who could identify the killer. The detective's tones were polite, but condescending.

I had to find Larry Cunriff. It was a silly notion to think that I could find him if the police couldn't, but I had nothing better to do at the moment. I called Damian Hesk's number. He wasn't there. I didn't leave a message, feeling foolish for not having spoken to him more about this when I'd had the chance. Then again, maybe I shouldn't leap into trusting him. I'd believed that he was uninvolved in the under-the-table dealings with Larry and his wolf, yet I'd only just met the man. He might simply be using Larry as a convenient foil for his money-making schemes.

I used the only other connection I had to Larry and headed off to visit Business Images, where Damian's ex-wife worked. The receptionist there was a startlingly pretty woman with a flawless olive complexion, black hair, and green eyes.

"Hi, I'm looking for Janine Hesk."

"You found her. What can I do for you?"

"My name is Allida Babcock. I ran into trouble yesterday with one of your ex-husband's wolves."

"Oh, yeah. I heard about that on the news. You were the wolf-bait woman, hey?" She scanned me at length from her seat behind her receptionist's desk.

"Yes, that was me. Do you know Larry Cunriff?"

"He works for Damian, my ex. Why?"

"I have a theory that the victim, Ty Bellingham, was actually trying to set up a fight between his dog and the wolf. I just wondered whether you thought it might be possible that Larry could have assisted."

"Yeah. It's possible. He's a bit of a sleaze."

"Do you know where I can find him?"

"Larry?" She shook her head and scoffed at the suggestion. "No, but believe me, you're better off not finding him. He's not one the world's most engaging creatures, and once he latches onto you, he's hard to shake."

"Would Damian have been involved himself in a dog fight?"

"No. Damian loves his animals more than he loves anything. He wouldn't have subjected them to that." She crossed her arms, leaned back, and gave her hair a haughty toss. "So, are you romantically involved with Damian?"

"No," I answered immediately, caught off-guard at the question. "I'm just looking for his employee because I'm concerned about dogs. I don't want to see anyone get away with this kind of cruelty to them."

"Hmm." She visually appraised me. "Let me give you a friendly warning. Damian's and my marriage may be technically over, but we're still very much together emotionally."

What was I supposed to reply: I'm happy for you? Unable to come up with an alternative response, I merely held her gaze and felt a small triumph that she was the first to avert her eyes. She was wearing a sleeveless dress, and I saw no marks on either arm. That was strange. She was supposed to have been so badly bitten by Kaia that she wanted the wolf to be put to sleep.

"Is there anything else?" she asked, in what was obviously intended as a polite version of "scram."

"No, but thank you." I continued to study her arms. "I'm kind of concerned about what my scar from the wolf bite is going to look like, but I guess I needn't worry."

She pulled her elbows off the desk and dropped them below my line of vision. "If you'll excuse me, I've got work to do." She rose and started to walk away from the desk. The backs of her arms bore no noticeable scars, either. She said over her shoulder, "If you know what's good for you, stay away from Damian," then disappeared into a back room.

Her belligerence was interesting. Now that she'd made it clear she still had an ongoing relationship with Damian, I wondered if that meant she still had access to the animals. Maybe Larry Cunriff wasn't the only person who could have brought Atla to Ty after all.

I had another house call to make—a recently adopted mixed breed with separation anxiety. Panic attacks when the adoptive owner leaves the house is a common problem, and the damage the dog does to house and home can be very upsetting. We were making some progress, though, with my reconditioning therapy.

Afterward, I decided to swing by Ty Bellingham's neighborhood before returning to my office. Either Beverly or Paige might be home. I wanted to ask some of those people who'd attended the field trip to Damian's ranch if they'd seen a certain dark-haired, green-eyed woman there.

I drove slowly down the Bellinghams' street, checking for signs that either of the Atkinsons was home. Their front door was shut and there were no outward appearances to let me know either way. Remembering the man at the store, I located a yellow house on the opposite side of the street and saw that its garage door was wide open. It wouldn't hurt for me to introduce myself to Seth Melhuniak and see if he might be willing to answer some questions about Ty Bellingham and his missing pit bull.

I pulled over and parked the car on the street in front of the driveway. The angry elderly man from Cheshire's store was in the open garage. I called to him, "Hello, Mr. Melhuniak? Can I speak to you for a minute?"

He turned around, jaw agape, stuck something in his pocket, then fixed a hateful glare on me and punched the button to shut the garage door.

Yet another neighbor who, not knowing a thing about me, was willing to treat me like a viral infection. I'd had enough of this type of reception and stepped directly underneath the door, reached up and gave the door a push. My shove triggered the return mechanism, and the door reversed directions. "Wait, please. I just want to ask you a question."

He shook a finger at me. "I saw you at that store. You're a spy for the Bellinghams' Way Cool Collectibles! You people stole enough from me at the garage sale! You don't get to take the garage itself!" He punched the button again, and the door started to descend on me.

"No, I—"

For some reason, he punched the button a second time, and the door started rising again. "The last guy Bellingham hired already cheated me out of the only thing that was actually worth something to you people. I threw him out of my garage. Did he tell you that? Did he tell you how I wouldn't sell anything to him, so he went and paid somebody else to buy the stuff for him? You can go right back to the store and tell that silly little widow of his that I was onto you. And you can also tell her she got the only set I had!"

I heard him out, largely because it was interesting to learn that he wouldn't deal with the Bellinghams face to face. "Listen, Mr. Melhuniak, I heard about your losing your Beatle statues." He pushed the button and the door started to descend on me yet again. I paused, having to physically stop myself from shouting, "And I don't give a damn about them! Get a life!" Instead, I mustered my sympathetic voice. "I assure you, I had nothing to do with that." Once again, the door was just overhead, and I pushed it. "I don't work for Way Cool Collectibles and I really know nothing about it. That's between you and Cheshire Bellingham. I just wanted to talk to you about the Bellinghams' dog."

"About their dog?" he shrieked at me. "Now you want to talk to me about their dog! What are you, some kind of a sadist?"

"No." Sheesh! I think I liked it better when he was calling me a spy. "Ty Bellingham hired me to work with his dog, and—"

"Don't ever let me see your face again, young lady. You should be ashamed of yourself!"

He got into his car, slamming the door, and threw the engine into reverse. I had to jump out onto the sidewalk to keep him from running over me. He pressed his garage button one last time, watched me to make sure I wasn't going to bolt inside his garage, then drove off.

I stared after his car long after he'd already disappeared around the corner.

There was only one scenario I could concoct that might begin to explain his actions. Even then, it was quite a stretch. I had to go over to Beverly's and ask what she could tell me about Mr. Melhuniak—specifically, whether or not he once owned a dog. Perhaps one that had fallen victim to Doobie.

I left my car where it was and walked across the street. As I neared, I could hear Beagle Boy barking inside. The barks were unnerving—repetitive and shrill.

I tried to shake off my worries as I rang the bell. I'd only been with Beagle Boy a half dozen times. I didn't know him well enough to gauge his emotional state from his barking. At the sound of the doorbell, the barking grew even more persistent.

Beverly had been at my office less than three hours ago. Surely nothing horrible could have happened in the meanwhile.

I rang the doorbell a second time and followed it up by knocking on the door. No answer.

Finally I tried the knob. It turned. The house was unlocked. Now I was scared. Beverly was not the sort to leave her front door unlocked if she were away.

"Beverly?" I called as I pushed it open.

No answer.

The house was completely still. Then I heard a whining and Beagle Boy's claws clicking across the hardwood flooring.

Beagle Boy came running to the foyer. His paws were covered in blood.

Chapter 12

My heart was pounding. As I made my way through the house and toward Beverly's enormous kitchen, my mind refused to grasp what I was seeing. There were red smudges and paw prints on the hardwood flooring. Beagle Boy danced in front of me in crazed, darting circles, barking incessantly as I walked.

In the kitchen, blood was everywhere. *This can't be happening. I must be losing my mind.* Feeling as if my legs were under their own control, I continued further into the kitchen.

On the other side of the kitchen isle, I found Beverly. There were no signs of injuries from a wolf or dog, but the slash across her neck was all too apparent.

"No!" I'd arrive too late to help her. She was dead.

My ears were ringing, my heart pounding so hard I felt faint. I stumbled toward the phone to call 911, but found only the cradle; the portable phone was missing.

I heard a metallic sound from the living room. Someone, my sluggish brain finally realized, was turning the knob on the front door.

The door creaked open. Beagle Boy dashed away from me and toward the sound. He was barking at the intruder, who maintained a slow but steady pace. Somebody wearing hard-soled shoes was nearing.

The killer! He'd come back! I had to get out of here!

I lunged toward the back door and fumbled with the lock.

"Allida?" The female voice was a near whisper. I turned. It was Rebecca, Beverly's partner. The color had drained from her face. "What's happened? Did you cut yourself?"

I couldn't find my voice.

"Where's Beverly? She was supposed to meet me over an...." Her voice faded as she caught sight of the body on the floor.

She came toward Beverly and dropped to her knees. She moaned in despair, then started to cry, pulling Beverly's body onto her lap and rocking her. Without taking her eyes away from the body, she cried, "Who did this! Who did this to my friend?" Rebecca looked at me, her face a picture of despair and outrage. "Was it you?! Did you kill Beverly?!"

Seeing Rebecca in an even deeper state of shock than mine helped me to think more clearly. "It wasn't me. I got here just a few seconds before you did. We need to call the police. My cell is in the car. Do you have yours with you?"

She was sobbing so hard she couldn't speak. This was too convincing to be an act.

Rather than search through the house for the second phone, I pressed the page button. A beeper sounded from a cabinet nearby. I opened it and found the handset in a back corner behind some plates. I grabbed it with my good hand. My gaze fell upon the object on the counter. It was a butcher-block style of knife holder. One slot was empty.

My return trip to the police station was horrid. The detectives were having more than a little trouble accepting the fact that I was innocent and yet had twice been the person who discovered the body. Afterward I went straight home. I had another couple of appointments, but I couldn't go. My shock at discovering Ty Bellingham's body was tripled at finding a murdered friend.

Part of me wanted to go into a blind rage. Yet, these murders were the acts of just one individual. I was determined to do anything in my power to help the police find whoever it was and put a stop to this.

I called Russell's office number on the off chance that he'd returned at some point in the afternoon. He answered, and to my chagrin, just the gentle tone of his voice pushed me over the edge and I burst into tears.

"Allida?"

I managed to control myself enough to mutter, "Oh, Russell. Beverly's dead. Somebody killed her. I need you to—"

"What? Did you say Beverly Wood is dead?"

"Yes." I battled my emotions enough to force my voice to work. "I need you to find my appointment book. I think it's in the kneehole drawer of my desk. I've got two appointments, I think. Probably already missed them. Please call them and tell them I'll reschedule."

"Where are you now?"

"Home. At my mother's house. But I'm okay. I'm just..." I let my voice fade, losing interest in whatever line I'd intended to pass off as the truth. I wasn't okay. At the moment, it was all I could do to hold my head up.

"Is your mother there?"

"No. She's...she must still be at the airport or with a student."

"Allie, whether you want me to or not, I'm coming over. After I reschedule your appointments."

"Thank you. I'm sorry to ask you to do this."

"I don't mind. See you soon." He hung up.

I indulged myself in another minute's worth of tears, then went out into the backyard, throwing sticks for the dogs. That horrid image of Pavlov as a charging wolf wasn't gone, but I was too numb now to care.

Something weird started to happened. It was at last eighty degrees outside, but I was shaking and freezing. It was as if my body was shutting down. I could hear what was happening all around me, but I couldn't move. I sat shivering on the bottom step of the deck, hugging my knees to my chest.

The dogs soon sensed my distress. Pavlov came and lay by my feet, Sage on the step above me, his body pressed against me back, and Dobbler beside me. The dogs leapt up at the sound of the doorbell, but I was still in this position as Russell came around through the gate when I didn't answer.

Russell knelt, peered into my eyes, and said gently, "Allida, sweetie, you're in shock. I can't carry you with my arm in a sling." He grabbed my uninjured right hand with his left and pulled me to my feet. He put his good arm around me and led me inside and into my room. He pulled down the blankets and top sheet on my bed and I kicked off my shoes and lay down, feeling exhausted.

Still fully dressed himself, Russell pulled the covers over me and lay down on my bed beside me and warmed me with his body.

My teeth were chattering. "Bet when you wanted to go bed with me, this wasn't what you had in mind."

He kissed me on the forehead and murmured, "I also imagined if I made you tremble, it would be a good thing."

I slowly felt some warmth returning to me. I lay still, staring at the familiar ceiling, tears running unabated down my temples and into my pillow. "This was my room when I was a child. When my father died, I lost track of how many times I'd send my mom to check for monsters in the closet. But she'd always check. She'd never complain; she'd just tell me that there was no such thing as monsters. Finally, she gave me a spray can, which she told me was monster repellant. I'd spray that in my closet and under my bed before I got into bed. The kids in my kindergarten class probably wondered why my clothes always smelled funny. I figured out that it was Lysol Disinfectant by first grade. It took me much longer to realize that there really are monsters in this world. And they are us."

Russell hugged me.

I closed my eyes and slept for what felt like hours. When I awoke, it was dark outside. Russell was gone. Feeling groggy, I arose and shuffled my way into the living room.

I overheard Mom's voice in the kitchen, but hesitated at the serious tone. Something horrible had to have happened for her to be having such sorrow in her voice.

I wasn't sure who she was talking to, but she was saying, "...my fault, in a way. After her father died, I had no desire to meet another man. I just plowed ahead, doing the best job I could of raising my children alone. She hasn't ever had a man to depend on, and the one time she trusted someone, he turned out to be a total bastard. But all of her experiences with dogs were the exact opposite. It's like she can read their minds, and they hers. I wish there was something I could do to make her see what she's got in you."

"Don't pressure her, Mrs. Babcock."

It was Russell's voice. My mother was discussing my deficiencies with my boyfriend!

"She feels what she feels," he continued. "You can't force her to love me anymore than she can force herself."

What a sweet man! So kind and loving. If what I feel for him is anything less than love, surely this was close enough.

Unwilling to hang out in the living room pretending I hadn't overheard, I intentionally stepped onto the squeaky floorboard, entered the kitchen, and forced a smile. Russell and my mother were sitting across the counter from one another, drinking lemonade.

"Talking about me, huh?" My smile turned genuine when I gazed at Russell, whose face was a picture of loving concern.

"Hi, hon," Mom said, looking only slightly embarrassed.

The phone rang. I answered.

"This is Paige Atkinson. Is this Allida Babcock?"

"Yes, it is." She must have heard about Beverly Wood, I thought, and was calling to feign sympathy.

"Sammy is missing. Can you help us find her?"

Her dog. She was worried about her dog. "No. Not right now." I sighed and rubbed my forehead, ignoring my bandages in the process. "Have you asked Hank? Maybe she's with—"

"Hank's right here. We don't know where she could be. Sammy's so heavy now, she can barely walk! Where could she be?"

"Did you make a whelping box for her?"

"Whelping box?"

"Yes! You're trying to breed your dog. You should know what the word 'whelp' means. She might be off trying to find a place to give birth to her puppies. Was she inside the house when you last saw her?"

"I don't know. Everything was so hectic for a while. Police officers are all over the place. I'm sorry to have to tell you this, Allida, but something terrible happened to Beverly."

"I'm aware of that."

"I asked the police if our dog was over there, but they hadn't seen Sammy either. We've checked everywhere. She must have been stolen. Oh, please, Allida. You've got to help us find our dog."

What would they do when they found her? Wrench the puppies away because they weren't white wolf pups? Damn it! I wanted to stay here with Russell! If only I wasn't afraid that my refusing to help would put Sammy and her puppies at risk.

I set my jaw and said, "All right. But this time if there is the slightest possibility that there are any wolves running around loose, you call the police, you do not wait for me. Got that?"

"We will. I promise."

"I'll be there in an hour. In the meantime, look for low, secluded places, such as under your deck." I hung up.

Both my mother and Russell were staring at me with matching expressions of annoyance. Mom said sternly, "Allida, you just discovered your friend's body. Three hours later, you're going to help somebody look for their missing dog?"

"The dog's probably giving birth, and her owners are idiots. I don't trust those people to oversee the whelping. They're the sort that might bury the puppies and keep the afterbirth."

"They can't be that stupid," Mom said.

"No, but they are that untrustworthy. These are going to be mixed puppies that the owners didn't want their dog to have in the first place."

"I'd better be going," Russell said, getting off the kitchen stool.

"Can you come with me? Please? There's something I need to say."

He smiled. "Sure. To tell the truth, I'll feel better knowing you're not alone, after what you just went through. I'll even help you look for your lost dog." A look of alarm flashed across his features as he glanced at the clock above the stove. "I'm supposed to be at a client's office. We'd better take separate cars." He stopped at the door and said, "Goodbye, Mrs. Babcock. Thank you."

We walked out to our cars side by side. He surreptitiously glanced at his watch, his brow furrowed.

"Is this client appointment something you can reschedule?" I asked.

"Sure. It's nothing important." He gave me a smile, but his words and nervous mannerisms left me unconvinced. "Remember I'm going to be following, so don't run any red lights." He opened the door of my car for me.

"Russell, you don't need to come with me. I'm just going to help these people—" It suddenly dawned on me that Paige had said *Hank* was helping her look for the dog. No way was I willing to have Russell accompany me to Hank Atkinson's home, considering how badly he'd injured Russell last night. "I'm just going to find the dog and then come straight home afterwards. You go ahead and meet with your client, and we'll get together later today."

He searched my eyes, and seemed to find whatever sincerity or confidence he was seeking, because he nodded. "If you're sure you'll be all right."

"I will be."

"You...said you had something you needed to say to me?"

I gave him a passionate kiss, then said, "Thank you."

He smiled. "I'm not sure what you're thanking me for, exactly, but you're welcome."

As much as I wanted to augment the conversation with an "I love you," the words wouldn't come. And Russell wasn't going to prolong this sweet agony any longer. He got in his car, which was blocking mine in the driveway, and drove off.

As I rounded the Atkinsons' corner lot, I peered through this side of the fence opposite the Bellinghams' property. Here the Atkinson's privacy fence gave way to split rail and wire mesh, and I spotted Hank leaning against a tree, watching Paige who was kneeling on the grass, a short distance away. I came through the gate, rather than ringing their doorbell.

Hank straightened and looked at me. "Oh, good. You're here. Now maybe I can get going. Paige wanted me to keep her company, but I'm meeting some of the guys for softball practice."

"I take it, then, you found Sammy?"

He pointed at the stack of logs in front of Paige. The Atkinsons' dog had built an intricate den underneath the log pile by the side of the house. Sammy was nursing six brown-and-white puppies.

"This is quite a den," I said as I looked at it. "There's even a back entrance. Sammy must have been working on this for quite a while. Didn't you know it was here?"

"Nope. There's a back entrance?" Hank said. "Hope she didn't dig up any of the...." He knelt and looked inside. "What's that? It's too big for another puppy."

I joined him and saw a familiar-looking pointed muzzle. "Come here, boy," I called, "Come on."

Another dog came out of the den. It was Beagle Boy. I now had a vague memory of letting him out through the back door before the police came to Beverly's house. I'd lost track of him after that.

"How did he get in here?" Hank asked testily. "I thought I saw a tunnel under the fence, but it was too small for Doobie or for Sammy. He must have cut through Bellingham's lawn."

"The puppies are smaller than I thought they'd be," Paige said, looking in the front of the den. They'd probably been so worried about how to handle their nursing dog that they didn't even look this close till now. "Also darker. They have such narrow bodies. They look like wet rats."

Hank went back around to join her. "Yeah. Kind of like...baby Beagles."

I swept Beagle Boy under one arm. "I think I'll just take B.B. home with me for the time being."

"Wait a minute!" Paige shouted. "A Beagle? Is there some way...." Both Paige and her husband stared at Beagle Boy, mirroring each other's expressions of shock and disgust.

"Allida?" Hank asked. "Can a male Beagle and a female Samoyed mate?"

"Yes." And it was pretty obvious that the proof was in the puppies. "Listen, this isn't my area of expertise. You need to take the puppies and Sammy to your vet the day after tomorrow and get them all checked out. Okay?"

"Beagle-Samoyeds!" Hank grabbed his head in anguish. "I was hoping for white wolves! And now I've just got furry, white wieners!"

Hank stormed off without another word. I stashed Beagle Boy in my car for safe keeping, then Paige and I managed to set up a reasonably good whelping area in the Atkinsons' mud room. We carried the puppies in on blankets, and Sammy waddled after us. Paige seemed sufficiently impressed with how cute and helpless the tiny newborns were that I was sure she'd protect them. Just in case Hank had other ideas, my parting words to Paige were, "The puppies need to stay with Sammy for seven weeks. I'll keep checking in on them from time to time."

I drove home, Beagle Boy making quite a racket in my back seat. I should probably have taken him to the Humane Society, where they would keep him for a week until a relative stepped forward to claim him or they'd put him up for adoption. He was my last link to Beverly, though, and I could take care of him for a while. Unless Mom objected, that is.

I parked and carried him inside. The living room was quiet. The dogs must have all been in the back yard. "Mom? I've brought home a house guest," I called.

"Is he or she bigger than a breadbox?" she called back. Her voice sounded as if it were coming from the basement. She was probably doing laundry. Mom was fairly difficult to faze, and I'd been brought stray animals home many times throughout the years.

"About the same size, when he's lying down."

She came up the stairs and I let Beagle Boy get acquainted with his new environment. He ran around sniffing everything, including Mom's ankles.

"Is this Beverly's dog?" she asked gently.

"He used to be. His name's Beagle Boy. Or B.B. for short."

"Come on, Beagle Boy," Mom said, heading to the back. "Let's introduce you to the gang."

Monday morning, I drove to my office early. I wasn't expecting any clients for another couple of hours, but felt the need to check in with the couple of client calls I'd missed on Sunday afternoon to make sure everything was all right. Russell's car wasn't in his space, so I'd apparently beaten him to work.

I got out of my car and locked it. The morning had dawned bright and cloudless, the temperature already sixty degrees, even at eight a.m. There was somebody sitting on the steps, as if waiting for me to unlock the door. As I neared, I recognized the woman, even from the back. She wore the same dusty overalls and her hair was still pulled back into a pony tail.

"Rebecca. Hi."

She looked up at me. Her eyes so red and puffy it looked as though she had been crying nonstop for twenty-four hours. "Allida, hi. Sorry to bother you. I just didn't know where else to turn."

"That's quite all right. I'm so sorry about Beverly. She was a terrific person." I unlocked the door and held it open for Rebecca.

"Not really. If you knew her well, you'd know she was just who she was," Rebecca said as she brushed by me. "Someone with her fair share of both faults and strengths, like all of the rest of us."

I let the door swing shut behind me and offered to make some coffee. She shook her head and dropped into the nearest chair. I leaned back against the counter, watching her, trying to decide if I should ask the question that nagged at me. It wasn't any of my business, but might have had something to do with Beverly's murder. "Yesterday, I got the impression that you and she were more than business partners."

Rebecca stared at me with empty eyes. "Beverly was straight, if that's what you're getting at." Her voice was almost a growl.

"I didn't mean to imply anything hurtful. You obviously cared deeply for her, and I'd like to help the police hunt for any possible connections between the murders."

"Such as ex-lovers," Rebecca said, her voice more weary than anything else. "She was like a sister to me. She was everything I wanted to be. I didn't mean for it to happen. None of this. I don't know how everything went so wrong."

The words chilled me. "Do you know who killed her?"

"No. I just...it's my fault. I should have confronted her."

"About what?" When she didn't respond, I asked, "The lawsuit?" taking a reasonable guess.

She shook her head. "You can't possibly understand. Nobody could. I want her memory to be...." She bit her lip and paused. "The police, the press, they'll just vilify her. And me."

My mind raced. I had the inescapable feeling I was about to learn things about my late friend that I really didn't want to know.

"I set the whole thing up. In the Bellinghams' kitchen. I'm the one who did it, but it was her idea, too. I was hoping it would be Ty who got hurt, not Cheshire."

It took me a moment to unscramble my thoughts. Rebecca was talking about Chesh's accident, not Ty's murder. "Why would you deliberately booby-trap your own construction site? You were obviously going to be held accountable at some point."

"I just wanted to make him trip, maybe bruise himself up a little. Sprain an ankle, maybe. He deserved it. He treated everyone like dirt, and he was always threatening to feed Beagle Boy to Doobie. I couldn't take it anymore. So one day, I set a board on pencil rollers, figuring he'd step on it. But Chesh stepped on the board, fell on her ass, and cracked her tailbone."

"Having your kitchen under construction probably makes lots of people cranky. It's impossible to believe you'd booby-trapped your own construction site, just because Ty was a creep."

She winced and shut her eyes. "The police didn't believe it either. But he really was capable of throwing B.B. to Doobie and egging him on."

"Why did Beverly keep working for Ty? Why didn't she have him arrested for threatening to kill her dog?"

"The problem was bigger than that, but we didn't have any proof. We didn't know how else to stop him."

"Stop him? From the dog fighting, you mean?"

Her eyes widened and she gaped at me. "Yes. You knew about that?"

"I found out only recently, but I don't understand—"

"See, Beverly claimed she felt the same way that I did about it, that she'd already notified animal control. One day, about three months ago, I came over to her place, and she had a pit bull. She told me he was Ty's. That he'd adopted the dog and was angry to discover the dog wasn't a fighter. She'd volunteered to take care of it so that she could protect it from Ty. A couple of days later, she told me that she'd found a home for it."

"Are you sure? I asked Beverly about that pit bull just yesterday, and she told me something completely different."

"I know. She called me yesterday. She gave me a feeble excuse for calling, said that she wanted to go over today's schedule and 'make sure we're on the same page,' but she never does junk like that. Then she says to me, 'By the way, if Allida Babcock should happen to ask you about Ty owning a pit bull, tell her you don't know anything about it.'"

"But that's...weird. If she wanted to cover up for her own role in this missing pit bull, why tell you not to mention it? I believed her when she lied about the dog. I would never have thought to ask you, too."

She leaned forward, elbows on knees, to look directly into my eyes. "I know. That's what bothered me so much. When I asked her why she wanted me to lie about the dog, she said that you were such a straight arrow you'd insist on following up on the woman she gave the dog to, and she didn't want you to bother her."

"She used the phrase 'straight arrow?'" I asked, my stomach tensing.

"Yes."

That was the same wording Larry Cunriff had used to describe his boss, Damian. I began to worry that Rebecca's tale could have some truth to it; that Larry and Beverly had been familiar enough with one another that they were picking up on each other's pet phrases.

"So you concluded that Beverly did something illicit with the pit bull? Sold it to a dog-fighting ring herself?"

Rebecca frowned. After a pause, she said, "That was the only reason I can come up with for her to be so worried about you tracking down this pit bull. The more I thought about it last night, the more I decided Beverly might have played me for a chump. Gave me this whole song and dance about how despicable Bellingham was to turn dogs into a blood sport."

"Did you ever report this to the police, or at least to animal control?"

She shook her head. "I was going to, but, like I said, Beverly convinced me that she'd already called. Then, once I began to suspect she was part of it, I didn't want to tell the police and damage her reputation. So, I kept quiet." She stared at me, checking for my reaction.

Frankly, my emotions were in something of a tailspin. I didn't want to believe any of this. Was that because it was unbelievable? Or was it merely my natural reluctance to accepting something so heinous about a friend? "Why are you telling me this, Rebecca?"

"It's killing me to keep it to myself. I have to tell somebody, and I don't know who else to turn to."

I pulled out my desk chair and sat down. Dozens of images of Beverly playing with dogs back when we were in high school together or recently with Beagle Boy popped into my head. That kind of affection can't be faked; even if she could have fooled me, she couldn't fool her own dogs. "Rebecca, I admit that I never knew Beverly all that well, certainly not as well as I once *thought* I did. But I absolutely cannot believe she had anything at all to do with a dog-fighting ring."

"Neither can I. I think she was playing me for a fool, all along. Don't you see?" She wrapped her arms across her midsection, rocking herself from her position on the edge of the chair. "Beverly was in on it."

"In on what?" I asked.

"Ty's murder. But her partner in crime killed them both."

Chapter 13

Rebecca's eyes looked glassy. She seemed to believe her own words, but maybe she was completely nuts. I'd prefer to believe that, as opposed to my friend Beverly having been a murderer.

"Rebecca, do you have any proof that Beverly plotted with someone to murder Ty Bellingham?"

"No, but I'm pretty sure that's what happened," she said, her voice a dry whisper.

To give myself a reason to turn away from her, I rotated in my seat and snatched the first item my gaze fell upon—a paper clip. I mangled it between my fingers. "I can't believe that. Even if she was involved in dog fighting, which I also can't believe, she had no reason to kill Ty Bellingham."

My words seemed to shake her out of her zombielike state. She glared at me and said purposefully, "The booby-trapped flooring was her idea. There was this crazy power struggle going on between Ty and Beverly. I think she told me the whole story about Ty and Doobie and the dog fights just to enlist my help in punishing Ty."

"So who were her accomplices? And how did you know she was involved? Did she confess to you?"

"No, but I know that she'd been talking to some man that worked for the wolf owner. I think she was cooking up something with him."

"Larry Cunriff?"

Her eyes widened in surprise. "Yes. That's the name. She had to pay him off to get the wolf. I think she was the one who unlocked the dog door so that Larry could get the wolf inside, and she also cut his phone cords so Ty couldn't get help."

I froze for a moment. I could see how word of the unlocked dog door might have innocently spread to people within Ty's circle, but not of the phone cord having been severed. When everyone's grannie and child owned a cellphone, it took someone with Ty's sixties affinity to have been vulnerable to a land line.

"How did you know about the phone cord and the dog door?"

"Beverly told me. Yesterday, when she called. She claimed knew because she stepped into the kitchen while you and the wolf's owner were taking the wolf out the front door."

Beverly had stepped into the kitchen? Was that possible? I distinctly recalled Beverly already being at the front of the house when Damian and I came out with Atla. Was Rebecca lying about Beverly having told her about the phone cord, Rebecca having cut it herself? My thoughts raced as I tried desperately to argue myself out of my suspicions. "But the furniture in the living room. That had all been moved out."

"The furniture had been moved?"

I nodded. "Ty had to have done that prior to the wolf arriving on scene."

She leaned forward in her seat, elbows on her knees. Finally, Rebecca let out a big sigh of relief and smiled. "You're right! Ty had to have been preparing for the wolf to be there! Nothing else makes any sense." She chuckled, as if a huge weight had been lifted from her shoulders. "I'm so glad I talked with you about this. Maybe I'm completely off-base. Maybe she had nothing to do with any of it."

"That's what I hope," I said, too alarmed by Rebecca's story to feel reassured. Even if Ty did know the wolf was about to be delivered to his house, that didn't necessarily mean that Beverly was off the hook. Furthermore, if Rebecca was the killer and merely feeding me a story, it wouldn't take long for her to figure out that my next step would be to report all of this to the police.

Meanwhile, Rebecca smacked her forehead. "I'm such an idiot. You know, I didn't get any sleep at all last night, running all of this through my head. But there's no proof for any of it. She might have been telling me the complete truth all along. See, if Ty knew this wolf was coming over, his death could have been an accident. Or, I should say, it was caused by his own negligence."

I faked a smile and nodded. Ty might have expected the domesticated wolf Kaia, but had been tricked into meeting Atla. More importantly, the murder weapon was a knife. And, how could Rebecca miss the obvious connection that *somebody* had to have cut the phone cord?

Her face fell. As if she'd been reading my mind, she said, "But, what about the phone cord? Ty had to have been murdered. And I can't believe Beverly noticed the phone cord, just by stepping into the kitchen." Rebecca let her voice fade. She looked more crestfallen now than when she'd first arrived.

Rebecca's mood swing was convincing and reminded me of how grief-stricken she'd been yesterday at finding Beverly's body. Of all the people I'd met from Beverly's immediate circle during the past few days, Rebecca was by far the most likable, and the least likely, by my book, of being a killer. "Maybe she only thought she saw for herself that the chord was cut, after the real killer accidentally told her about it. If so, that might be why she wound up a victim herself."

Rebecca wrapped her arms around her chest. As if mulling the likelihood of my last statement, she finally nodded. In a near whisper, she said, "In which case, you and I could be next."

That was a chilling statement, and for a moment, it left me nonplussed. "You've got to tell the police all of this, Rebecca. Even if it does make Beverly look guilty. It's ridiculous to protect someone's memory at your own expense."

"True. I'll go there now."

Not willing to take any chances, I said, "Let me call Detective Rodriguez right now, and you can tell him you're on your way and why."

I dialed the detective and, after identifying myself, immediately asked, "Could Beverly Wood have heard from one of the investigators that Ty Bellingham's phone cord was cut?"

After a pause, he said, "I'll look into that. She said something to you about the phone cord?"

"Not to me, but to her business partner. She's here now and is just about to head to the station to talk to you."

"Put her on, please."

I followed his gruff instructions, thinking that if any officer had gossiped about the condition of Ty Bellingham's phone cord, it wasn't Detective Rodriguez. He seemed very careful to make sure that he was the one asking—not answering—all the questions.

Rebecca muttered a few words of agreement into the phone, then hung up, and said to me, "I'd better go. Thanks for listening, Allida."

The words made me wince. They were eerily similar to the last words I would ever hear from Beverly.

She headed out the door, just as Russell was coming in, giving him an appreciative double-take. Russell, however, acted oblivious to the fact that he'd just passed a pretty girl. His right arm was still snuggly held by its splint. In his left hand he carried his brief case plus a handful of what looked like stems.

"Good morning," he said, giving me a sheepish smile. He set his case down as he got his key out, switching his bouquet of stems to his other hand.

"Morning, Russell." Eying the paltry condition of his flowers, I chuckled and asked, "Have you been shopping at Cheap Flowers Are Us?"

He unlocked the door to his office, then held his stems out toward me. "No, these were daisies, petals and all, when I got them for you this morning. And, my dear, you will note that there is but one petal left."

Grinning, I came toward him, focusing on his stem bouquet. Playing along, I said, "Indeed, there is but one petal."

"And do you know what this last petal means?" He separated out the one-petal flower and dropped the other stems into my waste basket. "It means, 'She loves me!'" His face had reddened slightly, but he continued, "So you see, Allida, all you have to do is pull off this last petal to make me the happiest man in the world."

I half laughed, half cried. "Oh, Russell. This is the corniest, sweetest thing anyone's ever—"

My phone rang.

At the interruption, Russell leaned over my desk and stuck the all-important daisy in the vase with my roses. He winked at me and said, "You'd better make up your mind about me soon, or there's going to be a whole lot of petal-less daisies in Boulder. Their fate is in your hands." He went into his office and shut the door.

Feeling torn between answering my phone and going after him, I hesitated, then picked the phone just before my recorder would have activated.

A woman said, "Hey, Allida, wha's happ'nin'?" Unnecessarily, she went on to say, "It's Chesh Bellingham. I'm at work right now, but I'm closing shop early this afternoon to go pick up Doobie from the vet's. Can you come work with Doobie right away? I want to start a whole new training regimen with him from the very first time he sets his foot in my house."

"You're already back in your house?"

"No, I mean the place I'm staying at. It could still be a couple of days till I get back in to my own place, but my friend says she doesn't mind my having Doobie come live with us, as long as he's quiet. That means I need to get him quiet, fast."

I checked my schedule and agreed to work with Doobie as a house call, rather than at my office. She gave me the address, and we set an appointment for four p.m. I referred again to my appointment book, taking care to look at Russell's neat and copious notations about exactly what I was to do regarding the two appointments he'd rescheduled.

One of those appointments was with the quiet malamute—Hank's referral from his job installing the security system. She was now scheduled for Wednesday, the day after tomorrow. I called to double check, and the dog owner was fine with that. Not the case with my second reschedule. She was overwrought, and Russ had penciled her in for tomorrow. I told her I was free now if that worked for her, and she said she'd be right over.

This trio of one middle-aged, well-dressed woman and her two dogs were new clients for me. Twenty minutes later, they'd not only arrived at my office, but we'd finished with the preliminary set of questions. The dogs were a neutered male and a spayed Welsh corgi named Corgi and Bess. I silently mused that if I ever had room for another pair of dogs, I might just get a couple of Corgis and steal the names. I have a soft spot in my heart for Corgis. Maybe it's our mutual short-leggedness. Corgis have big, upright, pointy German shepherd-type ears, a tapered muzzle, and squat little legs that are way out of proportion with their solid bodies.

The reason this woman was having trouble with her dogs was readily apparent. The male, Corgi, was fighting with Bess. Last week, he'd gotten hold of one of Bess's ears, and the severity of the wound had motivated their owner to contact me. And yet, she was making the glaring mistake even now of holding Bess, while Corgi snarled by her feet and Bess cowered in her lap.

"What am I going to do?" she cried in exasperation. "I can't protect Bess from Corgi all of the time. I'm going to have to consider putting Corgi up for adoption."

"We've got to start by switching which Corgi you're treating as the alpha dog. That's what's causing this friction."

"I don't understand. I'm not...treating Bess as the pack leader. I'm just trying to protect her. If I were to put her down now, Corgi would attack her."

"No doubt that's true, and that's going to continue to be true until you make it clear to the dogs that you understand and support their self-assigned hierarchy." I reached into my drawer and grabbed a pair of dog biscuits. I handed one to the woman. "Tell Corgi to sit, and when he does, reward him with the treat."

"I'm supposed to ignore Bess completely? Not even give her a treat?"

"For the time being, that's exactly what you'll have to do."

She grudgingly followed my instructions. Corgi was playing up his getting a treat for all it was worth, giving Bess the nonverbal dog's version of "Nanny nanny boo boo. I got a treat, but not you you." Bess, meanwhile, did not beg or even look for a treat of her own. This was highly unusual dog behavior and indicated to me how severe the hierarchy problem really was.

"Now instruct Corgi to lie down," I told the woman. "When he does, give him a second treat, and while he's eating that, put Bess down a short distance away from both of you."

Just in case the dogs immediately went at it, I got my noisemaker ready—an electronic toy that made an obnoxious sound at the push of a button—which I was prepared to use to distract Corgi from hostile actions toward Bess. I then handed their owner the second treat. She followed my instructions. Bess backed away immediately, and Corgi trotted up to the woman.

Success! I had her pick up Corgi and put him on her lap.

"This is so unfair to Bess, though," the woman complained.

"Does she look upset?" I asked, gesturing at the very complacent dog sitting between us.

"Well, no, but...."

"When a pet owner interferes with their dogs' hierarchy, such as by doting on the lowest-ranking member and ignoring the top dog to greet the bottom-runger first, problems are created. The alpha dog instinctively works all the harder to keep the omega in his place, which sometimes injuring that dog."

"But it's so unfair!" she cried again.

"No, it's not. Dogs are not like humans. They simply need to know what their status is; they don't feel sorry for themselves or mope over the unfairness of a caste system that assigns them a lower spot on the totem pole."

The woman nodded and said, "Oh. I see," as if she meant it. From then on, we had no more snarling and cowering on the part of the dogs or either of us, and I gave the poor dog owner my full lecture on how to handle such common things as greeting the dogs upon her arrival. We set a follow-up visit, and she even included a sizable "tip" in the payment that she insisted on giving me today.

The rest of the morning passed with blessedly few hitches, and I managed to push my worries from the conversation with Rebecca as far into the back recesses of my brain as possible. To that end, I surprised Russell with a picnic lunch for two in the small yard behind our office building. The fare that I scraped together on short notice—crackers, apples, and some odds and ends from the vending-machine in the building lobby—wasn't exactly romantic, plus we had to sit on the furry blanket from my back seat. But Russell clearly appreciated the thought, and we made small-talk easily throughout our makeshift meal.

Just as I was warming myself up to tell him that maybe, just maybe, I was capable of plucking off that last daisy petal after all, he asked, "Have you seen Damian Hesk, lately?"

My spirits sagged. "No. Why?"

"Just wondering." He got up and brushed off his gray Dockers. "I've got to get back to work. Be sure and tell me if and when he's out of the picture."

"What makes you think he's in the picture?"

"I don't, Allida. But the problem is, you aren't sure that he won't be in the future. Are you?" He gave me a chance to answer, but I couldn't, because he was correct. I sat there feeling miserable, trying to remind myself that three months wasn't all that terribly long to be dating someone and vacillating about how serious the relationship really was. He ran his fingertips gently along my cheek, then said softly, "Have a good afternoon," and left.

I drove to meet Chesh Bellingham at four, as scheduled. Her temporary quarters were a condo complex in downtown Boulder. From the outside, the places were set up to look like a street in San Francisco, which was fairly attractive, though somewhat incongruous with the surrounding structures. Having such a large, energetic dog in these tiny quarters was never going to work.

I rang the doorbell and an exchange of frantic loud barks and shushes followed. The "shushes" soon gave way to "No! Down! Bad dog!" and banging noises. Finally Cheshire threw open the door.

Chesh's face was damp and her eyes wild, but she said in a lazy drawl, "Hey, man, thanks for..." She gave her head a shake, then said, "Sorry. Old habits die hard. Thank goodness you're here. I need your help with Doobie. He's uncontrollable." She grabbed me by the arm and pulled me inside, shutting the door behind us.

"Where is he?"

"I managed to get him out into the back yard, if you want to call it that. There's barely enough room for Doobie to turn around. I have to get him calmed down quick, or we'll get booted out of here. Somebody already complained. I got a warning from condo management. They say one more complaint, and I'm history."

She led me to the sliding-glass back door, where Doobie had his front paws on the glass and, in this position, resembled a bear rearing up to lunge at us. I felt that damned fear of mine returning, as I considered how physically superior this lumbering dog was to me. I set my jaw, grabbed my noisemaker and said, "Go ahead and let him in."

Doobie hopped down as she worked the latch on the door, then barreled straight past him toward me. I braced myself and pressed the button on the noisemaker just as he jumped up to try to put his paws on my shoulders. He hopped back down immediately, but, to my surprise, started barking wildly, looking around me and the room to try to find the source of the noise.

Meanwhile, Cheshire cried, "No, Doobie! Hush!" She looked at me pleadingly. "I'm gonna get kicked out of here before the day's out at this rate!"

"Chesh, you've got to exert authority over him."

"Easier said than done."

"I know. But it's the only way." I looked at the barking dog and called, "Doobie, come." He followed my instruction. "Doobie, sit." He stopped barking as he did so. "Good dog." I stroked his fur vigorously and explained, "Dogs always get up on all fours to bark vigorously. That's why the 'sit' and 'lay down' commands are so good to get them to stop, and then you can reward him for following your command. Positive reinforcement."

Doobie got up and dashed out of the room, nearly knocking Chesh off her feet in the process. A moment later, he dashed back in and toward me. Our eyes met and my heart leapt to my throat. My injured hand started to throb. Doobie looked like a vicious animal.

To my great relief, he darted on past me. "Is he eating okay?"

"No. I think he misses Ty."

"Probably." Bad pet owners were often as badly missed by their pets as if they'd been good ones.

I continued to try to work with Doobie, but couldn't even get him to sit for me. He was too anxious to concentrate on my commands. Finally, I turned to his human counterpart. "Chesh, I'm not a licensed veterinarian, and I can't prescribe drugs. Normally, I don't recommend them anyway. But all things considered, you need to speak to your vet about getting some Xanix to put in his dog food, for the next few days at least."

"Already got that. The vet happens to agree with you, 'cause he already gave me some samples and made out a prescription for more."

Again I looked at Doobie's eyes, which were clear and alert-looking. There was no way this agitated dog could be on any kind of soporific drug. "He's on Xanix now?"

"No. Like I said, he's not eating."

"Oh, right. Of course."

At length, we managed to hand-feed Dobbie a dose of Xanix by wrapping it up in a slice of ham. Within fifteen minutes, he calmed down and stretched out on the floor, doing a passable impression of a bear rug.

After we'd discussed the basics of how to work the aggression out of the dog and my appointment was officially over, I asked, "Chesh, I'm curious about something. How did you and Ty meet?"

"At his store. I worked for him. Then I got booted out of my house, and he offered to let me rent a room from him."

"And you fell in love?" I prompted, just to test her reaction.

"Love?" She snorted and shook her head. "He's not my type. It was a business deal. We were married legally only. He offered me a third of the store in exchange for my taking the vows."

"What happens now that he's dead?"

She shrugged. "I get the house and the dog in the will."

"Custody of Doobie's actually written into his will?"

"I guess."

I thought for a moment. This was all just so clinical and foreign to my way of looking at things that it was hard to fathom. "So, you agreed to marry him just so you could avoid paying rent and gain part ownership of a shop?"

"Yes," she answered testily. "I know it's not exactly politically correct, but it worked for us. In the process, Ty got to get back at his ex-wife, and reap financial rewards himself when I had that accident and cracked my tailbone in his kitchen. That's what gave him the idea to propose, I think. He realized, if I married him, he'd get half the proceeds of the lawsuit, plus he wouldn't have to pay me to run the store."

Must be hard to get good help these days. "Sounds as though you really came out ahead when he died."

"So would your friend Beverly...if I'd died instead of Ty."

I frowned, and Chesh lowered her gaze. "I'm sorry. I shouldn't have said that. The police interviewed me yesterday. She was a neat lady."

"Have the police been out to investigate your warehouse yet?" I asked.

She nodded. "I took them out there the other day. They didn't find the hidden room, and I didn't tell them about it, either."

"Did you check it out yourself, later?"

She shook her head. "Not yet. I guess I'm afraid of what I might uncover." She shrugged, which was almost a shudder, then slipped back into her carefree facade. "Things have been too crazy, what with Ty gone and only me to keep the business together."

"I'd really like to see it myself, if I could."

She got up, signaling it was time for me to leave. I had to admit that it did seem as though my work was done for now. Doobie was calm, but not too drugged out. "Thank you for helping with Doobie."

I rose too, and she walked me to the door.

"Allida, tell you what. My clerk is going to be running the store tomorrow while I'm working at the flea market in Westminster from seven till five. That's not too far from the warehouse. Afterwards, I'll take you over. You can see the place for yourself."

She wrote down the address for me. I thanked her, then she said, "Actually, since we're right in the area, why don't you come to the flea market yourself? You'll probably be able to get some great prices on used dog equipment: collars, leashes, bowls."

"Yes, but won't the stuff have fleas?" She raised an eyebrow in puzzlement, and I went on, "Since it's a flea market and all. It was just a stupid joke. Never mind. But I've never been to one, so I think I'll take you up on that."

"Great. My booth is in the back, directly opposite the parking gates."

I left, pondering if joining her tomorrow was a good idea. For all I knew, Chesh Bellingham could be the murderer. She could have killed Ty for his inheritance, then killed Beverly because of this lawsuit or something that Beverly had witnessed.

Rebecca's ominous words— *you and I could be next*—returned to me. My going alone to the warehouse with her would be a stupid risk. I had to find someone to accompany me. Preferably someone strong. And fully armed.

Chapter 14

I hadn't been spending enough time with my own dogs, of late. They needed and enjoyed their fifteen minutes of basic training just as much as did any of my clients. I drove straight home from Chesh's place, determined to give my pooches quality time.

Beagle Boy had gotten along with the others fine last night, but because it had been his first night at my house, he was understandably very submissive. That might not last more than another day or two.

I needed to find Beverly's extended family members and ask what they wanted me to do with the dog. Her parents had been older than the norm, or at least that had been my impression as a high school student. I was fairly certain she'd had an older sibling as well, though we'd never met. I would have to check Beverly's obituary to get the sibling's name.

Mom was home. After exercising the dogs and brushing up on their training, we sat on the cement porch out back and had a glass of lemonade.

"Did everything go all right for you today?" Mother asked. For the fourth time.

"Just fine, Mom." I finally decided to relent and gave her the answer she really wanted. "Russell was at work today, and we're still in a holding pattern." Mom raised her eyebrows, and I held up my hand. "That's not a double entendre. I use the term 'holding pattern' totally out of deference to you and your flying."

The phone rang. Mother went inside to answer, then called that it was for me. "A Damian Hesk," she added.

My throat felt dry as I said hello. "Hi, Allida," he responded, his deep voice sounding completely relaxed. "I know this is short notice, but I get my well-mannered animals out once a week on my ranch to get their exercise and all. It's Kaia's turn this afternoon, and I thought you might like to join us."

"I'd love to," I immediately replied. This would not only give me the opportunity to see these exotic animals of his, but to ask him if he'd mind accompanying me tomorrow evening when Chesh showed me Ty Bellingham's secret room in their warehouse.

"Great. In case you were wondering, Atla is not going to be joining us. Even before your troubles with her, I felt she was too unfamiliar with humans to be let out of her cage like the other wolves. But Silver, that's my other wolf, will be included. She's almost as calm as Kaia."

He gave me directions. It would be a long drive, but I made myself a quick dinner-to-go and headed out.

Damian Hesk's property was the proverbial "in the middle of no place." These were the flatlands of eastern Colorado, where the soil was too arid to grow much of anything, there were no immediate wind blocks, and the land was too far from a water source for businesses or houses to spring up any time soon.

I pulled into his long hard-packed dirt driveway. Inside a wooden fence there were two structures, one for humans and one for animals. It was clear where the majority of his money had gone. His house was just a simple one-story building with a carport. The other, more distant, building was an impressive-looking round structure, circled by a thick chain-link fence with electric wires on top. I watched a tiger walking along the confines of his pen. He stopped, turned my way, then strolled through a tunnel-like opening into the round building.

Damian must have heard me drive up, for he came out his screen door and through the gate. Two medium-size mixed breeds rushed outside as well, which he shooed back inside the fence.

"Glad to see you found the place okay," he said, a broad grin on his handsome features. His short-sleeved shirt had only the bottom two buttons fastened, and I had to forcibly keep my eyes from drifting down to his muscular chest and tight-fitting jeans. The wind was blowing slightly. Damian ran a hand through his blond hair, and it fell back into place just that easily.

"I hope you didn't have to wait too long for me," I said, thinking how bad I am at making small talk.

"Nope. Come on and I'll show you around."

He led me back through the gate and, after I'd paused to greet the two dogs, toward the animals' quarters. Up close, I discovered that this massive structure wasn't a true cylinder, but rather, was multiply sided. The chain-link fence surrounding the building was divided into individual pens, each of which had a tunnel leading inside. The outer pens appeared to start and end at either side of the building entrance.

"What material is this made from?" I asked, touching the rough exterior surface next to the door frame.

"It's cement over hay bales. The cement is sprayed on over the bales, and it sets that way. The hay within the walls is a great insulator. The building stays cool inside, even when it reaches a hundred degrees outside."

The door was made of thick, heavy wood, not unlike castle doors. He selected a sturdy key that was hooked on his belt and unlocked it.

We went through the opening and were soon in the cement-floored center. As I'd been forewarned, the temperature inside was chilly, and my eyes took a

moment to adjust to the limited natural lighting
permitted by the numerous long, narrow windows on
each side that were just below ceiling level, and by the
tunnels inside all of the cages to the surrounding pens.
My sense of smell also took a moment to adjust to the
pungent odors.

The cages were set up like slices of an angel food
cake, with this open area the cake center. Without
taking time to count, I estimated that we were
surrounded by twenty cages, each roughly the size of a
standard bedroom. Their inner walls were formed by
bars typical of a zoo, and beside the doorway were the
controls that could lift the individual gates, not unlike
twenty garage-door openers. Next to that was a rolled up
firehose, which I assumed Damian used to wash out the
cages.

"What happens in case of a power-outage?" I
asked as I looked at the controls.

"The gates can all be operated manually as well,"
he replied. "Both from outside and inside each animal's
den." The animals had all run in from their pens to greet
us. Let me introduce you to everybody."

"I'm surprised they're all awake. Is this
suppertime?"

"Not for another hour. Their daily schedules are
seasonal. In the summer, when it's hot during the day,
they sleep, then they wake up around this time and are
up all night."

He told me all of his animals' names, which
passed in a blur. There were two bears—male and
female—their dens had underground caves for when
they hibernated in winter; a dozen or so big cats ranging
in size from bobcats to a male African lion, these caves
were set up in small habitats with lofts made of thick
logs; and the three wolves, which also had lofts, though
these were only a couple of feet off the ground.

"The animals were obviously healthy and alert,
their fur in good condition. This was so much nicer than
standard zoos, which depress me, though I'm not such

an idealist as to insist that it's always wrong to keep wild animals in captivity.

As I circled the area with Damian, I felt myself tense at the sight of Atla, but wanted to face her again in this safety. I slowly returned to her cage. She stayed at the back of her cage—den, as Damian referred to it—but kept her eyes on me. "The animal-control officers let you keep Atla in your custody?"

"For now. It's really the safest place. They stepped up their observation schedule, though. Till this past year, Atla's spent her whole life in a zoo with substandard conditions, and she isn't used to human contact. She stays in her den when I take the others out. Considering how things turned out last Saturday, looks like she'll never be able to get outside with the other wolves." He frowned and slowly surveyed the place. "I could lose all of this if there's another incident."

"You mean, the authorities will close you down?"

He nodded. "My ex-wife got on some stupid radio show in Boulder with this idiot talk-show host and accused me and my wolf of being responsible for that man's death. If all these animals get put down because of this...." He let his voice fade.

I wondered if she had brought Atla to Ty's home. "Does your ex-wife have a key to this building?"

"Janine? No. The only two keys are mine and Larry's, wherever he is. I just hope he isn't—" He broke off.

"Dead," I completed for him. "Me, too."

Damian nodded solemnly. "Why are you curious about the key?"

I felt awkward and out of place for saying this, but I was too curious not to give voice to my suspicions. "If your ex-wife resented your animals, could she have been behind all of this somehow? The murders, I mean?"

"No." His voice was cross. "It's not like that between us. We have a friendly relationship. We can't live with each other, is all. To do something that...evil, she'd have to hate me and want to see my animals get killed. She loves animals, especially the big cats."

"Does she still get to see them?"

"She only comes out once a month or so, usually when I'm exercising Leo, there." He gestured with his chin at the male lion, which pawed playfully with the bars of his gate. "Not a very original name for a lion, I know. He was Janine's favorite. Used to ride in the passenger seat with her when she was driving."

"That must have raised some eyebrows around town. Bet nobody tried to cut off her car in traffic."

Damian chuckled. "It did make some folks nervous. That's why we got tinted windows on both our vans. Kaia, sit." The wolf obeyed perfectly, and Damian headed toward the controls. "Let me show you how—"

"Did Kaia bite Janine's arm once?"

He glanced over his shoulder at me. "You must have heard that broadcast. A friend of mine heard it, too, and told me what Janine said about Kaia."

"By the way, that 'idiot talk-show host' you mentioned is a friend of mine."

"Ouch. Sorry." He opened the gate, Kaia eying me with, I hoped, idle curiosity.

"No, it's okay. I only like her when she's off the air myself. So did Kaia bite her arm?"

"No. I don't know why she said that. It never happened. Maybe she just got carried away with the sound of her own voice and started to fabricate to make herself sound more exciting."

That was plausible. My first impression of Janine was that she was all too aware of her beauty and could easily be enamored of the limelight. I watched Damian go into Kaia's cage, leash in hand. My heart pounded a little with the stress of being this close once again to wolves. Damian roughhoused with Kaia, then fastened the leash on his collar.

The two came strolling up to me, and Damian held out the leash for me. "Would you like to hold this?"

I chuckled. He sounded like a proud parent assuming everyone would want to hold his baby. "Sure." I took the leash. Kaia acted attentive and anxious as Damian repeated his procedure and went in to get Silver. Watching Kaia stand at attention beside me, I realized that my agreeing to be out with Damian and his wolves was an important step in shaking my nightmarish fear of wolf-like dogs. I hadn't even stopped to think that this might be healing for me, but I knew it was. I felt so relieved, I was tempted to give Kaia a hug. Fortunately, I'm not that stupid.

Damian returned with Silver straining to sniff at Kaia, who stayed put beside me. Damian took the leash from me and the wolves led the way out of the building.

"How did you come to own all these animals?"

"I was raised on a farm, and we inherited this lion cub from a dimwit neighbor when I was a boy. Nowadays, I'm pretty well-known. Used to be when a zoo wasn't up to standards and there were no other zoos that could take an animal, they'd put them down. Now they know they can call me."

"Beverly Wood had told me you travel most weekends."

He nodded. "On weekends, I do various appearances with the animals, when I'm not bringing tour groups or photographers here. Then on weekdays, I work my regular job as an auto mechanic, just to meet expenses."

He'd given no outward indications that he recognized Beverly Wood's name. He probably hadn't even heard about her death yet. I decided I wasn't ready to talk about that.

"I'll bet you could get a lot of money for using the animals in movies and special appearances."

"I'm not in this for the money. Even though it's true that there's a lot of ways I could make a fortune. And, apparently, my soon-to-be ex-employee was into one of those ways...studding out my wolves." He led us all to a second gate and pulled out yet another key to open this padlock. "It's amazing how ignorant people are. They'll pay top-dollar for purebred or hybrid wolves when there are so many terrific dogs at animal shelters."

"Do your dogs get the free run of all this property?" I asked.

"Yeah. It's unfenced around its perimeter, as you can see, but you have to go more than twenty miles till you get to anyone else's property. I've never had a problem with one of my animals running away."

"Not even the wolves? Can't wolves travel something like a hundred miles a day when they're hunting?"

"In the wild, sure. But these wolves were raised in captivity and aren't used to roaming the countryside for their food. Even if you opened all my animals' doors, most of 'em would stay put. Their dens are their homes. I have to admit though, I've been keeping my dogs in the yard and the house ever since this weekend. I'm kind of gun shy, I guess you could say."

The wolves strained to run free, and once Damian had closed the gate behind us, he let them off from their leashes. They loped across the field away from us. It was such a breathtaking sight, my eyes misted watching them. It must be such an incredible thing to be that coordinated, that fast.

The pair of wolves veered into what looked like a ravine of sorts off to our left.

"Strange," Damian muttered, following them up the slight incline that bordered the ravine. "They usually go right out toward the back fields, then come back around when I whistle for them. There's a lot more room for them to—"

He stopped, seeing the same thing I was. The wolves were sniffing at a spot thirty yards or so ahead of us. The area was swarming with flies, even at this late hour.

Damian shielded his eyes as best he could from the sun, low in the sky. "Cripes," he muttered. "I've got to get down there." He dashed a few strides further up the incline, then paused to look a second time. "What the..." Damian's voice trailed off. I trotted alongside him. He held out his arm to block me. "Allida, you stay here. I'll go get the wolves on lead."

I had already seen enough, even from this distance, to know exactly what was happening. I took a step back down the hill so that only Damian and the wolves were in view.

The wolves had found what appeared to be a prone, fully dressed male body.

Damian's face was white as he returned with both wolves on lead, wanting to return to their discovery, but too obedient to protest more than by baying and tugging half-heartedly against the leash.

Damian couldn't meet my gaze. From the glassy look of his eyes and the perspiration on his brow, it was clear he was fighting the urge to be physically sick.

He walked right past me and said, "We have to call the police. Kaia and Silver just found Larry Cunriff."

Chapter 15

I couldn't get a signal on my cellphone. We went back into the shelter. The animal odor seemed more pungent than it had just minutes before. Damian got the wolves back into their cages, then rejoined me in the center portion. There was a phone on the wall.

He spoke in hushed tones. A chilling fear enveloped me like a rain-soaked sweater. Three people were dead. Why? What had I gotten myself into?

The only possibility that still made any sense to me was that these deaths were the result of the hideous blood sport run amok; that Ty had gotten himself involved with disgusting people who got off on watching others suffer. They might have started with dogs and now moved on to humans. Ty and Larry could have simply been dispensable members of their group.

But what about Beverly? Despite what Rebecca had told me, I could not believe Beverly had been a willing party to dog fights. She might have witnessed something, perhaps even unknowingly, that posed a threat to Ty's murderer. Was it the severed phone cord? If so, was Rebecca in danger? Was I?

Damian hung up. He turned, but still couldn't bring himself to meet my gaze. His face was a portrait of barely restrained emotion—anger and sorrow. He gestured at the door. "County sheriffs are going to meet us in the driveway. May as well go out and wait for them."

He and I sat down together on the scrubby grass near the head of the driveway, neither of us speaking.

Damian fidgeted with a reed of grass, shredding its seeds one by one. "Larry's body could've been out there since Saturday. I didn't let any of my animals out the gate between then and now. Maybe Larry gave Atla to the killer, who turned around and killed him."

"Could you tell how Larry was killed?"

He shook his head, which seemed partly an attempt to cover for a shudder. "His body wasn't...in the best of shape."

At length, he looked at me and said, "I want to figure out what's going on here. Tell me everything you can about Ty Bellingham's murder."

I gave him as complete a rundown on the events of the past weekend as I could, including my friend's death, and related this morning's confusing meeting with Rebecca, as well as her accusation about Beverly's involvement in the dog-fighting ring.

"You don't believe her?" he asked.

I shook my head. "You know how intuitive dogs are. I just can't believe she could have loved dogs so clearly, yet been aiding and abetting Ty."

"And this warehouse you were telling me about. The one with the secret room. Have you gotten the chance to check that out?"

"Not yet, but I will tomorrow. I was going to ask if you'd come with me. I'm meeting Chesh Bellingham around five o'clock at the flea market, then she's—"

"The flea market? My ex-wife will be there. She makes carvings that she tries to sell every so often. Maybe I'll go and see what she's up to. I'll meet you there." He furrowed his brow. "Are you going to tell the police about this hidden room? Have them take a look first?"

"Not till I've seen it myself. The police haven't shown much interest in my theory about dog fighting being connected to Ty's death. Taking any part in or even knowing about a dog fight without reporting to the authorities is now considered a felony, not just a misdemeanor. Maybe that's why..."

I was about to say that maybe someone killed Beverly rather than let her turn them in to the authorities for soliciting dog fights, but I didn't want to give voice to that theory. My quest to put a stop dog fighting could be making me a bigger target.

The sheriffs arrived and separated us to get our statements. I was glad to see that there were no detectives from either Ty's or Beverly's murders on hand to say, "You again?" But that was short-lived. An unmarked sedan pulled up, and out stepped Detective Rodriguez. His first words to me were, "Allida Babcock. Hello. Again."

The message light was flashing on my machine when I arrived in my office the next morning. I pressed the "play" button and immediately recognized Chesh Bellingham's voice. She asked me to return her call as soon as possible and that if I was hearing the message after nine a.m. to call at her store. It was well after nine, so I called her at the second number.

"I finally got back into the house," Cheshire told me when I had her on the line. "It's weird though. I found something at the house that just...totally floors me."

"Oh?"

"Yeah. I'll show it to you. I'd like to get someone else's opinion."

"What is it?"

"It's a long story. I've got customers."

I rolled my eyes. This struck me as gamesmanship on her part. "Before I let you go, how's Doobie doing?"

"Now that he's in his own element, he's a little better."

"Good." I glanced at my watch. "Our next appointment is for six p.m. this evening. Can this...mysterious thing you want to show me wait that long, or can I meet you over at your house a lunchtime?"

"Hey, yeah. Cool. Meet me at my house around one. That'll give me a chance to check on the Doobster."

"The Doobster?" I repeated sourly to myself after hanging up. I hadn't heard the "-ster" suffix added to names until the 'eighties or so. Chesh was mixing her decades' lingo.

After an uneventful morning, I found myself once again ringing the Bellinghams' doorbell. Despite the beautiful dry weather, a feeling of deja vu crept up my spine.

Doobie started barking, and I was soon looking at his big face pressed against the front window. Chesh opened the door for me, and I barely had time to grab my noisemaker and activate it before the time Doobie jumped up on me, flattening me against the wall.

It took me two shrill blasts of the noisemaker before he put all four paws on the ground, which was a slower reaction time than yesterday. I tried to silently assure myself that his behavior represented job security, rather than failure.

Unfazed, Chesh said to me, "Come take a look at what I found hidden in the back of the dresser drawers in Ty's bedroom."

"You had separate bedrooms?"

She ignored the question and crooked her finger over her shoulder as she led the way through the living room, which—I noted—had been fully restored with all of its former troll-like furniture. She continued down the hall and into the part of the house where I'd never ventured.

She opened the first door, and, to my surprise, it was a bedroom furnished in classy—meaning non-sixties-style—antiques: a four-poster bed, a very attractive oak dresser with a mirror, a hand-stitched quilt on the bed. What was not surprising was that Doobie nearly bowled us both over in his rush to enter the room first.

"Is this your bedroom?" I asked.

"No, Ty's." She hopped up on the bed, which squeaked with her weight, and grabbed what looked like the basic size and shape of a yearbook that had been on the nightstand. "This is what I wanted to show you."

"Someone's high school yearbook?"

"Not high school. College. Arizona."

"I didn't even know universities produced yearbooks." I glanced at the date on the spine. "Apparently Arizona did, twenty-five years ago."

Chesh patted the mattress, indicating for me to have a seat, which I did, after we got Doobie, who'd assumed Chesh's gesture was meant for him, to lay down on the floor by our feet. She had bookmarked a particular page and flipped it open. She handed me the book and tapped her black-painted fingernail on the specific photo she wanted me to see.

It was a picture of a young Ty Bellingham. Though the photo was not taken in the sixties, he wore bellbottoms and a shirt with big cuffs and poofy sleeves. The stocky young man beside him was a shocker.

Chesh scotted closer to me to peer over my shoulder and, again, indicated what she wanted me to see by tapping with her nail. "Recognize this dude?"

I stared, trying to verify the face beneath the phony afro. "Is that...Hank Atkinson?"

"Yep. It was from Ty's college days at Arizona."

"That's where Hank went to college," I murmured. "I remember him saying he used to be on their football team."

Chesh said, "Thing is, though, *Ty* told me he never went to college. Why would he lie? And it seems he and Hank were the best of friends back in college." She grabbed the book back from me, and flipped it open to a second bookmarked page. Look at how Hank signed Ty's yearbook."

I read: To the best friend a guy could have. Go 4 it, Monster Man! Hank.

"Did Ty ever mention his past relationship with Hank to you?" I asked.

"No, never."

"This makes no sense."

I sat on the bed and carefully scanned the yearbook, looking for a picture of someone else I might be able to recognize. Sure enough, I found a very young-looking woman with a distinctive, beaker-shaped nose. Paige Gunders, the former Mrs. Bellingham and current Mrs. Atkinson.

I showed my discovery to Chesh, still seated beside me on Ty's four-poster bed. "This explains the sudden marriage to Hank Atkinson," I said. "They've known each other for years. In fact, there's an inscription here." I read aloud, "'To Ty, the best third wheel a couple could hope to have. Love, Paige (and Hank!)'" She'd dotted the "i" in Paige with a heart.

Chesh grabbed the yearbook from me and read it again herself. "This is, like, Beyond Bizarre. In the, um, nine months I've known Paige, she never once said anything about her and Hank and Ty all having gone to college together. And like I said, Ty used to tell everyone how he was living proof that college was a waste of time and money. That he'd never gone to college and here he was a successful, self-made business owner."

She looked at me, waiting for my reply. Every time something surfaced that looked as though it should be a clue, it only confused matters all the more. "You'd better turn this over to the police. Maybe it'll prove useful to their investigation."

"I will, but I thought, you know, you're a psychologist. I mean, I know your work is with dogs and all, but you still seem to know a lot about human behavior. Can you explain this to me? Why wouldn't the three of them have admitted to knowing one another?"

This was a first—nobody had ever made the leap that my work with dog behavior could make me incisive with human behavior. I decided to take her remarks as a compliment and leave it at that.

"Maybe they wanted to forget," I answered. "Something had to have happened after this yearbook was signed that led to Paige leaving Hank and choosing Ty." Which begged the question: Why, if you wanted to forget about your college experiences, would you live next door to a former college buddy—or lover—more than a quarter-century later?

Chesh latched onto my unspoken question and said, "Yeah, but I mean...whenever I've broken up with a boyfriend, I'd just as soon never see him again. You know? But Ty marries his best friend's ol' lady, his best friend marries somebody else, and they get houses next door to one another. And *then* they swap who gets the girl, detest each other, yet they still live in the same houses. It's like a really bad soap opera."

"You're right," I said, thinking that the relationship among Ty and the Atkinsons did bear some resemblance to dog behavior after all, but this wasn't a train of thought I wished to dwell on. Instead, I continued to flip through the yearbook, looking for Hank on the football team. He wasn't listed. That was interesting; both Paige and Hank had mentioned his having been on the team. In fact, Paige had said how "he never lets anyone forget" about his football prowess in college. I checked his list of achievements to see if he'd been on the team in previous years. No listing. He hadn't been involved in any sports activities, but rather, was captain of the chess club.

Doobie suddenly shot up on all fours and galloped out of Ty's bedroom. He was now barking from what sounded like the living room.

I ignored the dog and asked, "Chesh, did Hank ever happen to say anything to you about being on his football team in college?"

"Yeah." She rolled her eyes as she hooked her long blond hair behind her ears. "I remember one morning he was limping a little when we both happened to be going out to get our papers at the same time. Just to be friendly, I said something to him like, 'Hurt your foot?' and he told me that it was a football injury from his college days that flared up from time to time."

"Did Ty overhear the conversation, or did you ever repeat it to him?"

"Ty wasn't there, and I certainly wouldn't bother to repeat the remark. I mean, college football? Who cares?"

"Apparently both Hank and Paige cared enough about Hank's having played football on a nationally renowned college team to lie about it."

Doobie's racket from the other room had still not let up. Chesh murmured, "He's at it again." She frowned and sighed. "Allida, I'm real concerned about Doobie's mental health. He probably...witnessed Ty's murder." Our eyes met and she said somberly, "The police told me Ty wasn't killed by the wolf. That his throat..." she shuddered.

I shook my head. "Doobie couldn't have been in the room. Ty had trained Doobie to attack people on his command. That means, if Doobie had been in the room at the time that Ty was being murdered, Doobie would have attacked the person. Unless the killer was someone...the dog trusted." *Such as you,* I added in silence.

"That's good to hear," she said pointedly. "Doobie must have already been locked in the bathroom, because I didn't kill Ty." She covered her ears. "You've got to stop Doobie from this infernal barking! What is the matter with him, anyway?"

"Tell me more about the pattern of this barking. Does it usually begin at this hour?"

Chesh shook her head. "I'm almost never here at this time of day. I wouldn't know."

"Maybe I can ask some of your neighbors about the barking."

We left the yearbook on the bed and went into the living room. Doobie was barking out the windows again, but this time, he was barking out the front. I looked out the window myself, but didn't see anything. The sidewalk was deserted. No squirrels on nearby trees.

I turned back to face Chesh, who had slumped onto a beanbag chair, looking forlorn. "I have some appointments this afternoon, but before I go, I'm going to see if there are any neighbors around who can tell me about Doobie's pattern of barking. That might give me some clues."

"Thanks. I really appreciate it," Chesh said. She looked miserable and in physical pain, as if she were battling a headache.

We said our good byes, then I headed down the front walk and soon spotted Seth Melhuniak, tying his shoe lace. He rose, the color rising in his cheeks as he recognized me. He started to walk purposefully away from me, toward his house.

"Hello, Mr. Melhuniak. Could I—"

"You again!" he barked over his shoulder. He made a gesture at me as if he were shooing a buzzing fly. "Leave me alone!"

I quickly caught up to him, despite his impressive clip for someone his age. "Please tell me why you objected so strongly the other day when I told you I was working with Doobie."

Seth tried to wave me off again and grumbled, "That'd be just like a criminal defense attorney askin' why I'd object to his getting his murderous client off scot free."

I stopped as he headed up the short walkway to his front porch and called after him, "Did Doobie injure your dog?"

"I don't have no dog no more!" he said as he slammed his door shut.

Could Doobie have attacked and killed his dog? The thought made me shudder.

Chapter 16

I headed back toward my car, my feet slowing as I had to pass Beverly's house. Moments before, I'd trotted past it without as much as a glance, and now that struck me as a betrayal. I couldn't let her be swept out of my life this easily. There was a reason behind her death; there was a killer who was still breathing while Beverly wasn't, and I would not have peace of mind till I found out why her life had been taken, and by whom.

I needed to talk to the Atkinsons. They alone knew the reason behind the subterfuge regarding their past relationship with Ty. In the process, I could make sure the puppies were still in good health. I rang the bell, and Paige opened the door. Through dull eyes, she stared at me. "Oh, it's you. Dog woman."

My second warm greeting in a row. This was decidedly not Mr. Roberts Neighborhood. "Doobie is barking again and I thought I'd—"

"No kidding," she interrupted. "His barking begins like clockwork around two p.m. and doesn't stop till six." A high-pitched bark began from inside the Atkinsons' house. "And there goes Sammy, too."

It was too early for the afternoon school buses, I thought, but maybe Doobie barked in anticipation. "Do you ever see any children, taunting one of the dogs, perhaps, as they get off the bus?"

She shook her head. "Not that I've noticed. It's always in this order, too. Doobie barks first, then Sammy, then..." she paused and grimaced and said through her teeth, "Beagle Boy, the illustrious sire of our dog's puppies."

If the barking truly was that predictable, I could always stake out the house, hide out in my car, and watch what happened.

"Speaking of your dog, how are Sammy and her litter doing?"

"They're fine. We even have a couple of buyers already, which surprised me. They're not exactly going to be pedigreed."

"Pedigrees aren't as important to everyone as they apparently are to you." She gave me a blank stare, so I continued, "Did you know that your ex-husband kept his college yearbook?"

She paled and stared at me in shock. "No. That's hard to believe. He didn't want anybody to know he was a college graduate. He liked to project the image of the self-made success story. Thought it made him look better."

"Even so, apparently he was too nostalgic to throw away his year book. It's unusual how you and Hank were once a couple, and you bought a house next door to one another. Have you already explained all of that to the police?"

She started to sputter a protest at the "impertinence" of my question, then paused, sighed, and said, "Oh, hell, there's no sense keeping secrets now. It's not so strange, really. Hank and I stayed in touch after college, in spite of my marriage. Our flame never really died. We had a bad fight, and we broke up. I married Ty on the rebound. That was a terrible mistake. Hank and his wife bought this house once it came on the market a year after Ty and I bought his. For years, we all lived with the silly notion that we could just be friends. We were wrong. Hank and I belong together, and we're happy now."

"Huh. I also noticed Hank isn't mentioned as a former player for the Arizona Wildcats."

She curled her lip at me, then said, "He would have made the team. He blew out his knee, his freshman year, horsing around with his roommate."

"Was Ty Bellingham that roommate?"

"Yes, he was, as a matter of fact. Now, if you'll excuse me, I have other things to attend to." She shut the door in my face.

I weighed the notion of ringing her doorbell again to ask her more questions. Yet, the bottom line was, I wasn't a police officer or any kind of an authority figure that could make a case for needing to know. Besides, I was due at my appointment in east Boulder with the new client to whom Hank had referred me.

My new client, a young female malamute, was a beautiful animal, and every bit as friendly as his owner had described. She had lovely washed-out blue eyes with dark rims. The owner, Henrietta, had led me into the back yard to meet the dog, which came right up to me and nuzzled me for a pat.

"You must be Titan," I said. Once again, I could feel myself tense up despite my appreciation for the animal's beauty. Titan had those same lupine features that set my nerves on edge.

I took a calming breath. In the meantime, Titan rolled over onto her back in the submissive position and sought a tummy rub. To discourage her submission, I stepped back and knelt and called her over to me again, then petted her chest when she obliged.

A bit of motion in the corner of the yard caught my eye. Titan, too, turned her head, and we watched a squirrel dart across the length of the yard and then up a tree. Titan showed no more interest in chasing it than I did.

"She's a beautiful dog," I said to her owner, a thirtyish woman named Henrietta.

"Isn't she though? But can you teach her to be a better guard dog?"

" *Better,* yes. But the best watchdogs are aggressive. So far, on a scale of one to ten, with ten being the most aggressive and one the least, Titan is ranking at a two." Maybe a two-and-a-half, I silently reconsidered; at least she hadn't run from me or piddled on herself. "There are three basic elements to aggressiveness: predation, territorial instincts, and dominance. Titan shows none of the three. I can show you ways to beef up her aggressiveness, which I think would be a good idea so that she's not overly dependent on you. And, if you want, you could post a couple Beware-of Dog-signs. She's big enough that those alone could be an effective deterrent."

The woman nodded. "Especially now that I've got such a good security system, thanks to Hank."

"So you're pleased with the work that Hank Atkinson and his employees did for you?"

"Absolutely. Hank is the most-thorough man. Would you believe he personally stopped by today, just to see if I was satisfied?" I said nothing, but she continued happily, "I told him how you were coming out here this afternoon on his recommendation."

"How did he respond?"

She gave me a small shrug. "He didn't say anything, but I'm sure he was glad."

Glad? I thought to myself sourly. Not likely, since my being here did nothing to benefit him directly. Though it was a close call, I disliked Hank Atkinson even more than I did his wife. The man struck me as utterly devoid of integrity. Which is why it struck me as odd that he'd recommended me. Maybe he'd considered that compensating for his despicable treatment of Russell.

"Do you happen to recall when it was that Hank Atkinson recommended my services to you?" If it was after Saturday's softball game, his recommendation probably represented his personal penance for injuring Russell.

She looked thoughtful for a moment. "Must have been a week or two ago. It was the same day he installed the security system."

"Are you sure it was that long ago?"

She nodded. "Yes. His dropping by today was the first time I've seen him since a week ago Friday."

"Huh. That's interesting." It was primarily interesting because, "a week ago Friday," I had never heard of Hank Atkinson, or even of Ty Bellingham.

That meant that either Hank Atkinson had crossed path with a former client of mine who, unbeknownst to me, recommended my services, or he—like Ty—had gotten my name from Beverly Wood.

I continued to work with Titan and his owner on basic training and soon found myself thinking that I knew why the previous owners had been willing to give up the dog to adoption. Titan was a typical malamute, which, depending on what you're looking for in a dog, was good or bad. Very much like their closest canine counterpart, Siberian Huskies, Malamutes are typically not as far removed from their wolf predecessors as other breeds are. Malamutes show strong pack instincts and independence from their owners, and low tolerance for the standard sit-stay-come training. You want me to sit? Maybe later. Gotta go check out the smells by the maple tree now.

Truth be told, a malamute can make even an experienced dog trainer look like a nincompoop—with the emphasis on "poop." Luckily, I had a couple of face-saving excuses at my ready disposal. The easiest was the standard: It won't do you any good for me to train your dog because I won't be living with him. I can show *you* how to train him, though. That was legitimate, but also translated to: You and your dog are the problem, not my brilliant training techniques. A second plausible demurral was: My specialty is as a dog behaviorist, not a trainer, but I can recommend a good trainer to you.

Then there was the upfront method, which I opted for in this case. I explained very carefully and thoroughly my evaluation of Titan and what her owner would be up against, recommended that she might be best off using the tidbit-reward style of training, right before dinner when Titan was most likely to be hungry; to keep the sessions under fifteen minutes but very focused and energetic on her part; and to do this training using a "Gentle Leader," or reasonable facsimile. The Gentle Leaders fasten around the dogs' muzzle and behind the ears, then fasten to the lead itself just below the chin. This puts the trainer in control of the position of the dog's head.

Henrietta was willing to buy one from me, so I showed her how to put it on Titan, warning that the dog was going to hate it. Titan immediately pawed at the contraption like mad and trying to get it off. But she eventually accepted the fact that she couldn't get it off, and I ran Titan through a typical training session. I would have ranked Titan's performance as so-so at best, but Henrietta was ga-ga over it.

After I took off Titan's collar, Henrietta asked, "I noticed you said 'lie down,' as your command. I've been told you should always make one-word commands, such as 'down.'"

"You just hit on my pet peeve: superfluous tips from trainers. You can just consider 'lie down' a two-syllable word. Dogs are certainly capable of treating it as such."

"I've also heard that you confuse your dog if you say 'down' when he or she jumps up on you. That you should always say 'off' instead."

"If you say, 'down,' when a dog jumps up on you, and the dog not only takes his front paws off you but lies down, is that bad? Of course not. In reality, I've never had a dog actually do that, because the dog does understand the difference between 'down' and 'lie down,' so the whole issue is moot. Furthermore, if the dog's on the couch and you want him off it, the dog can understand 'off,' but he can also understand the concept that 'down' means lie down on the floor, not on the couch. The verbal command itself is only part of the cues that—"

My cellphone rang, which struck me as perhaps a hint from above that I'd launched myself into one of my bombastic modes and it was time to shut up. "Never mind." I glanced at my screen. It was Russell. My mood immediately switched to worry, as he rarely called when he knew I was with a client. "Do you mind if I get this?"

"No, go right ahead," she replied.

I walked away and turned my back as I said hello.

"Allida, it's Russell." His voice sounded tense and as if he were out of breath.

"Is everything all right?"

"I'm not sure. I've been here all afternoon, with the door closed. I've got a big presentation to make to a customer at the end of the week, so I've been pretty...absorbed. Still, you'd think I'd notice if somebody came into your office and.... Anyway, the thing is—"

"Russell, what's happened?"

"Did you take your computer someplace, to have it repaired or something?"

"No! Don't tell me it's been stolen! I've got all my client records since I started my business on that computer! It'll destroy me if my computer's gone!"

After a sizable pause, Russell said, "You're not one of those hate-the-messenger types are you?"

Rarely before had I felt this low. Back at my office, my computer was every bit as missing as Russell had described it to be. Nothing else seemed to have been touched. My vase of roses and its single-petal daisy was still there, my papers, knick knacks, just no computer. Russell and I filled out the police report, and I decided to call it a day. A lousy, miserable one at that. Although I told the police that this could have something to do with three deaths in the last few days, they were not optimistic about my chances for recovery. Furthermore, the sergeant, along with Russell, asked me about my backup flash-drive, just to drive the nail in a little further about my not having performed a backup for six months.

The next day, Chesh Bellingham called me to make the arrangements for my meeting her close to five p.m., when the flea market closed. She explained that she had a booth toward the back of the place, and while "the place is a zoo," that her sign for Way Cool Collectibles was pink and orange and hard to miss.

I made the drive down to the Denver suburb, appalled at the heavy traffic and the unending stream of housing. Whenever I'd made this trip down the Boulder-Denver turnpike as a child, the view out my window had been long stretches of barren, slightly hilly fields, against the backdrop of the Rocky Mountains.

The parking lot of the flea market was at least half full. I paid my small entrance fee on the way into the parking lot and parked. The market was one huge paved area with some permanent booths set up like a cheap backdrop for a spaghetti western. I negotiated a path past the huge quantities of fresh produce, the crates of which were partially blocking the nearest entrance from my car. I wandered slowly down the first aisle.

Here boldly painted semi-permanent booths had been set up. They resembled carnival plywood flats of a midway, only the merchants in this row were selling hair-care products and sunglasses, leather goods, fake plants and silk flowers, and socks and undergarments in bulk. Personally, I couldn't see myself buying a gross of panties from a flea market.

As I scanned the crowds, I was reminded once again how insulated Boulder is. The cost of living is so high there and the influence of the college campus is so great that crowds there generally tended toward white, middle-class, youthful people. It was sobering how out of place I felt here, nervous and put-off by the cigarette smoke, the crying, shabbily dressed children.

Past those booths was an enormous garage sale, where people—who all seemed to be smoking cigarettes—picked through vast quantities of used items. Beyond this area, I spotted a few carnival rides, but these were under a tarp, apparently operating only on weekends.

Based on where Chesh had told me to meet her, I concluded that she was probably someplace in the garage-sale-esque portion of the place, and so I wove my way through there till I spotted her orange and pink sign.

The booth was empty. Her hippie mobile was parked in the back. Only the folding tables and the sign were still in place. I asked the woman at the neighboring hunk of turf is she knew where Cheshire was.

The woman shrugged and blew cigarette smoke my direction. In a gravelly voice, she said, "She packed up a few minutes ago. Said everything was too dead to make it worth her while. She went off to see the main attraction, like everyone else."

"What 'main attraction?'"

"Some lion or leopard or something." She gestured vaguely in a direction behind us. "It's all the way in the far corner."

"Thanks." Was this one of Damian's animals? It seemed strange that he would have brought one to such a carnival-like atmosphere. I'd gotten the impression he wouldn't do such a thing.

There was a huge crowd in the back corner, as delineated by chain-link fencing with barbed wire on top. I pressed my way through it and spotted a woman from the back wearing mini-skirt over silver go-go boots and a bright tie-dyed T-shirt. "Cheshire?" I called.

She turned around. "Allida. Hi! I'm waiting in line. I'll be a few minutes yet."

"What's the line for?"

"There's a lion in a van up here. For fifty cents, you can pet him."

"Great," I muttered. And how much would you pay for the opportunity to stick your hand in a piranha tank? I couldn't see the van or the lion through this crowd. Keeping up a constant patter of "Excuse me, please," I started to squeeze my way closer, cursing my lack of stature, which currently made the act of breathing in a hot crowd unpleasant and my ability to see over heads impossible.

"Hey, lady. The line starts back here." I turned and spotted the angry-looking woman who'd spoken. She had a little girl in her arms.

"You're going to let your toddler pet the lion?"

She clicked her tongue. "Of course. They wouldn't let all these people do this if it weren't perfectly safe."

"Who is 'they'?"

She clicked her tongue a second time. "You know. The government."

"Lady, this is a flea market. I'm not sure how closely the government is supervising."

Just then, the lion let out a roar and people started screaming.

Up ahead, the crowd parted and fled. A huge male lion was growling and making his way through the panicked crowd, straight toward me.

Chapter 17

From the din of the frightened mob, a girl's shrill voice arose. "Billy poked the lion with a stick!"

My heart leapt to my throat as the lion neared. This could only be Leo, I thought. I froze, knowing I couldn't outrun a lion anyway. "Leo, stay," I cried.

The lion hesitated, looked at me, then veered off to my right and stopped just ten yards past where I was standing.

My line of vision restored by the rapidly thinning crowd, I spotted Janine Hesk. She was seated at a small folding table cluttered with what appeared to be plaster carvings of animals. To one side of her was an empty van, its double doors on the back wide open, Leo's now-broken collar swinging from its tether on the van's trailer hitch. Janine was clasping a fistful of dollar bills and staring at Leo in disbelief as she rose.

To my horror, rather than go after Leo, Janine stuffed her bills into her fanny pack and turned around. "What happened?" she cried. "Did somebody hurt my lion?"

A boy who looked about ten years old, his face pale, hands behind his back, was cowering between the fence and the front of the van. At Janine's outcry, the boy took off at a dead run.

"You jabbed my lion with a stick, didn't you? Didn't you!" Janine shrieked after him.

In the meantime, Leo circled back. He was now a mere five yards or so away from me. He positioned himself between some other seller's rack of faded clothing and a table packed with dirty old glassware. Surrounding sellers had deserted their wares, and Leo looked from side to side as if prepared to pounce on the first stranger who ventured too close. Terrified, I forced myself to slowly sidestep so that I'd no longer be directly between Leo and his owner.

The crowd was still noisy and panicked. They continued to push their way out of the lion's vicinity. Soon a baseball diamond's worth of space was cleared, with only Leo, Janine Hesk, and me in the field of play.

"Janine," I pleaded, "you've got to get Leo back in the van! Now! Before someone gets hurt!"

Just then, a host of security people approached on carts, no doubt having been alerted by the sound of Leo's roar. My thoughts battled the sensation that this was too crazy to really be happening. It felt as though I were in some circus scene, or in Theater of the Bizarre. The guard that whizzed past me had a gun in his holster. The sight of the weapon brought home the immediacy of the problem.

The carts were pulling up between Janine and Leo, blocking her from view. I gestured and shouted at them to move to either side of Janine. My fear was that, with the guards actively blocking his access to his owner, the lion might feel he needed to defend her—a de facto member of his pride. My efforts were ignored as four guards—all of them burly looking men—seemed to peer straight through me at the lion.

"Stay away from my lion!" Janine was shouting. She pushed her way between two of the guards and tried to shove them back. "For God's sake, don't shoot him! He's completely tame!"

I looked around for a means to help her. A middle-aged man who looked out of place in his business suit and tie was walking past me, utterly absorbed by the conversation he was having over his cellphone. In the hand that covered his free ear, he held a burger that he'd already taken a bite out of.

I ran up to him and grabbed his arm. "This is an emergency. I've got to have that burger!"

He gaped at me as if I were insane.

I grabbed my wallet out of my fanny pack. "Please. I'll buy it from you. I need it for the lion."

"What kind of a—!" He froze as he saw the lion, who had two security men with their guns drawn and Janine trying to shield the lion with her body. He held up his hands and backed away from me. "Just take it, lady." He pivoted and walked away with purposeful strides.

Burger in hand, I ran over to Janine. A guard had pulled his gun and had it trained on Leo. "Don't shoot," I hollered. "Let the owner get him under control."

Janine looked up at me. Her green eyes flashed and her attractive features were tense, but her demeanor softened when she saw what I was carrying. "Oh, thank God," she cried. I gave the burger to her. She'd disconnected the leash from the trailer hitch. "If only the buckle on Leo's collar weren't broken."

I grabbed the leash from her and stuffed the end still attached to the broken collar through the handler's loop at the opposite end. "Just use the leash like a choke collar," I explained as I handed it back to her.

Five guards had formed a half circle around Leo, protecting the crowd. Their guns were drawn as they kept wary eyes on the animal.

Maintaining his stance a short distance away, Leo was growling and pawing at the air.

"Give her some room," I said to the security officers. "This is the lion's owner."

"Put your guns away," Janine demanded. "You're scaring him!"

"Feeling's mutual, lady," one retorted.

"Come on, Leo," Janine called in babyish tones. "Here, boy. Let's go."

Leo took a couple of steps toward her, then she tossed half of the burger on the pavement. As he scarfed that down in one bite, she flipped the lasso-like leash around his neck.

"You'll get the rest in your cage," she said. She kept a firm grip on his leash, her hand buried in Leo's dark mane, and he walked calmly with her to back toward her van

"You're going to have to pack up and take this animal out of here, ma'am," one of the security guards told her.

"No problem," she said, giving her black hair a haughty toss. "I don't like it here anyway." She opened the back door of her van. The lion leapt into it.

As she locked the back doors, Damian drove up. He was tailed by some angry security guards, shouting at him to stop. Apparently he'd heard about the lion somehow and drove straight through the gates without paying.

He charged out of his van. "Janine!" Damian shouted. "What the hell did you think you were doing?"

"I just brought Leo with me to generate some interest for my carvings. I didn't know some stupid kid was going to hurt him."

"He's hurt?" Damian asked, flinging Janine's passenger door open to check for himself, through the panels that separated the lion's cage from the front seat.

"He got jabbed by a stick," Janine said.

Apparently satisfied with his lion's physical state, Damian quickly reemerged from the van. "You should never have taken such a stupid chance, Janine!"

The security guards near me were now conversing about what to do. One of them nodded to the others and walked toward Janine with a self-important swagger. "Ma'am, we've put a call in to the police. They're going to charge you with reckless endangerment."

"That's ridiculous," she said. "Leo isn't dangerous."

"You didn't get my permission to take Leo in the first place!" Damian was so angry he seemed oblivious to the public setting. "You had no right to get him out of his cage like this!"

Around us, some of the crowd made a show of pretending to look at the used merchandise nearby while they eavesdropped. Not wanting to be guilty of the same infraction, I decided to look for Chesh.

Before I could get out of earshot, Damian called, "Allida, wait."

"Leo is mine!" Janine retorted. "He always has been mine."

"Not according to the judge, he's not." Damian turned toward me. He still looked furious. "Come on, Allida. Let's get out of here. I'll give you a ride to your car."

"Damian," Janine interrupted, "you had better learn to keep your nose out of my business. What are you doing down here anyway?" She gave me a haughty appraisal. "Are you two here together?"

Following Damian's lead, I said nothing. Janine grabbed my arm. "You better watch what you're getting yourself into, girlie," she said under her breath.

She let go of me and tried to open her door, but Damian refused to allow Janine back into her van, saying, "You think I'm going to let you keep custody of my lion after this?"

He reached into his pocket and pulled out his keys, slapping them into Janine's palm. "Give me the key to your van, so I can get Leo out of here."

"No, Damian! I'm not giving you my car keys! My artwork is in that van, too. Knowing you, you'll just ruin the—"

Damian grabbed two large plastic bags on the front seat and thrust them into her arms. "Here. Get your dumb carvings, and get out of here!"

She gave me a smirk. "See what I mean, Allida?" Casting an evil eye Damian's direction, she slowly packed up the statues that had been on the table, folded up the table and chair, tossed those into Damian's van, then left with a pair of the security officers, her nose in the air.

Damian, in the meantime, had his hands full with the other security officers, assuring them that he had nothing to do with this and only wanted them to move aside so he could get his lion out of here. Finally, the guards relented, amid my and other witnesses' assurances that he arrived well after his ex-wife and the lion. He got into his Janine's van, threw open the door on the passenger side and said, "Allida. Get in."

I scanned the crowd of lookee-loos, which, now that the lion was safely locked away, had enveloped us. Finally, I found Cheshire. She was regarding all of this coolly, standing with her arms crossed and a bored expression on her face. I called to her, "We'll meet you in the parking lot. All right?"

She held up a hand in acknowledgement, then called back, "I need ten minutes to finish packing everything up. You can follow me, okay? You'll be able to recognize my van, right?"

"Yes." *Unless we got it mixed up with all the other orange VW vans with gaudy, inept murals on the side.* I climbed up into the seat beside Damian and shut the door. Through the thick wire-mesh panels behind my seat, I could hear Leo's rumbling noises.

"Is he purring?"

Damian nodded. "He's really gentle. Thinks of himself as a house cat." He smacked the steering wheel with his hand. "I can't believe she did this. What was she thinking? She snuck my lion in here and actually charged people to pet him. That's so stupid."

"So apparently she has a key to the animal den after all."

"Apparently," he grumbled.

We ever-so-slowly drove through the crowd. People were jogging alongside and trying to peer through the tinted windows. Damian drove us out through the gate, then we pulled over.

My pulse finally almost back to normal, I asked, "You're going to have to take Leo home right away, aren't you?"

He nodded. "I'm sorry. You won't have any trouble at the warehouse with that woman, will you?"

I smiled at the dramatic tone he'd use to describe Chesh Bellingham. "That woman?" I repeated.

He grimaced. "I met her and Ty when they were out at my place on the tour that Hank arranged."

Damian's demeanor made it clear that he didn't care for Chesh, but that wasn't surprising. Considering that Damian had met her while in Ty's presence, she'd have been using her drug-head persona. "I'm sure it'll be fine if she and I go to the warehouse by ourselves."

"Where's your car?"

I pointed it out, and he drove me over there. He stopped in an empty space at the end of the aisle. "How 'bout I wait with you? Then I'll follow the two of you over there, just to make sure there are no surprises when you get there."

I had to grin at that statement. What could possibly be more surprising than a lion on the loose at a flea market? "Thanks. I'm sure you and Leo will be able to scare off any intruders."

I waited a moment to see if, without my prompting, Damian would explain how Janine had access to Leo. He remained silent, however. "Damian, if Janine could get Leo, couldn't she also gotten out Atla last Saturday?"

He frowned. "I guess it's possible, but...." He shook his head. "No. There's just no way Janine would have gotten Atla out of his cage. Janine's scared to death of wolves. You heard her on that show. She even made that bogus claim about Kaia having bitten her."

"But maybe she hired Larry Cunriff to handle the part about getting Atla into Ty's house. Is it possible that she hired Larry to kill Ty, then, once he was expendable, she killed Larry?"

"Janine? Murder someone? No way. I was married to the woman for six years. There's no way she'd turn into a ruthless killer in the year since we got divorced."

He was convinced of her innocence, but what little I'd seen of her had given me no reason to think kindly of her. Plus, no one could truly know what someone else was capable of doing.

"I noticed she knew your name," Damian said. "You two know each other?"

"No, I went to her office a couple of days ago to meet her."

Damian tensed. "Why?"

"I wanted to ask her about Larry Cunriff. I've been trying to find out if he was Ty's partner in the dog-fighting ring."

"Did she think he was?"

"She said it was possible."

He nodded. "Thing is, though, since both Ty and Larry are dead, it's going to be hard to prove." He gave me a sideways glance. "Have you come across any avid dog lovers who might've turned into vigilantes?"

"You think these murders might have been the result of some anti-animal cruelty crusaders?"

"It's a possibility, don't you think?" he replied.

"Sure it's possible. If we were talking about a really off-balanced animal lover." Perhaps, I considered silently, someone whose dog had been killed. Seth Melhuniak came to mind.

What about Damian Hesk himself? He'd devoted his entire life to rescuing exotic animals. Could he have found out what was being done to his wolves and killed everyone involved?

No, I decided immediately. I simply could not believe this man beside me was capable of murder. Then again, what if he looked at the deaths as self-defense on behalf of the animals? Furthermore, I didn't know Damian whatsoever and had just now been skeptical of his ability to assess his ex-wife's innocence.

"Janine warned me to watch out a few minutes ago," I said. "That I had 'no idea what I was getting' myself into." I studied his face in profile, but he gave no reaction. "Do you have any idea what she meant by that?"

He rolled his eyes and shook his head. "She must realize... I'm attracted to you. She's still holding out this hope that we'll get back together again. It's never going to happen, though."

Chesh drove up in her hippie van, honking and waving. I got out to head to my car just as she drove up alongside Damian's. "Hey, guys. You all set? How's the gentle giant cat doing?"

Damian glanced back at Leo. "Sleeping. He's really used to riding around in here. He'll be fine. I'm going to follow the both of you, then take off."

"Groovy, dude," she said.

The outside of the Way Cool Collectibles warehouse was unexceptional—basic brown clapboard siding, no windows. As I looked at it, I couldn't help imagining it during fights as filled with smelly macho males, titillated at the sight of a couple of unfortunate, abused animals fighting to the death. I could almost hear the men's shouts and smell the beer breath and cigarette smoke.

Damian pulled up behind us into the small parking lot, which was empty except for our vehicles. He got out of his vehicle and quietly shut the door behind him. "Leo's still zonked. I can't imagine how he could get into any trouble if I come in with you just for a minute or two."

"Suit yourself, dude," Cheshire said with a shrug. She unlocked the warehouse door and flicked a light switch, then led Damian and me inside. The place had aisles and was neater than I'd expected it to be. There were rows of boxed items all with inventory numbers on them. Then, as we went further into the room, the neatness broke down and it looked like someone's messy attic.

"Haven't gotten around to sorting through all the new stuff yet."

"New?" Damian repeated, looking at what I recognized as a plastic bottle of bath bubbles shaped like a bear. I hadn't seen that product in at least twenty years. "Where'd you get this stuff?"

"We do a lot of scouting at garage sales and flea markets, when I'm not trying to sell off stuff, like today."

"'We,' meaning you and Ty?" I asked.

She nodded. "Got to get out of the habit of saying that, I guess."

"I'm sorry about your loss," Damian murmured.

She scoffed and said, "Yeah. Some loss."

Damian stiffened, but said nothing.

Chesh led us to the opposite side of the building. Though this inner wall with its cheap, shiny paneling looked identical to the other three, the flooring had some unusual-looking scuff marks. "Watch this, man," Chesh said. She pushed against one panel, and the other side rotated out toward us. "The opening's pretty narrow, and there are no lights on the stairs, so watch your step. I'll go first."

"Isn't it unusual to have a cellar in a warehouse?"

"Beats me. I think this building used to be some kind of factory. Ty might've built the hidden entrance himself."

The three of us felt our way down the dark, narrow staircase. The light clicked on just as I was on my last step, and I found myself in a dank, claustrophobic space, more like an underground cave than anything else. The ceiling was only about eight feet above the cement flooring, and the walls were made of cinderblocks. Thick metal poles were present every few feet to support the weight of the warehouse above us.

It wasn't an arena at all. A desk and a pair of ratty-looking chairs sat on a filthy, tattered throw rug that needed to be thrown away. Beyond these rudimentary furnishings, the place was filled with merchandise, but not 'sixties collectibles. There were stacks of audio and visual equipment: DVRs, cameras, and television sets, all out of their boxes.

Damian crossed his arms as he surveyed our surroundings. "Chesh, it looks to me like your late husband had a side business, dealing in stolen goods."

I made my way through the room, trying to ascertain how recently this stuff could have been placed here. A computer in the corner caught my eye. It looked identical to mine. I examined it. There was the same smudge on the side of the display that I'd noticed the other day and hadn't gotten around to cleaning.

There was a sticker on one side with the face of a German shepherd. I checked the opposite side just in case, and indeed, found the sticker of the cocker spaniel.

I turned to Damian and Chesh. "This is my computer. It was stolen from my office just yesterday."

"That...can't be," Chesh stammered, coming over to look for herself, along with Damian. "Ty told me he had the only key."

"Someone's got a copy of that key," Damian retorted.

Chesh shook her head. "All I know is, it wasn't me. I had no idea this stuff was down here."

"Do any of your employees—"

"We only have the one. An elderly lady, who works the register part time at the store when neither Ty nor I could be there. She's got no access to any of this. Probably doesn't even know where this place is."

We returned to the carpeted area near the stairs. This felt like a set-up to me. My computer gets stolen from my office, then happens to show up in the very place I was checking out twenty-four hours later. I wanted to get out of here—escape from this claustrophobic setting and mildew-scented air.

Chesh's brow was furrowed. "Ty must have had a partner in this...moonlighting operation here."

"Hank, maybe?" I suggested, thinking out loud. "He's got that Safe and Sound business of his. Maybe he rips people off before he installs their security units. Drums up business for himself as well as padding his accounts with proceeds from stolen property."

And yet, the all-too-convenient coincidence of finding my computer here sure made Chesh Bellingham open to suspicion. "Chesh, did you talk to anybody about our coming here today?"

"Nah. It's not like going to a warehouse makes for scintillating conversations."

Hmm. Could Chesh have had the opportunity to convert this room from an arena into a warehouse of stolen goods? As I looked around, I had to discount that theory. There were dust patterns on the furnishings that couldn't be easily faked. This stuff had been right where it was now. Seemingly with the exception of my computer, most of it had been here for quite a while.

So what could this mean? If Chesh hadn't told anyone we'd be here, could she have stolen the computer out of my office and put it here? Could she have known about Hank and Ty's illegal side business, and stashed my computer here to implicate Hank in Ty's murder? Or was Ty's partner just stupid? Did he think I had some clues in my data base that he needed to look at?

"Let's call the police and—"

"Wait a minute," Damian interrupted. While Chesh and I had been talking, he'd squatted down to rifle through a stack of video tapes on the floor. He studied one particular CD and pulled it out of its container. "The label on this is 'Ty Bellingham: Pit Bull.' Maybe we should take a look at one of these now. Might give us some answers."

I looked at Chesh, who plopped down in her late-husband's chair, the color drained from her face. "We may as well. If Ty was running some sort of... What do they call this? Fencing operation? That might be on the disk. Maybe it's a video inventory or something."

"Are you sure?" Damian asked.

She nodded. "I never knew about any of this. But if my store and my home were purchased with proceeds from stolen property, I'm right back where I started. On the streets." She paused and searched my eyes. "How could he do this to me? I just don't understand how anyone can be this slimy."

One of the television sets and DVRs were plugged in and aimed at the desk, as if Ty had been in the habit of coming down here to watch tapes, perhaps the one we were about to watch ourselves.

I turned on the set and DVR on, loaded the tape, and pressed the play button.

A moment later, we were looking at an extreme close up of Ty Bellingham's face as he adjusted the camera. He was wearing that same war-paint makeup I'd seen when I'd discovered his body. He stepped back to look at the camera. He wore a black wig with a headband, no shirt. He grinned at the camera and said, "It's show time!" Then he let out a young-boy's interpretation of an Indian war cry, complete with the woo-woos and patting of his lips. He chuckled and mugged for the camera.

I looked glanced at Chesh, who appeared stricken. She was having a hard time keeping her eyes on the screen, as if repulsed by her late husband's behavior.

As Ty stepped out of the picture, the setting for his makeshift film was revealed. It was this room. The camera had been placed where the stolen goods were now, so that the backdrop was the barren wall beside me and this desk.

"Come on, King," Ty was saying, still out of the picture. "Show me what you've got."

He led a pit bull on a leash into a spot just in front of the desk, then unbuckled the dog's collar. My pulse quickened and my throat went dry. Wrapping my arms around my chest, I vowed that I'd leave the room the instant it looked as though Ty were bringing Doobie or some other dog in to operate a videotaped dog fight.

"Come and get it," Ty said, holding something pink on his fingers. As King gobbled it down, I realized Ty was feeding the dog some sort of meat. But then Ty started to feed King another bite, but then snatched the meat away with his free hand and all but jammed his fingers into the dog's mouth. King backed away and cocked his head to look at Ty in puzzlement.

"Come on, you can do better than that!" Ty said to King.

My jaw fell. I mentally replayed my hour-long visit with Ty and Doobie, recasting them in a different light. Was it possible that Ty had not been involved in dog fighting after all? Could he have had some sort of masochistic perversion involving dogs? I'd never heard of such a thing, but that's what Ty seemed to have been encouraging. Unless, for some strange reason, Ty thought the taste of human blood would somehow turn this sweet dog into a fighter.

Damian muttered, "What is this guy doing?" He pressed the pause button, then glanced over at Chesh. "This was your husband, right?"

"Technically," she answered, her face still pale. She held up her palms. "I didn't know about any of this. Believe me."

"Did he ever..." Damian cleared his throat, then continued, "ask for you to bite him, during intimate moments?"

She shook her head. "No. But it's not like we ever had sex or anything, so I'm not the person to ask. A couple months ago, he told me he was sleeping with someone, but I have no idea who."

Wearing an expression of disgust, Damian restarted the tape and turned his eyes back on the screen, as did I.

"Know what this is, boy?" Ty was asking the dog. "It's hamburger. Doesn't that look good?" He smeared hamburger on his left forearm. The dog tried to lick the meat off Ty's arm. As he did so, Ty rammed his arm against King's mouth.

King yelped and wrenched himself free from Ty's grasp. The dog dodged out of the picture. Ty glanced at the camera and shook his head in exasperation, then followed the dog.

"What's the matter with you, King? You're a pit bull! You're supposed to kill small children. You're supposed to be vicious and have jaws like a vice!"

The dog ran across the screen again, followed by an annoyed Ty Bellingham. "Stupid mutt. Stupid purebred, I mean. Doobie's got twice your smarts!"

Chapter 18

Ty led the dog back into the center of the TV screen. He had replaced the dog's collar and leash and stepped on the leash, keeping a taut grip on him. Then he knelt and started shoving his forehand repeatedly at King's face, so that he was pounding on the poor dog's lips. In an amazing show of restraint and good personality, King just kept backing away.

"You stupid animal," Ty cried in exasperation. "You're going to find yourself right back at the pound!"

"I can't take any more of this. Sorry." I felt sick to my stomach, grabbed the remote control, and scanned the rest of the tape in fast-forward, just to see if the subject matter ever changed. There were no appearances by wolves or of would-be murderers, just one additional scene with Ty and Doobie, during which Ty was much more successful at getting himself badly injured. Even at fast-forward viewing, I had to turn my eyes.

Afterward, I stopped the DVR and unloaded it, then looked over at Damian and Chesh. They appeared to be equally as appalled by what we'd witnessed.

"Is this for real?" Damian asked Chesh quietly.

She stared at the desk top, running her fingertip through the slight dust that had settled there. "Ty was...a strange man. I guess he got off on having dogs bite him. That explains all the bills to emergency rooms of various hospitals in the Denver area."

"It also explains why he didn't want me to train Doobie." Could Ty's perversion somehow led to his own and two others' deaths? Paige had been married to Ty for several years. She must have known about his peculiarity and probably told Hank about it. One of them could have used that knowledge to stage his murder, but it was highly unlikely that anyone wouldn't realize how easy it is to distinguish a knife wound from an animal-inflicted wound.

I grabbed my cellphone. "The Boulder Police Department needs to know about this room and dust my computer for fingerprints. I'd better call them now."

By now I had committed Detective Rodriguez's direct line to memory. He answered on the second ring. He sounded tired and his voice was rough.

"This is Allida Babcock again. I'm at Ty Bellingham's warehouse in Broomfield. I found my computer here."

There was a pause. "You mean, some friend brought it there for you?"

"No, I mean whoever stole it stashed it here."

"Where you happened to be, the very next day."

"That's right. I know it's odd. Also, there's a videotape here of Ty Bellingham and his dog that I think you're going to want to see. It seems as though Ty hadn't been into abusing dogs, but rather, forcing them to abuse him."

The detective sounded as if he were trying to stifle a sigh of weariness or frustration. "Miss Babcock, stay put. We'll be there as soon as we can."

I hung up, wondering how many officers "we" meant.

Damian was pacing by the stairway, his brow furrowed. "Listen, Allida, Chesh, I'm sorry, but I really can't stay. I'm not sure what the police would do if they arrived here and found out I had a lion in my car."

"True."

"I should really boogie myself," Chesh said. "You didn't mention that either of us was here, so you can just tell 'em I got so upset after watching the tape that I took off. Is that cool with you?"

I resisted the urge to reply: *It's so cool I can see my breath.* "No worries," I replied instead, in a deliberate attempt to remind her of the current century, although I had no intention of lying to the police on her behalf. The three of us left the building. Once outside, Damian immediately checked on Leo.

"Still fine," he said in answer to my questioning facial expression. "Sound asleep."

"Well, this has been real," Chesh said, getting into her van. She got behind the wheel, but didn't start the engine. "I can't believe I married that weirdo, just for a few bucks and a nice place to crash. It wasn't worth it, man." Still shaking her head as if to rid her brain of the images, she drove off.

"There goes my theory that Ty was killed by a partner in a dog-fighting ring," I muttered to Damian. "Maybe there's something on one of the other DVDs that identifies the killer."

"Maybe." He smoothed back his blond hair.

When his eyes met mine, I felt more of an attraction to him than I wished I did. I wasn't quite ready for him to leave me here alone; I needed a sounding board. "Whoever had access to the cellar and put my computer here might be the killer. Maybe this solo act of Ty's turned into some sadomasochistic game that led to Ty's death."

"Or maybe it's all unrelated," Damian said. "Maybe Ty was a sick puppy, who got killed for completely different reasons. Such as by his partner in the burglaries."

"None of this makes any sense. Maybe the whole murder sequence is backward. What if Beverly was the intended victim all along?"

He furrowed his brow. "I don't follow."

"Maybe the killer concocted this elaborate murder scheme involving your wolves just to disguise who the real victim was."

He shook his head. "If I were intent on killing your friend Beverly, I'd set it up to look like a random act of violence. I wouldn't kill two other people just to hide my tracks. Otherwise, she might have packed up and left town the moment she heard about Ty's death next door."

"True."

Our eyes met and there was an awkward pause. "I'm sorry about the trouble you're in. Wish we'd met under better circumstances. Are...you and that guy in the office next to yours dating?"

"Yes, though we're currently on break."

"So there's hope for me." He put his hand lightly on my shoulder. "We have so much in common. We might make a great couple."

This was my chance to say something wildly romantic, such as: *You might be my missing half,* or *you're the yin to my yang,* but both lines sounded stupid. "Maybe."

He waggled his thumb over his shoulder in the direction of his van. "I'd better get Leo home. See you soon, I hope."

I smiled. "Bye. Thanks for your help." *Wow. I sure knew how to lead a guy on.*

"You sure you're going to be okay here by yourself till the police arrive? I mean, what if the guy who stole your computer comes back?"

"I'll wait in my car, just in case, and run the creep over if he tries anything."

"Good plan."

"Thanks again. Drive carefully."

"You, too." He gave me a sexy smile that came all too close to melting my heart.

The next morning brought the realization that I had to start my day with a rabies vaccination. I went down to Boulder Community Hospital and took my shot in my posterior, resenting Atla, as well as Ty, Paige, and Hank, for that matter. I really, really hate shots. They checked my hand and redressed the wound, which the doctor assured me was "healing fine." It looked pretty grim from my vantage point, but I didn't want to argue with a positive prognosis.

Afterwards, I went to my office and was disappointed to see Russell's parking space was vacant. Just in from the door, I checked my messages. The first one was from Russell, saying he would be at an on-site meeting all day and hoped that everything was going well for me.

A new customer had called, the owner of a golden retriever. What caught my attention was she said her dog was "having trouble because of the new security system."

I pressed "stop" on my answering machine and dialed the woman's number immediately.

The man that answered had such a reedy voice, I almost couldn't tell for sure whether he was a man or a woman, but with the name "Richard," I was assuming this was a male.

When I said that I was returning his call, he said to me, "Oh, yes. I have a problem, or rather, my golden retriever has a problem with the new alarm system I had installed a few days ago. And this guy I work with, Brad Rodgers, said you did wonders with his dog who was having separation anxiety."

He'd named a recent client of mine. "Oh, yes. I remember Brad and his black lab. Why is your dog having trouble with your alarm system?"

"Well, see, it triggers when there are strong vibrations in one of the windows or exits. She's tripped it by accident a couple of times by scratching at the door to get out. Now she's petrified of passing through that back door, or even the front door. Sounds ridiculous, I know, but all I can do when I'm home is open a window wide enough for her to jump through so she can get outside to do her business."

"Just out of curiosity, could you tell me who installed your system?"

"Sure. It was Hank's Security Systems. Hank Atkinson himself installed it."

Odd coincidence. "I see. Since this happened, were they able to adjust the system such that the dog can't accidentally trip it?"

"Yeah, that much is fixed. But can you help my dog so she'll be able to get over her phobia about our doors?"

"I should be able to do what's called counter-conditioning with her...encourage her to expect positive results from passing through the doorway."

"Great, 'cause I'll tell you, she's one scared dog, between this thing with the alarm, coming right on the heels of the break-in."

"Break in?" I repeated, tensing.

"Yeah. See, the house was burglarized a couple of weeks before. That's what made me decide it was high time to invest in an alarm system, you know what I mean?"

"Absolutely," I said, fully prepared to call My Favorite Detective one more time. The new customer set his appointment with me. I hung up and called Detective Rodriguez. To my chagrin, when I told him "this is Allida Babcock," he answered, "Of course it is. How are you, Allida?"

After giving the detective the names and addresses of my two new clients who'd used Hank's security systems after having been burglarized, I listened to the rest of my messages. Paige Atkinson had also called, asking me to return her call as soon as possible. I dialed, and she said, "Thank goodness."

I could hear Sammy barking in the background.

"Doobie and Sammy are barking like mad again. I'll bet the puppies would be too, if they were old enough to bark. It just starts up suddenly, and both of them

bark, then just as if finally quiets down, they start up
again. Please. It's driving me crazy. Can you just come
out here? I'll pay you anything you want to just make
these dogs stop barking."

I drove to Paige's house, but at the sight of Seth
Mulhuniak tying his shoes in front of the fence that
formed the boundary between the Atkinsons' and
Bellinghams' property lines, I kept driving, all the while
watching to see if he'd recognized me or my car. His
back was to the road and he didn't look up.

The last two times I'd been here when the dogs
were barking, Mr. Melhuniak had also been tying his
shoes just as I appeared. He only lived a few houses
down, so frequent shoe-tying a compulsive behavior of
his, but this was a man who'd gone apoplectic at my
mention of Doobie. Maybe Seth was riling the dogs
somehow, just to be ornery.

I circled the block, this time knowing exactly
where to look as I rounded the corner. Sure enough, the
moment my car started down the street, Seth
Mulhuniak pocketed something and started working on
his shoe laces. This time I was certain that he'd look at
me through the corner of his eye, so I pulled over.

"Hello, Mr. Melhuniak."

He merely pursed his lips and glared at me.

To give myself an excuse for circling the block, I
said, "You wouldn't happen to know where house
number 2046 is, would you?"

He waved me further down the street. "Way up
that-a-way."

"Thanks so much." I gave him a pleasant smile.

His face didn't change.

I parked just around the corner, where Seth
couldn't see me. I waited at the corner of the Atkinsons'
cedar fence, then popped around it rounded the corner
at a dead run. Seth Melhuniak was facing the fence,
holding his fisted hand up to his lips. This time I got a
clear look at the object he'd pocketed.

He looked horrified at me and started to walk away, toward his house.

"Hang on a minute, Mr. Melhuniak. I need to have a word with you."

"What are you doing here? This isn't any business of yours!"

"I'm afraid it is, sir. I've been hired to do something about the dogs barking in your neighborhood. That dog whistle of yours is aggravating a dog that gave birth to six puppies three days ago."

To my surprise, he blushed and sincerely looked contrite. "Must be Samantha, the Atkinsons' dog. I'm sorry. I had no idea."

"Just stop this, Mr. Melhuniak. You're letting your anger control you. That isn't doing you or anyone else any good. Ty Bellingham is dead. So is Beverly Wood. This has to stop."

"You don't understand! Tyler Bellingham took my dog from me! That crazy wife of his was in on it, too! I'm sure of it!"

"You mean, Doobie was yours?"

"No. He'd get Doobie to bite him, then he'd run to the doctor for medical care, and claim somebody else's dog bit him. They'd have an out-of-court settlement rather than risk losing their dog. Only I didn't have enough money to suit him. The judge didn't believe me. He forced me to put my Ezra down."

"Oh, my God. I...had no idea."

"I'm not the only sucker he pulled this on. He did it to at least two other people. Course, he didn't pull it in the same town each time. He wasn't that stupid. He'd pull his routine in Broomfield once and another time in Denver. The guy was as rotten as they come."

"The Atkinsons have newborn puppies. If you're interested in one of—" He was shaking his head so hard, I stopped.

"Don't want a puppy, thank you very much. Just want my own dog back. But I can't get him."

"There are some wonderful full-grown dogs at the Boulder Humane Society, Mr. Melhuniak. You can get a dog that's been trained by volunteers, such as myself."

"Yeah. Maybe I'll think about that, one of these days."

"In the meantime, I've really got to ask you not to blow that dog whistle."

He took the whistle out of his pocket and studied it. "Gig's up. Guess I'll have to retire this thing."

"Thank you. And I truly am very sorry that you lost your dog over this, Mr. Melhuniak."

He took a couple of steps down the sidewalk, then, to my complete surprise, said, "If we ever run into each other again, call me Seth."

As I headed back for my car, I saw Rebecca, seated on the bottom step of Beverly's front porch, which had had its police cordoning removed. I shored myself up, and walked up to her. With a blank expression on her face, she watched me approach.

"Rebecca. Hi. What are you doing here?"

"I don't know. I can't seem to keep going, you know? The business. Everything. It's all falling to pieces."

"I'm sorry."

"Are you? I was hoping you'd get in touch. After I left your office, I went to the police, just like I said I would. They didn't tell me anything. I don't know for sure, but I still think they're pretty sure Beverly did it. Killed Ty Bellingham, I mean."

"I hope not."

"Meaning you hope she didn't, or that the police don't suspect her?"

"Both."

Her eyes were so dull-looking. I was uncomfortable talking to her. She made me nervous. "Can you tell me again exactly what Beverly said during your last phone conversation?"

"She said something like, 'Don't say anything to Allida Babcock about that pit bull I had for a while last winter. The police suspect me, and I don't know why. I didn't kill Ty Bellingham. He was a sick man and deserved to be put out of his misery.'"

"Didn't you say she also mentioned the phone cord?"

"What phone cord?" she asked.

"At Ty Bellingham's house. You told me she said that Ty's phone cord had been cut."

"I can't remember anything about that."

"Rebecca, I'm positive. You told me that Beverly said the—"

"Stop it! I said no such thing! You're harassing me, just like Beverly always used to." She dashed back to her car and drove away.

Chapter 19

The next morning, it occurred to me that Beverly's extended family might know about the pit bull. It was a long shot, but I had wanted to contact Beverly's family anyway to ask what I should do about Beagle Boy. The four dogs greeted me enthusiastically in the kitchen, and Sage let out a sharp reprimand when Beagle Boy tried to butt in line.

I let Doppler and Pavlov out the sliding glass door, but Sage and then Beagle Boy went trotting off the opposite direction in search of Mom. I looked in the Berthoud directory for a listing under the last name of "Wood." There was none. With Sage dutifully a step behind, Mom came into the kitchen.

"You don't happen to know where Beverly Wood's parents are now, do you?" I asked.

Mom grabbed a mug off the small wooden cup holder beside the sink. Beagle Boy dashed into the kitchen, sliding a little on the linoleum floor, and promptly whined at Mom for a treat. We ignored him, although, in a show of disgust and superiority, Sage sat down in the middle of the kitchen with his back to us.

"Sam Wood died eight years ago, and Millie moved to Greeley a few months later."

"I didn't realize you knew them that well."

"I don't." She filled her cup with sink water, Beagle Boy begging all the while. In spite of Sage's attempts to sulk, his head was turned so as to keep a wary eye on our canine guest. "Right around the time Mr. Wood passed away, the wife of their former neighbors bought flying lessons for her husband's fiftieth birthday. Want Millie's address?"

I found Mrs. Wood sitting on her front porch when I drove up. It had been some fourteen or fifteen years since I'd last seen her, and I wouldn't have recognized her. She was on an old wicker rocking chair, staring out with what looked like apathy as I approached. She looked to be in her late seventies, white hair in a bun, her skin seemingly folding in on itself.

"Mrs. Wood? I'm Allida Babcock. I called an hour or so ago. I was friends with your daughter."

She stayed seated, but stopped rocking. "Oh, yes. Allida." She smiled, and now I recognized some of the facial features Beverly had inherited: the angular nose and chin, the gray eyes. "I remember you. Last time I spoke with Beverly, she told me you two were on a team together, again. Softball, wasn't it?"

"Yes. She was our pitcher. I'm so terribly sorry that this happened."

She pursed her lips and nodded, her gray eyes clouding. "No parent should ever bury a child. It's not the way life should be. Are you coming to the service tomorrow?"

It felt as though her grief was pressing against my own heart, making it hard for me to breathe. "Yes. I'll be there. So will my mother. She asked me to pass along her condolences, as well."

She gave me a little nod. "I spoke with Officer Rodriguez yesterday about taking care of Beverly's house and everything. He told me you had Beagle Boy."

"Yes, that's one of the things I wanted to talk to you about. Do you know of anyone in the family who would want to adopt him?"

She shook her head. "We discussed the matter amongst ourselves. Her sisters and I all have dogs

ourselves and don't feel they'd get along with her Beagle.
I could take him in for a while, though, and put up
some free-to-a-good-home signs."

I automatically winced. Dog-fighter rings
periodically scanned free-dog ads sometimes wound up
as "If you're certain you don't want to adopt Beagle Boy
yourself, I'd be happy to find a good home for him
myself. I work with dogs for a living, and I could
thoroughly check out the adoptive family to make sure
it's a good match."

"That would be wonderful. Thank you, Allida. So
long as my daughter's pet finds a good home, one dog is
plenty for me." The slightest hint of a smile returned to
her features. "Would you like to meet my dog? He puts
all of those cliches about vicious pit bulls to shame."
She rose and pushed open the screen door. "King, come
here, boy."

Out trotted the dog from Ty's video.

My initial shock quickly changed into feelings of
concern and confusion. Why had Beverly lied to me
about King's whereabouts? I knelt on the gray-painted
wood porch and petted his flawless brindle coat. He sat
down beside me, lavishing the extra attention, acting
not the least bit territorial. Pit bulls had fallen
drastically in the court of public opinion from their
heyday as the smiling dog in the Buster Brown shoe
ads.

"He's a nice dog, all right. How did you come to
own King?"

"He came to me thanks to Beverly," she said with
a sigh, returning to her seat. "She'd rescued him from
that hideous man who used to live next door to her."

"Ty Bellingham," I prompted.

Mrs. Wood was now rocking nonstop, as if seeking
comfort from the repetitive motion. "He was an evil man.
Beverly told me that Mr. Bellingham got King to be a
watchdog at his warehouse. He was just leaving the dog
there, feeding him once a week. Then he was going to
get rid of King because he discovered that he wasn't

vicious enough and would never have attacked an intruder. So, Beverly pleaded with him to let her find a good home for the dog. Beagle Boy was too jealous to be around him, so she asked me."

"I wonder why she didn't explain that to me. I found out about Ty Bellingham adopting King and asked her whether or not she knew what became of the dog. She told me she didn't know."

Mrs. Wood stopped her rocking and shook her head. "I'm afraid that's my fault. This county considers pit bulls a potentially dangerous animal. So they insist that you register them. I could never bring myself to do that. I was afraid if there was an incident involving a stray dog biting some child anywhere in the area, the authorities would come for King. I asked her not to tell anyone in Boulder about King. My neighbors out here, they've all met King and they know how gentle he is, and we all just make a point of taking care of one another."

"That's as it should be," I offered lamely. "I'm glad you trust me enough to tell me about King's not being licensed."

She frowned and averted her eyes. "A lot of things don't seem as important to me, now that I've lost my child."

Her words instantly increased a sensation of pressure on my chest. "I would have understood if Beverly had told me, too. I was only asking about King because I was concerned about animal cruelty from Ty or his associates."

She rose slowly. I'd clearly overstayed my welcome. "That's nice of you. As you can see, King is healthy and happy, but I don't want to rock the boat by adopting Beagle Boy. Thank you for looking after him on our behalf."

"Again, I'm so sorry. There's just one last question I want to ask. You called Ty a 'hideous man.' Is that because of his treatment of his dogs?"

My question motivated her to return to her seat, so I prepared myself for a long answer. "A grown man, dressing up like a hippie, and marrying some homeless wretch of a girl, just to make his ex-wife jealous." She shook her head. "One time when I was at Beverly's house, this must have been, oh, two years ago, Mr. Bellingham came over to complain about Beagle Boy digging under his fence and leaving messes in his yard. He said he was going to get a 'real dog' himself to take care of the problem, and, let me tell you, did he ever! That dog of his was half grizzly bear."

"I understand Beverly and her partner, Rebecca, had quite a bit of trouble with Ty when they were remodeling his kitchen."

She chuckled, or coughed, I couldn't tell which. "That Rebecca was absolutely convinced Ty was running dog fights. She hated the man with a passion. My Beverly never fully went along with the theory, though."

"It was Rebecca who suspected Ty was operating dog fights? She told me it was Beverly's theory."

"I don't know why she would say that, unless she hasn't been taking her lithium."

"Lithium?"

"Yes. Rebecca's a good person and was a good friend to my Beverly. But Rebecca has mental problems and has to be on medication. Beverly used to have to remind her to take her drugs every day. And without those reminders, who knows what she has going on in that mind of hers." She let out that half-chuckle, half-cough noise, and this time, I was certain she was coughing.

"Beverly never told me about Rebecca's problem."

"No, she wouldn't have. She had too much firsthand experience with the pain of mental illness in her own life. One of her sisters, my oldest daughter, suffers from the same malady. That's how Beverly and Rebecca met, in fact, through the outpatient clinic. Beverly knows more than most anyone to respect the person's privacy. Knowing how sensitive Beverly was about the whole subject, she probably kept Rebecca's illness as a secret."

"What about you? Did you tell the police what you just told me about Rebecca?"

"Heavens, yes. I doubt Rebecca's dangerous, even when she's off her medication. But still, it was obviously something the police needed to know."

"Thank you for your time, Mrs. Wood. Again, I'm sorry for your loss."

"See you at the memorial service, dear."

I nodded and left. I got about two miles down the road before the tears were blurring my vision too much to continue. I pulled over. How could I ever have doubted Beverly? I'd seen everything in exactly the worst possible light. I'd suspected her of murdering Ty. Doubted her motives for not being forthcoming regarding the pit bull.

And yet, somebody had to have told Rebecca about the severed phone cord. Unless Rebecca had cut it herself. In either case, I believed every word Beverly's mom had told me. Beverly had not killed Ty Bellingham. Rebecca might have been lying about the phone conversation she'd told me about. Or she might have simply been mistaken. She didn't remember telling me about the phone cord. Maybe she'd mixed up the phone conversations in her initial story.

That thought took me right back around to my number one suspects: Paige and Hank Atkinson. Hank and Ty could have had their illegal side business operating for some time now, but the two men could have had a legitimate falling out. Hank might have killed Ty and, because he was an accomplice who represented the biggest liability, killed Larry Cunriff as well. Beverly might have witnessed something, so Hank killed her as well.

I decided to visit the Atkinsons again under the guise of checking on the puppies. Paige or Hank might say something incriminating.

I drove straight there. Along the way, my sensible side was berating the rashness of my actions. Yet I couldn't get past my anger and guilt for Beverly's death well enough to listen.

I rang the doorbell, shoring up myself for the anticipated rude greeting I'd received here to date. Hank appeared in the doorway. His normally attractive features looked haggard. His reddish brown hair was uncombed, and he wore a gray sweatshirt with the sleeves ripped off at the shoulders over brown pants that looked to be slacks from a business suit, and black court shoes. "Allida, I'm surprised to see you here."

My instincts were warning that I should have paid more attention to the little voice that had voted against my coming here. "Likewise. I assumed you'd be at work. I just stopped by to check on the puppies."

"They're fine. Mother and pups are sleeping."

Hank's mannerism was so hostile, I found myself worrying not only about the dogs, but for Paige's well-fair. "Can I just take a quick peek in on them?" I asked.

He stayed put, one hand gripping the edge of the door. "You were at Bellingham's warehouse yesterday. It'd be best for your health if you forget all about that place."

"You're threatening me?"

"More like warning you. You've got things all wrong."

I forced myself to stay put, though my imagination already had put me making a mad dash for the safety of my car. "It's too late to do anything to me, Hank. I had other witnesses. We've already notified the police."

Hank flung the door out of his way and grabbed my arm with so much force, it hurt badly. "Let's go for a walk around the block. Let me set you straight on some things. I don't want us to disturb Paige." He dragged me out to the sidewalk.

"You're hurting me!" I said. "Let go or I'm screaming so loud your whole neighborhood will hear!"

Hank's face paled as he stared at something past me, further down the sidewalk. Chesh was out walking Doobie, more like she was being dragged by the dog. She took one look at me and let go of the leash. Hank tried to turn to run back into his house.

In a flash, Doobie leapt onto Hank, bowling him over. "Help!" Hank cried. The dog was not biting him, but had three of four paws on his back, pinning him down on the concrete sidewalk.

"Chesh, call the police." She ran toward his house. I turned my attention to the dog. "Doobie, cease!"

Doobie merely looked at me and did what dogs often do when they don't understand a command: revert to the single instruction they first learned and know the best. He sat down on Hank's back.

"Get him off me!" Hank said, straining.

Doobie let out a menacing growl. He had an eye on the back of Hank's neck, and it was too risky that he might bite. I commanded Doobie to come, but he ignored me. I managed to get hold of the leash, but was no physical match for the dog.

I heard a familiar voice from somewhere down the sidewalk. "Allida. What's going on?" Seth Mulhuniak must have heard the commotion.

"Dog whistle," I cried, unwilling to divert my focus from trying to keep Doobie's leash too taut for him to reach Hank's neck.

I realized as soon as I'd spoken that the odds were against Seth having his whistle with him. But a moment later, Doobie jerked around to look for the source of, what for him, would be a piercing noise.

Hank managed to get out from under the dog, which promptly snarled and barked fiercely.

Hank leapt onto the roof of my car. "I didn't kill anybody, Allida," he yelled. "It wasn't me. You have to believe me."

"Your credibility is somewhat lacking," I called over the loud barks.

"Get Doobie back inside! I need to get to the hospital. My arm is killing me!"

"I'm sure it is."

Chesh ran outside to join me. "I called nine-one-one. Someone will be here in another minute or two."

"Help me get Doobie under control." She grabbed hold of the leash as well, but even between the two of us, we wouldn't have been strong enough to drag Doobie into her house. Even so, doing so would have allowed Hank to escape.

A police car arrived incredibly fast. It must have been in the immediate area. The moment the officer stepped from his car, Hank cried, "Oh, thank God. Arrest me."

The moment the police officer was through taking my statement and told me I could leave, I drove to my office in search of Russell. His car wasn't in his space. I felt completely overwrought by the morning's events and needed to see him. I called his cell, but got no answer. I left a message to call me back. I sighed in frustration.

We weren't the perfect match. We didn't have as much in common as I'd like, but we could work on that. But whenever the chips were really down, it was always him I thought of first, the one I wanted to be with. I cursed when I saw his car wasn't in his space.

In the slim hope that he'd taken RTD in this morning, I left my car engine running and went inside. He wasn't there.

Damn! Just when I'd finally decided I could say those three all-important words to him that scared me to death, he wasn't here. I spotted the bouquet on my desk and remembered. He'd made it easy for me. I didn't have to say them. Instead I pulled the last petal off the daisy he'd given me and Scotch-taped it to his door.

"Coward," I scolded. If I stayed here to await Russ's return, I'd be too scared to leave my "note" in place. I had to do this thing before my fears left me apoplectic. I checked my watch. A few minutes after noon.

Across from the YMCA building on Mapleton, just a few miles east of my office, is a climbing wall. Russell often went there during the lunch hour. Going to go look for him there beat wearing a hole in the floor with my pacing and in my stomach with my nerves. I drove there. My heart started pounding mercilessly at the sight of his green Volvo in the parking lot.

In a lousy cliche, my knees were knocking as I entered the lobby and searched the large attached room for Russell. No sign of him. Come to think of it, why was he here when he had a broken collar bone?

"Can I help you?" the young, muscular, lycra-clad woman at the counter asked.

"Is Russell Greene here?"

"Haven't seen him. Just a minute, and I'll get one of the guys to check the locker room."

She left, and another perky woman approached. "Hi, have you been here before?" she asked me.

I shook my head.

"In that case, you need to fill out our form first." She slid a clip board toward me.

I started to protest, but decided this was a sign. I was being given this opportunity to conquer my greatest fears, all in one day.

The young woman at the counter gave me a long form to fill out, which basically made you acknowledge that you knew full well that you were an idiot so that if you fell and shattered your body, you couldn't sue them.

I gave her back her form all filled in and my money for one climb, which I assured her would be at the little wall for beginners and that, no, I had no idea what I was doing, but no, I didn't need an instructor, just a spotter.

I got up the wall easily. The problem was, I couldn't get down. As soon as I looked down to where I needed to put the next peg in to lower myself, I had a vertigo attack. The ground started spinning and pitching in my vision. I instantly broke into a sweat and shut my eyes.

"Uh, Miss?" the spotter called. "Are you having a problem?"

"Only if you consider paralysis a problem."

"Allida?" a familiar voice from down below asked. I wasn't able to risk turning to see if this was my imagination, or Russell really was here, after all.

Moments later, Russell, sans his sling was on the wall beside me. "I'm going to help you down, one move at a time."

"But your arm..."

"I don't need it for this beginner's wall. We're not high. You're only one step up off the ground."

"But that's not—"

"Don't look down. Just do exactly what I say. Grab this peg in your right hand and move it down, like this."

He winced as he placed the peg in a hole for me. I followed his instructions, feeling like an idiot, but knowing it was important to get him off this wall before he aggravated his broken collar bone. One step at a time, he talked me down.

Once we were back on the ground, I sank to the floor, my face bathed in sweat. Russell sat down next to me. The other climbers did their best to ignore us and not make me feel worse than I already did.

"What were you trying to do, Allida? Did you forget you were scared of heights?"

"No, but I thought I might be able to get over it by facing my fear...the same way I got over my fear of dogs after the wolf bite, by facing Atla again."

"I've got to get my sling back on. I can't believe you did this. It was lucky I was here."

"Yes, it was." A thought hit me. He hadn't mentioned the petal I'd taped to his door. Could he have not been back to his office yet? Had he been in another room when I first arrived? "Russell, how long have you been here?"

"'Bout an hour. I had lunch with a friend. Why?"

Which meant, if I wanted to tell him how I felt now, I'd have to actually say the words. "I can only work on one fear at a time."

"What do you mean by that?"

"I have to go, Russell. I'll call you later, okay?"

I headed off. Russell followed me out to the parking lot. From my rearview mirror, I saw him standing there, looking after my car, as if in the hopes that I might return.

Chapter 20

Though immensely disappointed in myself, I drove straight to the office and removed the daisy petal from Russell's door. The moment it felt right to tell him had passed me by. More importantly, there was too much going wrong in my life to trust my emotions just now. When you're dangling off a cliff, no one could be more beloved to you than the person who pulls you back to solid ground, yet that doesn't mean those feelings will last.

I couldn't stand to throw the petal away, and so I folded its tape on itself and put it in my pocket. I drove off to my first appointment and made a point of not returning to the office at the end of the day, merely went through my thankfully short work day in something of a daze.

Afterward, as I started on my long drive home, it occurred to me that much of my confusion regarding Russ had started with my attraction for Damian Hesk. Seeing him again might help me to put things in focus. I drove to his ranch, pondering what to say.

By the time I got there, my stomach was in knots. I decided to be upfront for once and blurt out my reasons for coming. Then I would make a hasty exit.

"Damian. Hi, I was hoping you'd be back from work. I'm sorry to drop—"

"Hey, Allida," Damian interrupted. "Good to see you. You can help feed the animals"

"I have something to tell you. Yesterday you hinted that you'd be interested in dating me. That made me face up to my feelings for Russell Greene. The guy who shares my office space?"

"And?"

"And I think I'm in love with him."

"Oh. I'm sorry to hear that. For my sake. I hope he makes you happy. Get the door for me, would you?" He tossed me the keys.

I hadn't been expecting a big reaction on Damian's part. It's not as though he should be groveling at my feet and pleading with me to give him a chance, or anything. But a frown might have been nice. Or a sigh. A blink, even.

Demoralized, I unlocked the door to the animal's house and swung open the heavy wood-plank door. Damian, his muscular arms struggling with the weight of the two huge plastic buckets of meat, followed me into the center of the animal shelter.

"What'd the police have to say about the contents of the warehouse?"

"Not much. They tend to spend their words on questions. But they arrested Hank Atkinson earlier today"

"On what charges? Do they think he's the murderer?"

I shrugged. "I guess so. They're awfully tight-lipped about their cases"

"Must be who was behind all of this. I have to say, he's paid me quite a bit of money over the past couple years for my work on his commercials, but I never liked the guy the much"

"Neither did I."

Damian was slowly scanning his animals, who were all inside the building with us. He seemed tense.

"Do you think all of this could have been Hank Atkinson's doing?" I asked. "That he took the keys from Larry and stole the wolf?"

"Something's wrong," Damian said under his breath. "The animals are agitated"

I followed his line of vision, immediately chilled by Damian's words. I'd assumed that they were acting this way out of hunger, but on second look, Damian was right. All of the big cats, wolves, and bears were pacing and "talking," the tigers and lions roaring. Kaia was prancing from side to side in his cage and was salivating. The two bears kept rising to full height and growling.

Damian's brow was furrowed. "What the hell is going on?" he muttered.

"Maybe a stray animal wandered in here and upset them," I suggested cautiously.

"No." He shook his head. "That wouldn't set them all off like this." Damian threw a switch by the door and a florescent overhead light came on. He stared at the cement floor ahead of him, then paused and checked each cage. He stopped at Kaia's cage and peered through the thick mesh. He pointed. "There are shoeprints in Kaia's den. Somebody's been in his— Damn it! He's limping!"

Damian pivoted and returned to my side. He took a big sniff of the slightly acrid air. "Allida. Do you smell that?"

I inhaled deeply. "What?"

"It smells like singed hair. Or fur. I think somebody's been in here with a cattle prod! That's the only reason..."

He let his voice fade. I sniffed again, but the odor of animal waste was still too strong for me to detect anything else.

He ran to the switches, shoving me toward the door. "I've got to help Kaia. Call the vet. His number's right there over the phone."

"Wait, Damian. Should you go in there? If Kaia's injured—"

"I raised Kaia from a newborn! He's as gentle and well-trained as any dog!"

"Yes, but an injured, scared dog can badly hurt its owner. Shouldn't you wait until the vet can come give you a hand?"

"Yeah, you're right, damn it all." Damian crossed his arms as if to hold in his anger. "How the hell could this happen?"

The same way somebody got Atla away from where he belonged and over to Ty Bellingham's, I thought. I picked up the phone. The line was dead. "Phone's out. Someone cut the line." I grabbed my cellphone, just in case. Not surprisingly, there was no signal.

"Shit! Kaia's limping badly! Go to the house. Check that phone. If that's out too, just drive to the nearest gas station and call nine-one-one." He pressed the button to open Kaia's cage.

"Damian, don't!" I grabbed his arm, but he pulled away from me as if I were a five-year-old child clinging to him. "This is a trap! Can't you see that? Somebody's trying to lure you into that cage"

"Yeah, but I've got to see if I can help Kaia. Whoever's done this is going to have to get through me first before he hurts one my hair on my animals' hides!"

"Oh, for—" I stopped. I was wasting valuable time trying to argue with him. I ran toward Damian's house, patting my pockets for my keys in case, as I strongly suspected, the phone lines to the entire residence had been cut.

My pockets were empty. I remembered then. I'd planned to make a hasty exit and had left them in the ignition.

I bolted through the front door and raced toward the first phone I could locate, in the austere living room. I picked up the handset. No dial tone. "Shit!"

Could I really leave Damian here with a wounded wolf while I drove off for a phone? A trip to the nearest gas station and back would easily take half an hour. But what choice did I have? I just didn't have the physical strength to be of much help.

I ran back to my car, cursing my physical shortcomings. I grabbed the handle on the car door. Locked! How could that be? I peered through the window. No keys in the ignition.

Dear God! What was happening?

I raced into the carport and tried the door of Damian's van. His doors were locked as well. I had to get the keys from Damian, if he was still all right.

I ran to the animals' building, but then approached the doorway on tiptoes. Waited by the door, listening. The animals were still making a racquet, but I heard no human voices. "Damian?"

No answer.

I knew it! I knew it was a trap! But there was nothing for me to do now but step into it myself. I couldn't go the ten miles on foot to reach the highway. Couldn't run and hide and leave Damian in the cage with an injured wolf.

The lights were out inside the circular open space. I stepped quietly into the shadows, giving my eyes a minute to adjust to the muted darkness. "Damian?" I whispered.

The door on Kaia's cage was shut. Damian was inside, crouched against the wall. He'd been gagged and his hands were tied behind his back. His forehead was bleeding, but he was conscious and breathing, struggling to work his hands free. Kaia was beside him.

"Oh, my God. Damian. I'll get the door." He shook his head, grunting at me, pointing with his chin at the doorway behind me. Just as I started to turn, I spotted a padlock on Kaia's cage that hadn't been present moments ago, locking Damian and Kaia inside.

I automatically flinched and took a step back as someone stepped briskly through the doorway. I recognized the shapely figure and long black hair.

"Allida, is that you?" she said, her eyes not yet adjusted to the muted lighting inside.

"Janine. I should have known. It was you, all along!" I said in answer. "You killed all those people!"

"What are you talking about?" Janine asked. "What's going on, anyway? I just came out here because you called me and said Damian was hurt and needed help. What's the matter with—"

Somebody rushed up behind her and conked Janine on the head with what looked like a baseball bat. Janine crumpled to the floor.

I gasped, horrified, then found myself gazing at Chesh Bellingham, who stood over Janine, bat in hand, breathing deeply as she watched over her.

I cursed in silence, but hoped for the best. "Chesh, thank goodness you're here. That woman was trying to kill us. She knocked out Damian and locked him in the cage. Help me find her keys, so I can go call the police."

Chesh laughed. "Now, why would I want to do that, Allida? I've finally got both you and Damian exactly where I want you."

"You trapped us? Not Janine?"

"'Fraid so. See, the police would have gotten 'round to figuring it all out sooner or later, if I just killed my husband. That's the oldest crime in the book, right? I needed more victims"

"You killed Larry and Beverly just to throw the police off the trail?"

She shrugged. "Larry could identify me as the one who bribed him to get Atla and the key to this place, so that was a no-brainer. And it was high time I got even with Beverly for breaking my tailbone. You gave me the idea for the perfect person to frame—Janine. It'll look like you came in and found what she did to Damian, struggled with her, and you both bit the big one." She chuckled. "That's something of a pun, isn't it? Sorry it has to end this way, Allida. I'll give Doobie your regards."

"You'll never get away with this. No one—"

"I'm going to step outside the door till this is over. Course, if you do make it out somehow"—she reached behind her back and pulled out a long, dark object that had been strapped in place by her belt—"I've got a stungun. You won't get far."

She pressed the buttons and opened all the animal cages.

I jumped over Janine and raced toward the doorway as it slammed shut and the lock was thrown. Just as I reached the panel of switches, the overhead light went out. She'd thrown the circuit breaker.

Chapter 21

Atla dashed out of her cage and into the open space. My first thought was to distract Atla by throwing some meat for her, then duck into her cage and close the gate. Yet Janine was still unconscious and unable to defend herself.

I needed to feed Atla in the open space and all of the other animals in their individual cages. Since Atla was already nearly upon the plastic industrial-sized barrel full of meat, I tossed her the first piece I could grab, which were rock hard because Damian fed them their food frozen.

Reserving a club-like piece of meat-on-bone to use as a weapon, I worked at a feverish pitch, hurling food over the animals and into the backs of their cages. The bucket probably weighed as much as I did, but my adrenalin was pumping, and I could now lift it by the handle.

Damian, meanwhile, was rubbing his tethering in a sawlike motion against the bars. In the cage with him, Kaia was more agitated than ever at the sight of me feeding his companions. There was no feeding-slot on his cage, however.

A bear came out of his cage toward me. He was enormous. I felt like Jack of the beanstalk to his Giant. Bears are omnivores. They prefer nuts and berries to meat. I didn't know what to feed him.

"Where's the bear's food?" I cried to Damian. I dropped some meat by the bear's feet, unwilling to risk trying to pitch it past him.

Damian grunted and gestured with his chin in the direction of his house. The bear got down on all fours to sniff at the meat, and I kept going, hoping for the best.

When I was only two-thirds around the circle, Janine started screaming. I'd had a concussion once. Screaming upon awakening was common.

With no time to gamble on the animals' reactions, I dropped my make-shift club and flung the rest of the bucket contents in the general direction of the remaining third of the cages.

"It's all right," I cried to Janine as I ran to her. I grabbed her under the arms and dragged her as best I could toward Atla's empty cage, next to Damian. Janine tried to fight me off. I managed to pull her to her feet and get her stumbling with me in the direction of Atla's cage.

Atla started to head toward us. "Atla, stay," I demanded. I began to manually crank the pulley-driven gate mechanism. Atla followed us as far as the threshold to her cage.

"Stay," I said again. Fortunately, she held her ground just outside the gate as it shut.

Though Damian's legs were bound, he managed to hop toward the bars that separated Atla's and Kaia's cages. Beside me, Janine lay sprawled on the floor where I'd unceremoniously dropped her. Kaia was howling, but did not impede Damian's progress.

Through a series of head jerks and noises, he indicated he needed me to reach into his pocket. I had little space to work with between the bars and it was slow going, but I eventually managed to pull out a Swiss Army knife. I flipped open a blade as he turned himself, and I soon managed to cut through the rope on his wrists.

He yanked off the red bandana gag in his mouth and said, "Give me the knife. I might need it." He started to untie the ropes on his legs. "We can't leave the animals like this. They've never been out together, except within their own species. Sooner or later, they'll start fighting."

Indeed, some of the big cats were venturing outside of their cages, looking to poach some more meat from their neighbors. There was a general clamor of warning growls and snarls.

Janine, meanwhile, had sat up and some semblance of cognizance had returned to her features. "Where am I?" she said, her words slurred. "Why are we in a cage?"

"Chesh Bellingham trapped us," I answered. I returned my attention to Damian. "She threw the circuit breaker." I glanced in the direction of the tunnel, which led to the exterior circle of pens. "Does that mean the electric fencing above the pens is off as well?"

He shook his head. "Separate circuit. We can't climb over it with the power on." He yanked on the padlock. "I have to get out of here," Damian muttered. "I can't leave the animals like this."

Janine started crying and whined, "Damian, help me. My head hurts."

The padlock Chesh had fastened was a combination-style, which she'd fed through an old-style bicycle chain. Damian quickly cut through its plastic sheathing, then began sawing on one of the links. In the meantime, I noticed that Atla and one of the female tigers were in the initial stages of squaring off. Atla was poised to claim the mostly empty bucket and the entire open space as her own.

"That's going to take forever," I said. "Do the electric wires outside extend between the pens? Can you climb into Atla's pen with us?"

Damian promptly pocketed his knife and scrambled through Kaia's tunnel to the outer pen. Ignoring Janine's whimpering beside me, I knelt to watch through the small tunnel in Atla's cage as best I could. The only view was directly ahead and not of the fence separating the pens.

I gasped as I spotted Chesh on far side of the pen, brandishing some sort of stocky rifle. Before I could react, she fired.

An instant later, there was a thud as Damian dropped to the ground. Then he rose and staggered through the tunnel toward me.

Reflexively, I grabbed his shirt and helped pull him inside.

"Shit!" he said. "She's got my tranquilizer dart gun. Hit me in the thigh." He dropped something he'd been gripping, which rolled across the floor.

There was another report from outside, and a dart wedged itself in the bottom of the thick meshed gate to the cage. Chesh had shot a second dart at us through the tunnel.

"You think you can outsmart me, hey?" Chesh screamed. "I'll shoot a dozen darts into each of you and kill you myself!"

At the noise, a cougar and a black leopard emerged from their cages. They both dashed past us, both Atla and the tiger letting out warning protests.

Damian slumped over. I shut the mini-gate to the tunnel, a solid guillotine-like sheet of metal.

"Damian! No!" Janine started sobbing and rushed beside him, pulling him down into her lap.

He let out a small grunt, then lost consciousness.

Damn it all! We'd be sitting ducks if we stayed in this cage until Chesh came in after us. What the hell could we do? "She's not going to just barrel in here, knowing all the animals are loose," I muttered, thinking out loud. Then again, she had the cattle prod to fend off the animals.

At least four big cats and Atla were set to do battle. My only hope to stop Chesh from shooting us with darts, was to enter the cats' arena. Shit! How had I gotten myself into this mess!

Beside me, Janine sputtered and cried, rocking herself with Damian's head and shoulders in her lap. "Janine," I said coarsely. "We have to save ourselves. I'm going to have to go out there again. Surprise Chesh as she's coming through the door."

"You'll never manage," Janine answered, catching on to what was happening. Her words were still slurred. "The animals. The dart gun."

"Then help me! We'll get on either sides of the entrance!"

"I can't go out there like this!" she whined. "I'm bleeding. I'm seeing double. I can't do it."

"You have to! She's going to come in here and shoot us! We either stop her now, or we're dead!"

"I can't." She burst into tears.

I didn't have time for this. I reached through and flipped the latch into the open position, then started cranking the door back up.

"Janine," I said through a tight jaw, "pull yourself together. Grab a meat bucket. You hear her rattling the lock, you get ready. When she comes through the door, drop the meat bucket over her head."

I cranked open the gate just far enough to crawl through. Atla was half whining, half howling. The bear, too, was in the center of the open space, playing with the meat bucket like an overgrown toddler. Mercifully, this seemed too much for the leopard and cougar. They'd returned to their respective cages to defend their meals.

Janine, still sobbing, lowered the gate behind me. "I'm sorry," she cried. "I can't help you."

I walked past both of the animals in a slow gait, not looking at either of them to portray a confrontation. If they attacked, it would only shorten my life by a few minutes.

I grabbed my hideous club of meat and flattened myself against the wall alongside the door. I heard a key in the lock.

I raised my club, the flesh of my unbandaged hand sticking to its icy surface. A moment later, the lights went back on, the door was kicked open, and Chesh charged into the room, the rifle in one hand, the cattle prod in her other.

I'd been surprised by how fast she'd entered. I swung at her head with the full force of my fury. She saw me coming enough that she dodge a little. My blow landed on her shoulder.

She cried out in pain and dropped the rifle.

I scrambled after it and swept it up, just as I felt an unbelievably horrible pain in one leg. The Taser felt at once as though my leg had been crushed and stabbed.

I managed to keep my grip on the dart gun and whirled toward her.

She dropped the prod and got both hands on the rifle before I'd gotten a strong grip myself.

She screamed as Leo trotted close to us. He wanted to claim my "club" before any of the others did. I kicked it his direction, still wrestling with the gun, but she pulled it free. All I could do was hold onto the rifle barrel and prevent her from aiming it.

"Let go!" she hollered. She spun around with so much force I couldn't hold on any longer. It felt as though my fingers were broken from the force, and I fell.

She aimed at me. I scrambled to me feet.

"Look out!" Janine cried.

Chesh automatically flinched and turned to look back. I tackled her, launching my shoulder straight at the back of her knees. She got a shot off as she was falling, the rifle once again dropping from her grasp.

I fought for all I was worth. The bear ran back into his cage as Janine and I flailed away at each other on the hard-packed dirt floor.

She clawed at my injured hand. The pain was excruciating, but I elbowed her in the breast. There were some metallic clicks behind us. I prayed that the sound was of a gate being cranked open.

Chesh managed to roll on top of me. She got both hands around my neck. I pushed up desperately, but couldn't get leverage. I grabbed her wrists and tried to pull her hands off of me, but she had her full weight on them. I couldn't breathe, couldn't last much longer.

From the corner of my vision I saw a flurry of motion. A gunshot echoed. Janine's grip loosened.

Chesh collapsed on top of me. Gasping for air, I slithered out from under her. My neck hurt horribly. I tried to speak, but couldn't. Janine sat down on the ground, dropping the rifle from her hands in the process.

I pulled the dart out Chesh's back and dropped it, then staggered toward the still open door. I flipped the switch on the circuit breaker on the outside wall, then went back in and lowered all the gates. As I did so, I realized that the door to the open space had been wide open this whole time. To the best of my knowledge, all of the animals had stayed inside, as Damian had once told me they would.

Only Leo and Atla remained outside of their cages. Leo was contentedly gnawing away on my former club. Atla was pacing in the open space, near the opening to where Damian still lay.

Janine looked like a character from a horror film. Blood was matting her hair. Her face was totally white. Her eyes looked like black holes. She stood stock still, gripping the tranquilizer gun, staring down at Chesh.

Supporting my throbbing throat with one palm, I said in a cracked voice, "Janine. We've got to go get help."

To my surprise, she shook her head. "Can't leave Damian." She reached into the pocket of her shorts and tossed me a set of keys. "There's a cellphone in my van. You can get coverage about ten miles toward the city." She picked up the cattle prod from where it lay, a short distance from her feet. "I'll keep watch."

I shut the door behind me and got out to my car as quickly as I could, hurting with every step. I drove as fast as I could, while keeping an eye on my phone until a bar appeared. I pulled over, called nine-one-one, and told the dispatcher to send an ambulance and police to Damian Hesk's ranch.

She kept asking more and more questions. My throat was killing me with hen I spoke. Finally I pretended we'd just gotten cut off and hung up in the middle of one of my answers.

I dialed Russell Greene's home number, my heart pounding at the sound of his hello.

With my hand supporting my throbbing throat, I said, "Russell, I love you."

There was a pause.

"Allida? Is that you?"

My throat hurt too much to laugh, but I smiled. "Is this Russell Greene?"

"Yes."

"In that case, yes, it's me."

"Ah," he said with a smile in his voice. "In that case, I'm the luckiest man alive."

Author's Note

If you enjoyed this book, I hope you will enjoy all four mysteries in the Allie Babcock Mystery Series: *Play Dead, Ruff Way to Go, Give the Dog a Bone,* and *Woof at the Door.* You also might enjoy my humorous Molly Masters Mystery Series: *Death Comes eCalling, Death Comes to Suburbia, Death of a Gardner, Death Comes to a Retreat, Death at a Talent Show, Death on a School Board*, and *Death Comes to the PTA.* To find out more about these and other books by Leslie O'Kane and Leslie Caine, please visit my website at LeslieOKane.com or my Facebook page, Leslie O'Kane Books.

Acknowledgments

Much of my knowledge about dogs and publishing come from Edie Claire, my wonderful friend who is also a wonderful writer. Thank you, Edie! Thank you from the bottom of my heart to my wonderful, talented, writer friends, especially Francine Mathews, Claudia Mills, Phyllis Perry, Elizabeth Wrenn, Marie Desjardin, Christine Jorgensen, Lee Karr, and Kay Bergstrom. I couldn't write anything at all without the support of my family, especially Mike, Carol, and Andrew. There are dozens more people whose names aren't listed herein and deserve mention; please forgive me and know that your names and many significant contributions are written in my heart.